GAME OVER

GAME OVER

M.C. ROSS

SCHOLASTIC INC.

DEDICATED TO MY MOM, FOR
BEING A COMPUTER WHIZ WAY
BEFORE EVERYONE ELSE WAS
A COMPUTER WHIZ, AND FOR
TELLING PAT WHEN IT WAS MY
TURN ON THE COMPUTER. AND,
YOU KNOW, FOR EVERYTHING
ELSE. IN THAT ORDER.

ISBN 978-1-338-53811-3

10 9 8 7 6 5 4 3 2 1   22 23 24 25 26

Printed in the U.S.A.   40
First printing, December 2022
Book design by Christopher Stengel

TUTORIAL

Hello! Congratulations on purchasing your first HIVE™ headset. Just by reading these words, you've already leveled up.

To begin gameplay, please strap your High Integrity Virtual Environment (or HIVE) headset firmly around your head, making sure your goggles are securely in place. If your BrainSTIM Card has been properly implanted, simply pinching the bridge of your nose will grant you the ability to see, smell, feel, taste, and touch in the wonderful world of HIVE.

To choose a game, merely walk through the clearly labeled hexagon of your choosing. We have games for players of all ages, tastes, and experience levels. Some higher-level games may require payment to play, but don't worry; your BrainSTIM Card gives us access to your bank account. Paying is as easy as thinking!

If you have questions at any time, tap the side of your headset, and a help screen will appear. You can also feel free to ask NPCs, or Non-Player Characters, for help—if you think they're the kind of characters who'd be likely to help you! If you are lost, you may also receive assistance from our friendly worker Drones.

Please do not harass, tease, or upset our NPCs or your fellow players. Harassment is a violation of HIVE rules.

If you violate HIVE rules, you may receive assistance from our friendly worker Drones.

If you intend to use HIVE for purposes other than gameplay, please exit this tutorial and select our Business Tutorial.

If you intend to use HIVE for purposes other than gameplay or business, please exit this tutorial. You should know what to do next.

Before we start, please accept our Terms and Conditions. Remember: You don't actually need to read our Terms and Conditions to complete this step! You do not have to understand our conditions. You just need to accept them.

Now, please prepare to enter the world of HIVE. And remember, if you are

- pregnant,
- elderly,
- suffering from recurring heart conditions,
- prone to nausea, or
- a player with a disability

. . . please feel absolutely free to play HIVE regardless.

Everyone belongs in HIVE.

Game on!

PART ONE

LEVEL 1

A lot of people will tell you I had a problem with HIVE, but that's not true. I liked HIVE. I was good at HIVE. It's just that, if I'd had it my way, I'd have been given the option to sit somewhere and read instead. As it turned out, this would have been very bad for the fate of the entire world. But it would have been pretty great for Kara Tilden, which is to say, me.

Okay, maybe it would have been bad for me, too.

Hard to say.

Let's start again.

At its peak, this is how popular HIVE was: Some days, the teachers didn't even bother to show up to school.

This was not as fun as you might think.

It *could* have been fun; I really think it could have. Case in point: I had the option to sit somewhere and read. Like right now, Elizabeth Bennet and Mr. Darcy were about to get married again. Well, for the first time in the book, but this was my second or third time reading *Pride and Prejudice*, so for me, the weddings were starting to stack up, and even though I was sitting in the front row of a practically empty chemistry classroom, I could just about hear church bells chime.

Then, instead, I heard someone threaten to light someone else on fire.

"I'm gonna light you on fire!"

I tried to ignore this. This was not my problem. I only wanted to read, as discussed. And frankly, as far as threats went, it just wasn't great dialogue.

Then I heard the flick and *hiss* of one of Mr. Teigen's butane lighters being switched on, and with a sinking in my stomach, I realized it had been less of a threat and more of a very blunt promise.

"Get off me!"

"What's the matter, Cornball? Forget what it's like to have to deal with another human?"

"You can't—"

"I can. Welcome back to the real world, Hivehead."

With great regret, I marked the page in my already well-marked book and put it down. I knew, on some (most?) levels, I shouldn't get involved. But I also knew no one else would. It was twenty minutes into eighth period and Mr. Teigen was nowhere to be seen. Most likely, he'd ditched school early to run home to his HIVE headset. This in turn meant that more or less the whole class had felt free to do the same. I hadn't looked up from my book in a while, but a few minutes ago, Gracie Garner had stood up and announced she was going for "boba and HIVE," and as Gracie Garner went, so went the rest of the class. So there was a good chance I was the only one left in the room to intervene.

And I know what you're thinking: That's ridiculous, teachers can't just leave, there'd be an uproar, et cetera. But I'm telling you: This was peak HIVE popularity. This happened.

And anyway, of course I was going to get involved. I had it on good authority that I'd always had a tendency to assume it. Authority, I mean. Dad said I got it from Mom. My older brother, Kyle, agreed. But Gus, my boyfriend, said I got it from always sticking my nose in books.

"It's like practice," he'd explained, grinning. "Y'know, for sticking your nose into other people's business."

I'd punched him on the shoulder, and then we'd kissed. It was like that with Gus.

But Gus wasn't here right now. In fact, as I stood up and turned around, I discovered I'd been right: There were only three people left in the room. One was me (hello). The poor sucker stuck in a headlock was another. And, of course, administering that headlock, there was the bully with the butane, Markus Fawkes.

This was not good. Markus Fawkes had been held back a few times over the years, and it showed in the way he towered over his peers—a group that, regrettably, included me. At five foot three in boots, I may have been a Good Samaritan, but I was not exactly the *ideal* Samaritan.

"I'm not asking for much," Markus said, leering, too busy with his victim to look at me. "Just every cheat code you know for the next time I'm in HIVE. I know you know them. You spend so much time in there, I'm amazed you haven't turned into a little worker Drone."

"HIVE doesn't have cheat codes!" spat the kid under Markus's arm, struggling to get free and hissing like a cat each time his fingers met open flame. "And even if it—*hnss*—did, why would I tell a moron like you?"

Markus looked genuinely surprised by the question.

"Because otherwise I'll light you on fire," he said. "I thought I was really clear about that."

"Get *off*!"

Emerging from under a dangling mess of brown hair, the victim's voice cracked. In that moment, I realized I knew that voice. And what's more, I knew that if I didn't do something right away, I wouldn't be able to live with myself.

"Hey, Markus," I said, taking a step forward. "Why don't you pick on someone your own age?"

Trash talk wasn't my normal go-to, but I felt you were allowed to aim a little low when the person in question was trying to barbecue your classmate.

Markus turned to look at me with faint surprise but never for a second loosened his grip. If anything, his smile only got bigger, and his already-ruddy cheeks turned the same bright shade of red as the curly hair that blazed on his head—and, for that matter, pretty much everywhere else on his body.

"Nerd," Markus said, the way other people would have said *hello*. "You into HIVE? You wanna get in on this?"

I shook my head because, y'know, no.

"Just let him go, Markus," I said, taking another careful step forward. "You can't afford another summer of detention."

Markus snickered.

"You see anyone here who's gonna give me detention?" he asked, sweeping his non-headlocking arm out in a grand and jeering gesture at the empty classroom. "Consequences only happen in HIVE now. And as soon as this nerd gives me what I need, I won't even have to worry about— *Hey!*"

I'd been waiting for Markus's arm to reach the end of its long arc. As soon as it was fully extended and the lighter was as far out as possible, I hurled myself forward, a move Markus had clearly not expected. I'd never been anyone's idea of an experienced athlete, but I was a *very* experienced little sister, and years of Kyle playing keep-away with my books had taught me exactly what to do in situations like this, which was, unfortunately, to go for the armpit.

"Oof!" With a grunt and a clatter, Markus dropped the lighter to the classroom floor as I essentially headbutted him in the underarm, sending him and his hostage reeling. It was a gross maneuver, made even grosser by the ionosphere of spray-on deodorant that surrounded Markus Fawkes at all times. But it was an *effective* maneuver, and with bullies, as with older siblings, I figured you had to play every card you had.

Another card in my favor: being closer to the ground. As Markus crashed into a table, scattering and/or shattering a row of test tubes, I dove to the ground, snatched up the lighter, whirled around, and held it between us, trying as hard as I could to keep my hand from shaking.

"Let him go," I said, "or you get a taste of your own medicine."

"You won't use that, dork," Markus spat. "I've seen you. You just read books all day, right? You're not gonna *burn* someone."

"You'd think," I said, wiping what I hoped was just deodorant from the side of my face. "And yet."

We stared each other down. The funny thing was that he was absolutely right: I was just playing brave, acting the way I thought someone in one of my favorite books would act. And yet, when I looked into Markus's eyes, small and beady though they were, I got the sense that he was playing, too.

And I played better.

"Whatever," Markus said, breaking off his gaze to roll his eyes, as if he had suddenly become bored. "You two dweebs deserve each other, anyway. Let's see how brave you are when you meet me fully equipped in HIVE." And with that, he dropped his gasping captive to the floor and made a break for the hall.

"I'm honestly sort of a casual player," I called after him, "so I feel like we won't—"

But Markus's footsteps were already fading into the distance, presumably taking him to the Bullworth Apiary, where he could intimidate other HIVE players in peace.

As soon as I was sure he was gone, I turned back to the grumbling boy on the floor.

"Geez, sorry about that," I said, extending a hand to help him up. "But, hey, Jason. Long time, no . . . Jason?"

My hand froze in midair, which turned out to be fine, since the boy was making quite a show of pushing himself up to his feet without accepting my help. This was not exactly surprising behavior for Jason Alcorn, the resident loner of Bullworth High.

It was, however, sort of rude, considering we went way back.

We had met reaching for the same Dr. Seuss book in the children's reading room of the Bullworth Public Library, where even at the age of six we were both already seasoned regulars. After a brief standoff, we'd agreed to share the book, and a tentative friendship had begun, made slowly less tentative over hours spent in the comfy beanbags and stained-glass lighting of the reading room. We never spoke very much (it was a library, after all), but I think this had almost made me feel a closer bond with Jason than if we'd been chattering away the whole time. It was the bond between two people comfortable spending lots of time together without saying anything at all.

But that same silence was probably why it took me a few years to realize that we were there at the library for different reasons. I came back again and again because, duh, I loved books. But it turned out Jason, with his worn-down clothes and his rumbling stomach—extremely noticeable in a silent reading room—came to the library because of something else.

He didn't really have anywhere else to go.

Around the time I figured this out, Jason must have found

somewhere else after all because he started coming to the library less and less, and then stopped showing up entirely.

And now Jason was fixing me with a glare that was *not* the look of someone who had once helped me to sound out the words *Truffula Tree*. It was not even the look of someone who had just gotten their skinny butt saved and who should probably say thank you. It was more the kind of look that made me slowly retract my outstretched hand and fold my arms across my chest.

"Hey, are you . . . okay?" I asked.

It was an effort to fill the awkward silence, but it was also a genuine question. As long as I'd known him, Jason had been kind of skinny and . . . unconcerned with his appearance, to put it nicely. But the Jason standing in front of me now seemed to have gone even beyond that. His cheekbones jutted out severely in a way that shot just a little past handsome and landed at malnourished. His brown hair had always been fairly long and frequently messy—and, to be fair, it had just been rumpled up by Markus Fawkes's *other* armpit—but it was clear that he'd not had a haircut for several months. And just as I was wondering why it had taken me so long to notice any of this, I realized that I couldn't actually remember seeing him in class for several months.

With a pang of guilt, I wondered if he really hadn't been there. Even worse, maybe he *had* been there and I just hadn't noticed.

"I'm fine," Jason said, in exactly the tone of voice fine people never used. "You can go."

I could tell when I wasn't wanted, but that voice in my head that always voted to step in and help out, regardless of whether anyone had asked, was practically jumping up and down on the ballot box.

"I don't have to go," I said, carefully sitting myself down on the edge of a desk. "We could hang out, for old times' sake. You know, like at the library? I haven't seen you since . . . since . . ."

Jason's incredulous stare tripped me up midsentence.

"Well, in a while," I finished weakly.

"Yeah, and I wish you still hadn't," Jason said, nodding at the butane lighter in my hand. "I don't even know why I came here today. Should've stayed in HIVE."

Okay, that stung, but I was ready to plow through it.

"Is that where you've been?" I asked. "Is that why Markus called you Hivehead?"

Jason's look shifted into utter confusion, which was at least an improvement from outright resentment.

"Do you really not know?" he asked, looking at me as if I'd just asked if gravity was still, like, a thing.

I just shrugged and repeated what I'd told Markus: "I'm more of a casual player."

Jason's expression shifted for a third and final time, but this shift was the most unsettling of all. His brow furrowed, his head tilted to the side, and if I didn't know better—which, to be fair, I didn't—I'd say he was looking at me with pity.

"Ugh. That's so depressing," he said.

Yep. Definitely pity.

"I mean, I *play*," I continued, taking one last stab at polite conversation. "Mostly simulators. You know, like *The Skims*? There's this historical pack you can add, *Mind Your Manors*, that I've—"

I stopped when his head tilted farther. (I hear you begging to know more about *Mind Your Manors*. Don't worry, we'll get to it.)

"And, uh, my boyfriend definitely plays," I tried. "Do you know Gus Iwatani? He loves the big fantasy games. If you ever play *Family Feudalism*, you may have seen him."

"Ugh. *Normals*." Jason threw his hands up as if he were being subjected to something unspeakably beneath him and stalked away from me, making a beeline for his backpack. "And people say *I* seem like a Drone? Level up already."

So much for reconnection.

"Okay, I have to be honest with you," I said. "That kind of talk is *exactly* why people try to light you on fire."

"Yeah, well, next time, you can let them," Jason said. "Now, if you'll excuse me, I have to get to the Apiary before the big Update."

"Wha— You too?" I knew Jason could be odd, but this was beyond all expectations. Instead of answering, Jason just stormed past me. His backpack smacked me on the shoulder, but as I grunted and whirled in disbelief, he didn't look back—just tossed up a sardonic wave and disappeared through the door.

"That's . . . that's where he's going to be!" I yelled after him. "The guy who was *just trying to light you on fire!*"

But he was already gone, and I was the only person left in the room.

Come to think of it, I might have been the only person left in the whole school.

At its peak, this is how popular HIVE was: Some days, I felt like the only person left in the world.

LEVEL 2

Again: I did *not* have a problem with HIVE. But if I *did*—this moment in time, with me cleaning up the torch and test tube pieces all around my feet, in a school spookily abandoned before the final Friday bell had even rung—*this* would have been a perfect moment for me to reflect on why I *did* have a problem with HIVE. Which I did not.

Maybe, as I swept up all that broken glass, I would have thought about how HIVE had seemed so innocent when it first started. How it began as an arcade game, born just as arcades were dying, where for too many quarters you could sit on a giant throne with some Velcro gloves and goggles and play one of a handful of mini-games, or just wave hello to someone in another run-down arcade in another far-off country. Quarters, if you're wondering, were like those coins you're supposed to unlock in HIVE treasure games, except you could exchange them for real human things, like gumballs or the ability to play HIVE treasure games. Look, I know it sounds weird, but this is just what my mom told me, and she should know.

After all, she was the virtual reality pioneer who helped turn HIVE into what it became.

That's something else I could have thought about.

But I didn't. Because I didn't have a problem with HIVE.

Instead, I thought about the final Friday bell, which now actually *was* ringing. I thought about putting the broom back where I'd found it and figuring out how to click the butane torch back into its holder. I thought about Gus, and how the next time I saw him I'd pick his brains about what I was already deeming The Jason Incident. I thought about—

Wait a second.

Gus.

Click.

I snapped the butane lighter back into place just in time to recall: If it was Friday, then Gus and I had date night, which always began with us meeting in the parking lot by my car. And if the bell had already rung, then I was already late.

I snatched my copy of *Pride and Prejudice* off the desk and bolted for the door. Then I realized I'd forgotten my backpack, bolted back, picked it up, slid it on, and re-bolted, flicking off the lights and taking off down the hall in that terrible elbows-out run that is the curse of any backpack wearer. My braid slapped up and down furiously as I ran, and my favorite black boots sent echoes through the halls, making me sound like a one-woman stampede.

At least there's nobody here to see this, I thought, huffing down the stairs two steps at a time. Then: *Wow, there's really nobody here to see this* as I ran through a completely empty foyer and burst through the front doors. Seen through a squint in the bright afternoon sunlight, the parking lot looked like the outskirts of a ghost town, with my lonely little car parked at the back of the lot like the world's laziest tumbleweed.

This, of course, would have been another perfect moment for me to think about HIVE, and how everything had changed when it went portable. Kyle and I had come downstairs one day in December to find that our mother had snagged us a pair of prototypes—two headsets and some strap-on gauntlets. I'd never been a huge gamer, but even I had to admit: It was cool to stand in my own living room and play something my mother had worked on. And if you found the right games for your personality, it was almost as fun as getting lost in a good book. Almost.

For the rest of the world, there had been no "almost."

When the home headsets hit wide release just a few weeks later, HIVE became the hottest thing on the planet. It was the best gift for your family, the best way to spend time with your friends, the best way to spend time if you didn't have any friends, and certainly the best way to spend money. It didn't take HIVE long at all to announce their first pay-to-play games, showing up within the world of HIVE as new golden hexagons that, upon closer inspection, turned out to be made of gold coins. And then, before anyone had much time at all to worry about that, the first big Update rolled out, and the whole world pretty much vanished into HIVE—including, it seemed, just about everyone in and around Bullworth High.

And my mother.

Absolutely none of which I was thinking about. Because I was late for a date. And was fine with HIVE.

Except: A sinking feeling stole over me as I closed the distance between me and my car in the self-driving car section. There really was absolutely no one in the parking lot, and the thing about there being absolutely no one was that Gus was absolutely someone, and therefore—spoiler alert!—not in the parking lot.

I pulled out my phone to make sure I hadn't missed a text. Nothing. And nothing pinging or dinging in the half-dozen or so messaging apps Gus may have used to get in touch with me, either.

Well.

There was one I hadn't checked.

As I unlocked the car with one hand, I pinched the bridge of my nose with the other and tried not to think about how the easiest way for me to log in to HIVE was also a gesture of exasperation.

Bzzzzz. The familiar sensation-sound of a bootup rose from the back of my neck and tingled around my ears. As I slid into the driver's seat, my vision didn't change (I would have had to be wearing my headset for that to happen), so I was acutely aware of how silly I looked when a chipper voice announced, "Hello! Welcome to HIVE. How may we help you?" To which I responded, out loud, to no one at all, "Check messages from GoodGusNoRe, please."

Right. So. That first big Update: That was the BrainSTIM

Card. It wasn't nearly as cheap as the headset, but it bought you, in this order: some local anesthetic; an extremely micro microchip; two minutes in a surgeon's chair; and then a miracle. The miracle was the ability to really feel like you were in HIVE. This wasn't just having your gloves vibrate across your knuckles when you punched a virtual villain; now you could feel textures like you were using your bare fingers, talk to people as if they were standing right next to you, and even smell.

Weirdly enough, it was that last thing that really caused HIVE to blow up. If you could smell, you could taste, and if you could taste, you could eat. The first HIVE businesses were the HIVE restaurants, blue hexagons popping up between the increasingly vast selection of games, serving foods and tastes that had never existed in the real world, or that hadn't been tasted for years—foods like fried dodo, or glowing ice cream with pixel sauce, or giant cheesecakes that had zero calories (because all digital food had, when you got down to it, zero calories).

And with the HIVE restaurants came the HIVE economy. And with the HIVE economy came . . . just about everything. Special HIVE chairs for people who played so long it gave them back problems. Special HIVE nutrient feeds for people who bought those chairs and then didn't want to get up to eat. And finally, for people who didn't want to get up after they'd—how do I put this?—used those nutrients: completely immersive chambers, located in centralized clusters called Apiaries. Like arcades, except you weren't hanging out in the physical world—you were in your own chamber, next to your friend in their own chamber, both hanging out in HIVE. And so everything had come full circle. Folks still had the option to play whenever and wherever, but HIVE was once again something people could go somewhere else to do.

Possibly people like your forgetful boyfriend on your Friday date night.

Or maybe not. Maybe Gus had *also* just rescued a long-lost acquaintance from a bully, and was even now racing toward me from, I don't know, the woodshop room! No need to blame HIVE (which I was okay with). Everything was (probably) fine.

But it couldn't hurt to check.

"No messages found," said whichever Drone was inside my head that day. "Would you like to send a message?"

"Yes," I said. "'Hey, everything okay?' Send."

There was another *Bzzz*, this one made to sound as if it was rapidly flying away from the car, carrying my message into the digital expanse like so much pollen. Then, before I even had time to turn on the engine:

"Message read at two forty p.m.," said the Drone chipperly, as if it wasn't spitting in my eye.

"Oh, you're kidding me," I muttered, quickly turning around to fish through the flotsam and jetsam of my back seat.

"Send 'Oh, you're kidding me' to GoodGusNoRe?" asked the Drone.

"No!" I said, throwing a Bones & Narble bag to the side

and digging through what was underneath. "No, I'll— Where is— Ah! I'll tell him myself."

Finally, I had found my headset, the same one I'd had since that day in December. Any devoted HIVE user (so basically anyone alive, really) would have been horrified to see such precious cargo buried in the back of a dirty car, but I wasn't quite so delicate with my tech. I basically kept it around for social gaming, meeting up with friends, and times when I wanted to play *The Skims*.

Well, and times like right now.

It was that new Update, was what it was. As I turned back to the front of the car, sliding the headstrap under my braid and letting the goggles rest on my forehead, I suddenly remembered what Jason had said: *I have to get to the Apiary before the big Update.*

Now that I thought about it, I'd been hearing about this all week, from snatches on the Digicast as I drove to school, or from excited murmurs in the halls as kids speculated about what Eric Alanick, the famed founder of HIVE, had in store for them this time. Previous updates had brought beloved features like Sidekicks, cute and customizable buddies that could follow you from game to game, or Modifiers, which allowed you to exchange game points (or your good old actual money) for cool upgrades to your HIVE self. Like horns or wings or, say, cute black boots that looked just like your real-life favorite boots (shut up). Or—

Suddenly, I was gripped by a memory.

"Double jumps," Aaron had said, gesturing emphatically with a chicken tender. Like a lot of Aaron's gestures, it got a bit out of hand, and the chicken finger wound up falling into his strawberry yogurt.

None of us flinched. For one thing, we all knew Aaron's cerebral palsy, mild as it was, still resulted in the kind of spasticity that could lead to small spills. For another, Aaron had often been known to dip his chicken in his yogurt of his own free will. We had been watching him eat his cherished strawberry-chicken concoction for several minutes now.

"We already have double jumps," Sammi reminded him, picking up a napkin and dabbing yogurt from the lunch table while Aaron fished his tender back out again. "Like, half the games you play have double jumps."

"Yeah, but . . . but imagine if *all* of them did," Aaron said, throwing both his arms wide, and everyone laughed. Even me, and I only had half a clue what we were talking about. I had just decided to reread *Pride and Prejudice* that morning, and I was at that moment tearing through the second chapter. Still, I was in my happy place: book in hand, lunch on table—and on chicken tender day, no less—plus Gus on my left side and our friends on my right. And also my left. It wasn't a huge lunch table.

Gus squeezed my hand lightly, and I looked up just long enough to make eye contact with him and smile.

"You wanna know what I think it is?" asked Sammi, waiting absolutely zero seconds for anyone to respond. "A universal language app. How cool would that be? We already play with people from all around the world. Imagine if we could *understand* them." She brought her hands up to her head and then flicked them away in the universal sign for *mind blown*.

"You *can* understand them, Sammi," Gus pointed out. "You speak, like, eight languages."

"Gus, buddy . . . there's more than eight languages." Sammi knocked on Gus's head, took a baby carrot from his tray as if it were a fee for slowing down her thought process, and then turned and tapped her baby carrot on the edge of my book.

"What about you?" she asked, happily gnawing at the pointer/carrot. "What do you think the big Update is gonna be?"

I'd just gotten to a good part, but I didn't want to be rude, so I quickly marked my page and looked up. "What are we talking about?"

"HIVE," Aaron said. "This weekend there's supposed to be a— *Ow!*"

Aaron cut himself off quickly, almost as if someone had kicked him under the table.

"Oh, right," he said, "Sorry, Kara, I forgot your mom— *Ow!*"

"I think Kara's not as hopelessly nerdy as we are, guys," Gus said in a loud, determinedly cheerful voice. "Well, she is, but in a different way. I'm sure she doesn't care. Anyway, it's probably just gonna be some update to the privacy policy or the Terms and Conditions or something. You know how no one ever knows what's going on with those. Hey, does anyone think Mr. Mulsoff and Ms. Bailey are dating?"

Sammi and Aaron jumped on this conversational bait instantly, and I briefly considered steering the conversation back—*Wait, no, I can talk HIVE, too, I'm cool!*—but Gus squeezed my hand like he'd done me some big favor, and I would've hated to burst his bubble. And I really *was* getting to a good part of my book. So I squeezed his hand and went back to reading.

That was one of the things that I liked about being in the same room as Gus: He loved to talk to people, real people who weren't just in books, or talking about books, and he was happy to do enough of that talking for him and me combined.

Of course, we had to actually be in the same room for that to happen. And now, sitting in my car, I had a pretty good idea why he wasn't here with me. He, like everyone else in town, had gotten so excited about this new Update that he'd forgotten about the rest of the world completely.

Which would have been fine, except the rest of the world happened to include me.

Now I did a cursory check to make sure all my car doors were locked. As far as I could tell, there was nobody around—like, to an almost spooky degree—but better safe than sorry. Everyone knew that going full HIVE in public was practically an invitation to get yourself mugged. Everyone went ahead and did it anyway, but still.

There were, of course, other ways to handle this. I could have just sent Gus another message, or even made a voice call. You didn't have to be all the way inside HIVE to talk to someone who was playing (otherwise, moms would never be able to call their kids to dinner), but I couldn't think of anything more cliché than literally being the nagging voice in my boyfriend's head.

So I sighed, chucked my copy of *Pride and Prejudice* onto the passenger seat, lowered the goggles over my eyes, and thought something that maybe, arguably, could have been described as the *slightest* grievance against HIVE, which was:

Elizabeth Bennet never had to deal with this crap.

Then I gave my nose a second, much harder pinch, and entered the world of HIVE.

LEVEL 3

The first time you enter the High Integrity Virtual Environment is dazzling. That buzzing in the back of your head gets louder and louder until suddenly it spills and flows down your whole body, a sound you can feel all over, like your entire body has fallen asleep but you're still awake and vibrating on some impossible frequency. Then all of a sudden you *are*—that is to say, you exist—somewhere other than where you existed before. You stand on a horizontal hexagon in a vast chamber full of *vertical* hexagons. In fact, you realize, it's *made* of them, a swelling and bulbous structure as large as a moon that you are somehow flying inside of, all wallpapered with glowing and colorful six-sided doors connected to one another by cat-walks and stairways, launchpads, and landing ports, one of which you're headed to now, on your floating self-propelled hexagonal loading-level platform. If you know where you want to go and speak it aloud, the hexagon will smoothly change direction and take you there. If you want to take the long way around and see the sights, you can just step off onto the nearest landing pad and start walking your way there, passing other players and Sidekicks and floating gray Drones, carrying messages and bits of code and who knows what else, hurrying from game to game, or game to business, or business to place of worship (congregations that were no longer able to afford real-life real estate had taken happily to the opportunities of *not*-real estate). Below you, the doors and ports and pads drop to a bottom so far down you can't even see it's there; above you, the same soars up in reverse. It's the Grand Central Station of video games, and it's all up to you and your stash of points, or just your checking account, to decide where to go next.

The first time you enter HIVE, you are born anew.

The four thousand and eighth time you enter HIVE, you're totally over it, and you just want to know where the heck your boyfriend has gotten off to now.

I was pretty sure I had a good idea where the heck my boyfriend had gotten off to now.

"*Family Feudalism*, please," I said, and my loading platform obeyed, floating me through the void until we reached a yellow hexagon emblazoned with a medieval font, decorated around the edges with ravens and pitchforks. It was, at least, a free game, so all I had to do was take a step forward and the game opened up right away, the hexagon splitting apart into two halves that slid to each side like automatic doors. Behind them was an eternal yellow glow.

I entered the game.

I was bathed in light.

I was standing in mud.

Correction: I was sinking in mud. I'd been dropped into the middle of a sprawling expanse of heavily trampled farmland, the kind of scene you always saw in paintings of peasants in fields, except normally the peasants weren't disappearing ever more swiftly into a patch of muck that was up to their shins and climbing. It was like quicksand—very squelchy quicksand—and if I didn't move fast, I would be stuck there, or worse.

It wasn't painful to die in HIVE. You could be drowned in mud, pushed off a cliff, squished by a dinosaur, zapped by a laser, or, in the case of one aggressively realistic dating simulator I'd played, contract mad cow disease from a haphazardly run steak house. All this and more could happen to you, and the result would always be the same. First, you'd feel a warm and comforting sensation, like being zipped all the way into a sleeping bag stuffed with goose down and anesthetic. Then, much less comfortingly, you'd find yourself dumped back out into the world between games, sprawled across your loading platform like you'd been pushed down by some faceless bully. It was all in good fun, and you were allowed to reenter whichever game you'd been in pretty much immediately, but it was undeniably frustrating. More to the point, I did not intend to exit this game fifteen seconds after I'd first entered it, especially since I was a player with a mission.

"Hello?" I called out. "Can anyone help me?"

"Mayhap anyone can," said a voice. "Or mayhap just me."

Oh, *great*. In a fantasy game, hearing a cryptic reply from a mischievous voice just outside your field of vision could only mean one thing: elves. Or gnomes. Or whatever pointy-eared breed of NPC populated this world. If you asked me, they were all insufferable, they were all untrustworthy—and they were all I had to count on right now.

"Okay, let's cut to the chase," I said as the mud swallowed my knees. "What do you want in exchange for helping me?"

"Oh, I could never put a price on a fair maiden's life," said the elf/gnome/whatever. "But I do know one thing about Hungry Mud . . ."

Ugh, you could just *hear* the capital letters.

"The first step to escaping it is removing any heavy, extraneous, or *expensive* items from your person," finished the NPC.

"Okay, first off, not a fair maiden," I said, pointing at my braid. "'Fair' means blonde. This is 'Dark Umber.' I know because they make you choose off a customizable menu. Second: I don't have any equipment on me, so don't think you're making off with anything valuable."

All this was correct. It was a fair gambit on the NPC's part; for other players, loading up on weapons and equipment was a way to show how many points they'd earned and spent in HIVE, or just how much dough they had to blow in the real world. I'd stacked up my fair share of points over the years—it was almost impossible to spend time in HIVE and not do so—but I'd never felt much of an urge to splurge on anything. The most expensive purchase I'd ever made was the boots I was wearing now, purchased because they'd looked pretty much exactly like my actual boots. And if I'm being honest, because I'd just met this cute junior named Gus Iwatani at the time, and I'd had a sneaking suspicion I was about to be playing a different type of game than I was used to—one that called for more durable equipment than the default athletic shoes every HIVE avatar was given.

I'd clocked some good hours with Gus in these boots. I was glad they were hidden in the mud right now, or I might have been asked to give—

"Mayhap you could give me your boots," said the NPC.

Frick. That was the problem with artificially intelligent opponents. You could never tell how intelligent they were going to artificially be. Especially the magic ones.

The mud was up to my hips now, but with some effort, I was able to turn the top half of my body to face my harasser head-on. He was grinning like the cat who ate the canary, if said cat had lots of tiny, terrible, tapered teeth, a sickly green-ish hue, and giant pointy ears the size of palm fronds. In short, he was a textbook gremlin, down to his being four feet tall, tops. And yet, perched comfortably as he was on a berth of mud that had been baked into a solid crust, and sinking as I was into an inescapable pit, he was still taller than me.

"Heavy shoes cause extra suction in the Hungry Mud," the gremlin continued, looking down at me. "You'd be helping yourself as much as me. Lose the boots."

"Nope," I said, even as the mud bubbled up to my shirt. "Try something else."

"What else is there to try?" the gremlin asked, his tone quickly becoming much more exasperated and much less medieval. "How else do you intend to get out of there?"

I didn't have an answer. Yet. But I believed I could figure this out. Being smart was just a matter of noticing things, and noticing things was just absorbing information, and if I was good at nothing else, I was good at that.

But currently, there wasn't very much for me to absorb. Just the gross brown farmland. And the gross squelchy mud. And the gross little gremlin. And the gross, slightly less squelchy mud that the gremlin stood on.

Wait.

"How'd you get up on that mud?" I asked. "Can I get up there, too?"

But even as the gremlin opened his mouth to answer, I raised a hand to shut him up. It was the wrong question. I could feel it. The gremlin was magic, so for all I knew, he'd teleported there, and anyway, anything he said was bound to be annoying. So, different question. But as the mud rose and a light rain started to fall, it was getting harder to concentrate on what the right question could—

Oh.

"It's raining right now," I said, looking at the baked earth where the gremlin stood, where drops were starting to spatter. "And it looks like it's been cloudy all day—no sun. So . . . how did that mud get like that?"

The gremlin looked down at the ground.

He looked up at me again.

"You know," he said, "I'm actually not sure."

And then a massive, moving column of flame ripped across the plain, missing me by just a few yards and missing the gremlin by no yards at all. The fire was followed swiftly by an enormous shadow that passed over the earth, and when it was gone, there was no gremlin—just a pile of ash, a dry heat in the air, and a *lot* more baked mud.

And in the sky, a huge ruby-red dragon was reaching the end of a terrible, lazy loop, and beginning to make its return.

"Oh," I said weakly, watching as smoke rolled out of the dragon's nostrils. "*That's* how the mud got like that."

Luckily—by a significant stretch of the meaning of *luckily*—the new swath of baked mud came right up to where I could just reach it. Now torso deep, I thrust my arms out as far as I could, preparing to push myself up and out. I hesitated for just a second when I saw that each raindrop hitting the freshly scorched earth instantly evaporated with a menacing *hiss*. For all intents and purposes, I was about to slam my hands down on a sizzling-hot fajita plate.

Then the flap of leathery wings beat at the air above me, and I decided very quickly that I'd rather be sizzling than burned to a crisp.

"Nggh—*ahh!*"

My palms seared and steam rose in billows between my fingers, but I pushed through the pain and slowly began to rise out of the mud.

Too slowly. The wings were getting louder by the second, approaching from the south, or whatever counted as south inside HIVE. I focused on pushing, refusing to look up and see how close the dragon was getting. But I didn't really have to look; it became all too clear as a shadow fell over me, sliding up from . . .

The north?

"Kara! Take my hand! Also, hi!"

A metal-gloved hand thrust itself in front of my face. Too relieved to question it, I grabbed the glove, which instantly set about helping me by trying to yank my elbow out of my socket.

"Aargh!" I yelled, which I think was fair.

"Keep pushing!" my new friend encouraged me while enthusiastically trying to rip me in half. Was I imagining it, or was the air getting warmer? The dragon must have been right on top of us. Despite the burning in one hand and the wrenching pain in the other, I closed my eyes, gritted my teeth, and pushed.

Squeeeelch!

The mud let me go.

"Whoa!" I toppled forward onto solid ground, taking my helper down with me.

Whoomph! Another blast of fire tore past us, missing the bottoms of my mud-covered boots by mere inches, as well as the metal boots of—

"Sammi?!" Now that we were at eye level, I could see that my new friend wasn't so new after all. It was the same face I saw every day at the fifth-period lunch table, albeit with a few Modifiers: bright violet eyes, a suit of lightweight armor that managed to beautifully complement Sammi's turban, and a nose piercing that I knew for a fact Sammi's mother would *never* let her get in real life.

"Thanks for the help," I said, pushing myself up to my knees. "Hey, do you—"

"Laddu!"

Ah, of course. There was Laddu, Sammi's virtual Sidekick, tumbling adorably over Sammi's shoulder. Laddu looked more or less like a smallish peregrine falcon, if they were a lot fluffier, a lot more orange, and a lot more willing to be petted gently on the head without tearing your throat out.

"Hey, Laddu," I said, providing the obligatory head pat. "Listen, would you guys—"

"Laddu!"

"Happen to know where I could find—"

"Gus!" Sammi's violet eyes went wide as they beheld something shocking over my shoulder. I whipped around and, sure enough, there was Gus, dashing madly over the mud. In fact, he was racing directly toward the dragon in a move that contradicted pretty much all my assumptions regarding the right direction to run around dragons (i.e., away).

"Don't worry, Sammi!" Gus yelled. "I got this!" As he ran, he kept his eyes focused on the dragon, even as his hands moved down to his belt and detached a large and spiky object—a grappling hook, I realized with a flip of my stomach.

The dragon, frustrated by its two failed attempts to secure some oven-baked human, was bearing back down on us now with smoke in its nostrils and a look in its eyes that said *Third time's the char.*

"Just watch this," Gus said, swinging the grappling hook in rapid circles and turning back to flash a cheeky grin. "Flamebreath's not gonna know what hit— *Kara?*"

The cheeky grin became a stunned stare. The grappling hook slipped from suddenly slack fingers. The dragon pounced, and hook met scale, but not around the neck, as Gus had presumably intended. Instead, the poorly thrown grappling hook sank deep into the corner of the dragon's wing, and with a bellow of pain, the dragon hurled itself back into the air.

Taking Gus along with it.

LEVEL 4

"Oh *no*."

Sammi and I said this at the exact same time, which was a bummer, since in different circumstances that would have been totally cool. In *these* circumstances, we craned our necks to watch in horror as Gus flew off the ground, clinging to his end of the grappling hook like the string of a runaway balloon, if balloon strings were prone to screaming and flailing their legs a bunch. Every few seconds the dragon would roar and release a great guttering jet of flame. Swinging wildly under the dragon's belly, Gus was safe for now—but one swing in the wrong direction and he'd be literal toast.

"We have to get him down from there," I said, wincing as the dragon pulled a tight turn and slammed Gus into its flank.

"Totally," Sammi said. "Got any ideas?"

"Working on it." I had never slayed a dragon, but I'd spent hours reading about people who had. My mind raced as I tried to pick something out of the dozens of stories that might have been useful.

"Laddu?" Laddu inquired, flapping his wings tentatively toward the sky.

"No way," Sammi said. "It's too dangerous. You'd be roasted in a minute."

"Who needs a whole minute? Watch *this*!"

The voice came from behind us, but I would have recognized that cocky tone anywhere. Whooping with undisguised glee, Aaron leaped right past us—emphasis on *leaped*.

There were two principles by which you could largely predict Aaron Ridley's behavior in any given game of HIVE. The first went something like this: Ever since the BrainSTIM Card had come along, players with physical disabilities in the real world could, if they chose, play without those disabilities in HIVE. Amputees could regain limbs; the near- or farsighted could become just plain old sighted; and Aaron's CP, previously a constant throughout his life, suddenly became optional. Not everyone chose to take advantage of this; not everyone wanted to. But Aaron did, and did so with relish. His playing style within HIVE was as exuberant as his personality was in real life—and seemed calculated to incorporate as much impressive coordination as possible.

The Second Principle of Aaron was this: More than anything else, the kid loved to double jump. And *Family Feudalism*, like all Aaron's favorite games, allowed double jumps in infinite measure. Accordingly, he had worn his beloved Springheeled Jackboots, and now, as Gus dangled above us, Aaron put his boots to use. With another whoop of joy, Aaron leaped up once, high into the air. Then, just before he would have fallen onto his and/or our faces, Aaron leaped *again*, bouncing *off* the air and soaring higher still.

Just high enough, in fact, to grab on to Gus's legs as the dragon swooped low. Aaron's added weight pulled the grappling hook even deeper into the dragon's wing, causing the dragon to bellow in pain as it tumbled to the earth.

"Oh, I don't think that's going to be helpful," Sammi said, staring as the dragon's jaws unhinged.

"It's not," I said. *"Look out!"*

We leaped, rolling in opposite directions as another gout of flame blasted the earth. Laddu took to the air with a squawk, just narrowly avoiding getting roasted. And Aaron and Gus crashed down hard, rolling like bowling pins across the mud and coming to a bruised finish a few yards away from us. The dragon, temporarily distracted, stayed where it was and twisted its long neck around to snap at the hook buried in its wing.

"I saved Gus," Aaron said. "Everyone saw that, right? Hi, Kara. I saved your boyfriend."

Gus shot to his feet, and then practically fell over himself again in his hurry to help me up.

"Hey!" he said. "Nice to see you. I don't suppose I get any handsome swashbuckling points for riding a dragon?"

I knew I had come here to track him down, but I smiled despite myself.

"Oh, was that riding?" I asked. "I've been taking the bus

all wrong. Next time I'll lasso the tailpipe and let it drag me down the road."

Gus laughed, flicked me on the shoulder, and kissed me on the cheek. It was like that with Gus.

"So what are you doing here, anyway?" he asked.

Huh. That, I did not expect. "Did you not get my message?"

"Oh!" Gus squinted, as if recalling a slightly hazy dream. "I saw something, but I was distracted. Dragons. You know how it is. What's up?"

I stared at him, dumbfounded.

And then the dragon, finally fed up, reared back on its hind legs, crying out to the sky with a ground-shaking roar.

And everything became clear to me at once.

"Quick!" I yelled. "Get back in there! We need that hook!"

Now it was Gus's turn to look dumbfounded.

"I'm on it!" Aaron jumped and then jumped again, vaulting over the dragon's right wing. The beast twisted its neck again, hoping to take a bite out of its harasser, but Aaron had already grabbed ahold of the grappling hook and, with a grunt and a heave, pulled it out from its leathery sheath. You had to hand it to him: He may have been a show-off, but at least he had the skills to back it up.

He also, as of that moment, had nothing holding him to the dragon. There was a Wile E. Coyote stretch of seconds in which he held the hook close, looking vaguely stunned to have succeeded so easily. Then, just as the dragon lunged down to snap him up, Aaron remembered gravity, or gravity remembered Aaron, and he toppled down the back of the dragon's wing and onto the ground.

That was my cue. "We need a distraction."

"All right, Laddu," said Sammi. "Now's your turn to— Oh, wow, he's already doing it. What a pal."

The Sidekick bobbed and weaved around the dragon's snout. The dragon, diverted from its quest for an Aaron hors d'oeuvre, snapped at Laddu like a dog attempting to catch a fly but to no avail. Aaron took advantage of the moment to scramble to his feet, still clutching the grappling hook to his chest.

"Hey, Aaron!" I called. "Do you think you can muzzle that thing?"

Aaron looked from the dragon, to me, and then back to the dragon. For the first time since he'd raced onto the scene, he seemed to be feeling a flake of doubt.

"I mean," I continued, "if you think it's too *hard* . . ."

My reverse psychology scheme seemed to instantly backfire, as Aaron's jaw dropped. "Are you *patronizing* me?"

"Oh my gosh, no," I stammered. "I didn't mean—that wasn't about—"

"Dude, I'm messing with you." Aaron grinned devilishly. "Do you know how good these games are for my hand-eye coordination? Check this out."

He turned, spun the grappling hook until it was a circular blur, and then released—and I was reminded, not for the first time, that Aaron's cherubic blond curls so often threw off adults and strangers from seeing the ebullient mischief-maker who lay beneath.

Poor Laddu nearly got speared as the hook shot past, but otherwise, Aaron's aim was on point—the hook fell around the dragon's snout, swung back up, and then wrapped around and around again until the mouth of the beast was clamped firmly shut.

"Aw, man," Gus grumbled. "*I* was gonna muzzle it."

"Now," I said, ignoring this, "does anyone have anything big and sharp?"

"I do!" Gus pulled a sword from his belt, just as Aaron proclaimed "Me!" and did the same.

"Great," I said. "When the dragon reared up just now, I saw a purple patch. I think it's got a soft spot."

The others stared. The dragon swung its head this way and that, trying to free itself.

"You know," I said, "a soft spot? Like in *The Hobbit*? You pierce the soft spot, you kill the dragon. Come on, they made three movies about this. Four with the cartoon."

Gus nodded. "I trust you," he said. "If you think it'll work, I'll do it."

"I'm closer!" Aaron protested, making determined but not very effective attempts to get nearer to the squirming dragon. "I should do it!"

"You just want the points!" Gus shot back. "Let me do it!"

"Uh, guys?" Sammi said. "You know how we can all breathe

out of our noses? My big concern is, presumably, dragons can, too?"

Indeed, the dragon's nostrils had begun to glow red. Despite the heat of the baking earth around us, I suddenly felt a chill pass through me.

"Of course I want the points. At least *I* can admit it," Aaron said, brandishing his sword accusingly. "You can't admit you just want the adrenaline rush!"

Ruby rings of light blazed at the tip of the dragon's snout.

"What's that got to do with anything?" Gus took a step toward Aaron rather than the dragon. "Anyway, my sword's bigger."

The dragon, ready to make its move, reared up once more on its hind legs. A dark patch of violet flashed into view.

"Oh, for the love of— *Fine!*"

I stepped forward, grabbed Gus's sword from his hands, and ran.

It's just like going for Markus Fawkes's armpit, I told myself as I sprinted into the shadow of the dragon. *Except now Markus can breathe fire. And is about to do so. At you. With his nose. Which feels worse than the armpit. Maybe.*

"Yeah, Kara!" Sammi cheered.

"Whoa, *Kara*." That was Aaron.

"Kara!" Gus called. "Be careful!"

Somehow, this was what broke me.

"*Rrrraaghh!*"

I plunged Gus's sword deep into the dragon's soft spot. When I pulled it back out, dragon blood gushed from the wound, sizzling and spitting like acid where it hit the earth. I probably should have backed away, but instead I kept plunging the sword in, grunting wildly with every stab.

"I wouldn't! Have! To be careful! If you didn't! Skip! Our date! For this stupid! *Game!*"

With that last stab, I drove the sword in all the way to the hilt, and in doing so felt something shift. Even though the dragon towered over me and must have weighed ten tons or more, it began to tip backward like it had been pushed by some sort of Mega-Kara. The ground around me seemed to tilt, as if the whole world was shifting so I could be at a more dramatic angle. And the light, once gray and muddy, suddenly turned golden as a great and sourceless voice rang out across the plain:

"Absolute slayage! Maximum points! You win: control over dragons!"

And with all the creaking gravity of a toppling redwood, the dragon fell, slammed into the ground, and exploded into a shower of gold coins.

The ground un-tilted.

The light changed back.

I stood in front of a mountain of gold, a few fallen weapons— including Gus's sword—and a constellation of hissing puddles of dragon blood.

"Laddu?"

I turned to see Laddu, Sammi, Aaron, and Gus staring at me, jaws (and beak) wide open.

Finally, Aaron broke the silence, pumping his fists into the air.

"Way to go, Kara!" he hollered.

Sammi reached over and pulled his fists down.

"Did I—did I forget our date?" Gus asked. "Oh man. I forgot our date. I'm so sorry—we were all just so excited for the big Update, we thought maybe it would happen today, so we came here and—I must have lost track of—why didn't you say something?"

I said nothing.

"Oh, did you— Oh man. You said something." Gus put his face in his hands. "That was what the message was. I'm sorry, I totally didn't take it in. Why didn't you *call*?"

"I, uh." I crossed my arms. For some reason, I suddenly felt very silly. "I didn't want to make it a whole thing."

A light breeze caused an avalanche of gold to slide down to the back of my feet, kicking up more blood steam around me.

There was a moment of silence. Except for the sizzling.

And then, once again, despite myself, I felt it rise within me: First, a single giggle. Then a chuckle. And then it was a full-on laugh, as gold and blood pooled at my feet and the ridiculousness of the last few minutes set in. Gus, whose face had been twisted up in genuine regret, now broke out in a broad and relieved smile.

It was, as it had been since the first day we met, a terribly handsome smile. In HIVE, as in real life, Gus had a jawline you could light a match on, a lean but compact build, and dark hair just short enough for minimal maintenance (but just long enough to get charmingly mussed up due to minimal maintenance). Some in the past had called Gus "nerd hot." By "some in the past," I pretty much just mean "Sammi."

Speaking of which: Sammi must have seen an opportunity to bring things to a happy end because she chose this moment to straighten up and clap her hands.

"All right," she said, speaking in the same loud and cheerful tone one might use to address a kindergartner who has just asked why Harry the class hamster is no longer moving. "Great work, everyone. Good game? Good game. Seems like the Update's not gonna happen tonight, but maybe, uh, a regular date possibly can? Aaron, let's get out of here, huh? Sound fun?"

"The Update could still hap— *Ow*," Aaron said, in the same tone one might use if an armored boot had just stepped on one's foot. "Yes. Okay. Great. Let's go."

As she pinched her nose to leave, Sammi winked at Gus and said, "Good luck. Be careful what you say! Remember, she's got control over dragons!"

And then she was gone. Aaron, though, hesitated.

"I'm going, too," he said. "Except, uh . . ."

"Except what?" I said, breaking eye contact with Gus for the first time.

"We've all been playing for a few hours," Aaron continued,

at least having the decency to look down bashfully. "Y'know, down at the Apiary. And you know what they say about, uh, HIVEing and driving. So . . ."

I did know what they said. As far as coordination went, every hour spent in HIVE was equal to one drink of alcohol. They called it *getting buzzed*—and they called driving while buzzed a felony offense. Which meant—

"Right," I sighed. "Of course. I'm in my car right now. I'll come pick you guys up."

LEVEL 5

Aaron lived closest to the Apiary, so we dropped him off first. Next was Sammi's town house on the outskirts of Bullworth, but I found myself wishing she lived even farther away because there's no such thing as an awkward silence as long as Sammi Khanna is in your car. There's no such thing as silence, really.

"I heard Mr. Mulsoff came by Ms. Bailey's third-period class today," she said from the back seat. "Just to 'swing by.' It's like they *want* us to know. And speaking of—"

But soon enough we were pulling into her driveway. Sammi wormed her way out of the back seat—mouthing *good luck* first to me, and then to Gus, as if neither of us could see her doing it to the other—and then she was punching in the code to her garage door, and there was no one left in the car but Gus, me, and (though I may have just been imagining this part) the two-thousand-pound invisible elephant between us.

"So, uh," Gus said at last as I pulled out of Sammi's cul-de-sac and onto the main road. "Sushi? Do we think sushi sounds good?"

And honestly, it did sound good. I'd always loved the family sushi joint a few blocks from Gus's place. For one thing, their sushi reminded me of my grandmother's, which she had loved to make for us, even decades after immigrating to the States from Japan. Second, Hiro, the owners' son, was a senior at Bullworth and a family friend of the Iwatanis, and always slipped us a few extra rolls when he was working front of house. Real, nondigital food, served by real friends in a real and comfy corner booth sounded much better to me than fighting in, fighting over, or even spending one more minute thinking about HIVE.

BACK IN A MINUTE, read the handwritten sign. I'M IN HIVE.

"Well, at least he's honest," said Gus.

"I mean, presumably we'd have noticed," I said.

Hiro sprawled out in front of us, flopped over a chair he had clearly dragged from the main floor. His right cheek was squished up against the greeters' podium. His headset was strapped firmly over his eyes. His mouth was open and, yes, definitely drooling.

"C'mon, let's seat ourselves," Gus said, stepping carefully over Hiro's feet and heading for our usual booth, which was currently unoccupied—along with every other booth in the restaurant.

"Where are his parents?" I said, glancing toward the kitchen as I grabbed two menus. "Where's *anyone*?"

Gus took one of the menus and examined it carefully, which was odd, as I knew that both of us knew this menu back to front.

"I mean," Gus said sheepishly, still not making eye contact, "everyone's probably waiting for . . ."

"The Update," I sighed, pinching the bridge of my nose. "Of course. Hold on a second."

"Hello! Welcome to HIVE. How may we help—"

"Send message to HiroOfTheWeek," I said. "'Hey, California rolls, please.'"

There was a *Bzzzz*, and then there was a pause, and then across the room there was cursing and the *thump* of a headset being detached so quickly that it smacked into the podium.

"Hey, guys! Sorry! California rolls coming right up!"

Gus laughed, and I cracked at least part of a smile as Hiro dashed across the dining floor and disappeared into the kitchen.

Leaving us alone, once again, in a quiet room.

A very quiet room.

It seemed like the elephant had come in from the car and joined us in the corner booth.

"So, about the—" I began, at the exact same time as Gus said, "I'm *so* sorry."

"You don't have to be sorry!" I said quickly. "You already said you were sorry! So we're fine."

"You were just about to say something un-fine!"

"You don't know that!" I protested. "I was just going to say—uh . . ." My brain raced for something fine to say. "I had the *weirdest* conversation with Jason Alcorn today."

"Okay, one, Jason Alcorn doesn't have conversations,"

Gus said. "Second, I know you, Kara. And I know you have a problem with HIVE, which is fair, especially because of your mo—"

"I don't want to talk about that," I interjected. "And I *don't* have a *problem* with HIVE. I just— You're smart, Gus. Really smart. And forgetting our date—our weekly, standing date—feels . . ."

"You're looking for a nicer word than 'stupid'?" Gus suggested.

"If you know any, that'd be really helpful," I admitted.

Gus laughed again, and again, I felt some of the tension inside me melt away.

Or maybe that was just the elephant shifting in its seat.

"I don't know," Gus said. "I think, in some ways, I may be pretty stupid. Like, did you see me get wrecked by that dragon?"

I winced and suddenly found that I, too, was very interested in the menu.

"Yeah, but that wouldn't have happened if I hadn't been there to surprise you," I said. "I always have to stick my nose in things. Just like you're always telling me."

"Correct." Gus smiled. "And I love that about you. But wait, why are we blaming you for things now? I thought we were mad at me."

"I'm not mad," I said, still looking at the menu.

"Then why," Gus said, still smiling, "are your cheeks turning so red? Why would you say you're not—"

"Because I don't want to be mad at you!" I slapped the menu down on the table with a laminated *thwack*. "I don't want to have an argument!"

"She argued," Gus deadpanned. "Madly."

Finally, I looked Gus right in the face. In his stupid, smart, handsome face.

"I don't want to argue with you," I said. "Because in arguments there are winners and there are losers, and if we're winning or losing, then we're not really hanging out together. We're just playing another game. Like we're still in HIVE."

Gus held my gaze, his smile slowly fading.

"Which I still don't have a problem with," I added.

"Uh," said Hiro, looming over us awkwardly. "Hey, guys. California rolls?"

After a truly ridiculous number of rolls had been placed on the table—a silent apology to go with all the audible ones Hiro offered—Gus topped a roll with wasabi, popped it in his mouth, and regarded me thoughtfully while he chewed.

"Can't it be both things?" he asked eventually. "I mean, playing a game can be hanging out. It *is* hanging out. And who says we have to win or lose whatever we're playing? Look at *Family Feudalism*. That's an open-ended game. No winners, no losers, just players. Really, my favorite games are the ones you can't win."

I paused, chopsticks halfway to my mouth.

"Just so I'm clear on this," I said slowly, "you're comparing our relationship to a game you can never win?"

"Oh. Ah. I." Gus squirmed in his seat. "It seemed cute at the time?"

I shot a look over at the other side of the restaurant. Hiro was already back inside HIVE. We were, more or less, alone in the room.

"Okay," I said, putting down my sushi roll. "Look. I get it. I play HIVE games, too."

"Sure, like *The Skims: Mind Your Manors*," Gus supplied helpfully.

"Right," I said. (We'll get to it!) "And those games are open-ended, too. And pretty addictive. So I understand, and I don't want you thinking I'm, like, sensitive about it. But . . ."

"But you *are* sensitive about it," Gus cut in. "And that's okay! It makes sense! Because . . ."

I knew in that moment exactly where Gus was going, and I did *not* want to let him get there.

"Because the whole world's obsessed with HIVE?" I asked. "Because the bookstores are all closing down, because no one wants to read anymore when they could just play the first-person shooter version of *Les Mis*?" (Okay, I'd played it. It was awesome. Moving on.) "Because Dad has to spend all day inside a HIVE office, because digital real estate is cheaper for businesses, so Kyle and I have to cook for him every night cuz he's too buzzed to walk? Because my *boyfriend* and my *friends* totally lose track of our *date ni—*"

"No! Because of your *mom!*" Gus blurted. "It's okay, Kara! It's okay to talk about it! It totally sucks that she left you guys, but that's not HIVE's fault, and it sucks that I wasn't there today, but I'm not her! I love you, Kara, and I'd never— *Oh*."

I had squeezed my chopsticks so hard that a roll had exploded between them, spattering rice and avocado all over the table. Something somewhere far back in my head reminded me of the dragon exploding into a thousand gold coins.

"I mean, oh, shoot, Kara. I didn't mean to imply that your mom, like, didn't love you, I— Oh, that's not— I just meant— Look, do you want help with that, or—"

Woof. Okay. Let's talk about this.

It had happened six months after the December day with the headsets, and just a few weeks after the release of the BrainSTIM Card. I had come downstairs on a bright summer morning and found Dad sitting alone at the breakfast table. That wasn't unusual—Kyle tended to sleep in, and this was well before Dad's job was relocated to a corporate Apiary, so I was used to seeing him relax around the house most mornings before work.

Not like Mom, who hadn't been around half as much recently. In the months since she had brought those head-sets home, my mother had become convinced that this crazy HIVE startup was about to take off, and that she had to be there when it did. Which it did. Soon she was rushing from coding marathons to tech expos, working around the clock with Eric Alanick and the other biggest names in virtual real-ity to stay one step ahead of the world's ravenous demand for

HIVE. And ever since the BrainSTIM Card came out and changed the game, I was more likely to see my mom on the news than at home.

It thrilled me, watching interviewers stick microphones in Mom's face and ask something inane about stock prices or sales numbers, only to be met with one of Mom's highly passionate, completely incomprehensible rants about software patches and immersive reality theory. Sometimes it seemed like Mom had an easier time talking about virtual reality than actual reality, and as someone who was used to hearing these disquisitions over the dinner table, I loved watching someone else have to try to keep up. Sure, I missed having her around all the time; Dad was great but didn't know the right ratio of butter to peanut butter in a butter-and-peanut-butter sandwich, the way Mom did. But if it meant she could be recognized publicly as the amazing woman she was, then I was proud to be a part of that exchange. I was happy to stand back and watch Mom go.

But that day, when Dad looked up from the table, some part of me had known right away, somehow, that the exchange had gone wrong. Mom had gone too far.

For one thing, my father, the most stoic man in the world, had red rings around his eyes.

For another, there was the note.

She hadn't left the note on the table. Years later, that was still the worst part.

She had left the note in HIVE.

To Robert, and to Kyle, and to Kara,

I'm sorry to leave so abruptly, but something has come up at work. In fact, things have been coming up at work for a long time now, and it seems certain that things are going to come up more and more in the future. I'm sure you all have noticed: Balancing the demands of home and HIVE these past few months has been hard. I pray you all believe me: Writing this note is harder. I don't know how long it'll be until you see me again; I just know that I need some time to give all of myself to this work. That way, someday, I can give all of myself to all of you. I pray that day is soon, and I pray you understand.

I love you.

As it turned out, none of Mom's prayers came true.

If it had been anyone else, it might not have seemed possible. But Mom really was that passionate, and HIVE really had gotten that big. And sure enough, she made good on her word. She didn't come back to the house that evening, or the next day, or the day after that, and soon it became clear: The woman who'd always had one foot in the world of technology had just upped it to two feet, and then some.

Because she hadn't just left her family to focus on her work; she had left everyone else, too. She stopped wasting time on interviews or even polite appearances at public fundraisers and showy sales panels. In short, she disappeared, and most of HIVE's top team of programmers did as well, becoming invisible just as HIVE itself became increasingly inescapable. Only Eric Alanick, it seemed, remained willing to deign us unwashed masses with public appearances, and even then, he only did it rarely, and you always got the sense that he'd rather have been hidden away like all the rest of his friends. His fleeting appearances at tech conferences and investor meetings merely fueled his sense of mystique and added to the world's hunger to know more about him. Rumors spread around him like viruses through source code: He slept in a HIVE chamber. He was secretly married to an incredibly advanced Sidekick. He was actually a vampire (this one didn't have any HIVE twist to it; the guy was just handsome and pale).

It wasn't long until the only time you heard about HIVE architects other than Eric—that was to say, architects like Mom—was when new updates were released. If you scrolled all the way to the bottom of the patch notes, you could find the names of the coders involved, written in the smallest font imaginable.

For a while, I scoured these notes obsessively. Sometimes I felt like a one-person bomb squad, sweeping for an explosive, except that whenever I found my target—the name "Kimi Swift," attached with terrible nonchalance to the end of a long and dry document—the bomb would go off immediately, and

I would be filled with an explosion's worth of emotions: excitement, sadness, anger, confusion, and still, terribly, way deep down, the smallest spark of pride.

But that spark got smaller and smaller, and HIVE got bigger and bigger, and eventually updates stopped crediting individual coders—I guess there were just too many minds involved in HIVE for credits to be feasible. And then a year went by, and another, and another, and I came to accept that I had lost my last connection to my mother.

But please, don't start going all "Oh, poor Kara" on me. I gained other things along the way, after all. Gus, for example. And a sense of perspective.

Because of course I didn't have a problem with HIVE. Why would I? If I wasn't so busy cleaning up rice and seaweed, I would have told Gus this: I didn't blame HIVE for the monster it had become, demanding my attention, my time, my patience, and my mother.

That would be ridiculous.

I blamed Mom.

I blamed Mom when Gus apologetically offered to walk himself home from the sushi restaurant, seeming to think I wanted to be alone in the car with a two-thousand-pound elephant.

I blamed Mom when I got home and found Dad passed out on the couch, with a microwave meal sitting on the carpet below him—a sure sign he was incapacitated from another day in HIVE.

And I blamed Mom when I crawled under the covers that night, too exhausted from a day of dragon slaying to finish *Pride and Prejudice.*

But as I drifted off to sleep, I thought about all the other people in the world right now, tossing in their beds, waiting for the big Update. And I realized I really couldn't judge them.

Because I also prayed that somebody could update my life.

As it turned out, all my prayers were about to come true.

LEVEL 6

The next morning started with the sun shining through my window and a fire burning in my belly.

It was the fire—no—the *blaze* of purpose. The morning was beautiful. My boyfriend was rash, but very sweet. My mother was terrible. I would not let that last fact ruin the first two facts. Life was not a game, but I was going to *win*.

I sprang from my bed and began preparing for the day with an intensity and eagerness almost unheard of in teenagers before eight a.m. Before long, I was tying up my braid, tucking my book under my arm, and slipping on my favorite black boots.

They had once belonged to Mom.

No. No! I did *not* have time for this. I pulled the laces so tight my toes scrunched, and then bounded out the door. I did not have *angst*; I did not have *backstory*; I had only a *future*, in which I thrived, and told my boyfriend I forgave him, and loved him, and would even join him in HIVE on the day of the big Update to show how totally cool and angstless I was.

Which meant I also had a future in which I took the bus. Dad was working overtime today, and I never drove if I knew

I'd be spending more than an hour in HIVE. Luckily for me, there was a bus stop right at the end of my street. Of course, there was a bus stop at the end of just about everyone's street these days. Eric Alanick must've had some powerful friends, because right around the time folks started getting buzzed on a daily basis, buses and food delivery programs started receiving a *lot* more government funding. As a result, all I had to do to get into town on this glorious day was stroll through the crisp morning sunshine, pull up at my usual spot on the bench, open my book, and wait.

And wait.

And wait a little bit more.

And eventually look up from my book and scan down the street, wondering how much longer I was going to have to wait.

Don't get me wrong. I love having time to just sit somewhere and read (we have discussed this). But the bus had never taken this long to arrive before, and if I sat and read any more, I was going to run into every bookworm's worst nightmare: finishing the book I was reading without having a new one on hand.

And that wasn't all. Now that my fire and/or blaze had been given some time to cool down, something about the morning felt . . . off.

I just didn't know what. The weather was perfect; another in a string of cloudless fall days, cool enough not to sweat but warm enough not to shiver. My street looked normal—like, aggressively normal, with piles of obsessively raked leaves in every yard and funny little faces painted on the mailboxes. And somewhere in the distance, as always, the soft sound of . . .

Nothing.

That was it. That was what was off: the volume. Instead of cars purring down the nearest county highway or kids yelling in unseen backyards, there was just nothing at all, as if someone had hit a mute button for the entire world.

I didn't realize I was holding my breath until a bird tweeted once into the silence, at which point I gasped, jumped two feet in the air, and fell from the bench onto the ground.

This seemed like a pretty clear sign that I had lost control of the plot. I needed to regain some of that momentum I'd felt upon waking, with or without a bus to help me—and it seemed pretty clear it was going to be without, since it didn't sound like a single vehicle was on the move in Bullworth today. So I stood up, brushed a few leaves off my butt, and set off down the road into town. I was still in control of my destiny; I would just have to walk a little to reach it. It was still a beautiful day; there just happened to be some slightly creepy vibes afoot, if you cared to notice them.

Okay, maybe the vibes were more than slight. As I reached the outskirts of my neighborhood, I kept expecting to hear something—I wasn't sure what, exactly, but *anything* would have made more sense than this endless hush. There should have been trucks rolling by, or music pouring out of open windows. But the only things I could hear were the occasional calls of the birds that hadn't flown south for the year, and the crunching of leaves under my boots. *Did everyone* else *die*, some part of my brain thought, *or just you? Where* is *everyone?*

Well, I mean, obviously I had a hunch. It just wasn't the kind of hunch I wanted to think about right now. But as I approached the main road into town, I have to admit I started to walk a little faster.

Then I saw the pillar of smoke, and my walk turned into a run.

As I ran, the pillar became a plume, roiling and black. For a terrible moment, I had a clear image of the dragon I'd slain yesterday, having somehow escaped into the real world and lying in wait just around the corner to catch me in a rematch. Then I turned onto the main road and discovered something much worse.

There, smoke billowing from its crumpled hood, was a bus that had veered off the road and into a streetlight.

See, it's good you didn't catch the bus after all, thought a distinctly unhelpful part of my brain. The rest of me concentrated on running as fast as I could toward the crash. Since there was absolutely no one else in sight, it was up to me to check if there was anyone still inside.

Which, again: unfortunate. We've established that I'm not the tallest heroine around, so even as I hopped over the curb and ran along the half of the bus that had ended up on the sidewalk, I didn't have the best view through the high windows. That said, the shapes flashing by above me looked distressingly like the prone forms of passengers. By the time I reached the front doors, my eyes were watering from the fumes, but when I leaned up against the glass and squinted through the smoke, I was able to make out a driver slumped over the steering wheel, as if she had just decided to take a short nap between stops.

"Hey! Come on! Wake up!" I yelled, banging my fists on the doors. "Please!"

Maybe it was my asking nicely, or maybe it was the particularly hard *thwack* I gave the bus door just then. Whatever it was, as a thick belch of smoke rolled up from the hood, the bus driver's head jerked up with a start. There was blood dripping down her face, and her features screwed up in confusion as she looked forward into a world that must have been pure black with streaks of red.

"Hey!" I shouted again, and she turned and saw me. If she was confused before, she was entirely lost now, but she opened the bus doors and I stumbled inside, wrapping my arm around her to help her out of her seat.

"Come on!" I said. "We gotta go before this thing goes— I mean—is it going to explode? I don't actually know how buses . . ."

I stopped speaking then—one, because I was panic babbling, and two, because I had looked up into the mirror over the bus driver's seat.

Behind me, there was a passenger in every single seat of

the bus. Well, not every seat—some riders had been flung out of their seats when the bus crashed; still others had been slammed into walls. Almost every one of them was wearing a HIVE headset.

And absolutely none of them were moving.

"Are they . . ." I began, frozen in shock. It was now the bus driver's turn to push me toward the door.

"I don't know," she said, hustling us down the steps and onto the grass. While I'd been staring at the chilling tableau of bodies, she'd grabbed a plastic jug from under the dashboard, and now she ripped at the safety cap with her teeth. A drop of blood fell from her forehead and spattered onto her uniform's name tag: Sheila.

"But should we get them out?" I asked helplessly. "I mean, is the bus going to explode?"

"No," Sheila said, spitting the cap onto the sidewalk and striding around the front of the bus. "The engine is just over-heating. But smoke inhalation is still very bad."

She popped the hood, releasing a mushroom cloud of fumes into the air, which seemed like a weird way to not inhale smoke. But as she wheezed and waved away the smog, she tilted the jug into the reservoir, and bright blue coolant poured out into the engine, turning smoke into hissing steam.

Sheila spoke as she poured. "I was driving," she said, "and everyone was on their headsets. Which isn't that unusual. But it can get creepy when it's *everyone*, you know?"

I did know. More than once, I'd stepped onto a bus where almost every passenger was staring into a void, getting in a quick HIVE session during their commute.

"The intercom's hooked into HIVE, so normally they know when to get their stop," Sheila continued, pushing the jug up to empty it out. "But today, I noticed we were making great time. I mean, *too* great. No one had asked to get off in a few stops. And no one had gotten on, either. I looked in the mirror and saw what you saw—no one moving. Like they couldn't be bothered to get out of HIVE. Hey, call nine one one."

She added this to me almost as an afterthought, as the last drops of coolant trickled out and she tossed the jug onto the grass. While I fumbled frantically through my pocket for my phone, Sheila scrubbed the blood away from her eyes and looked out at the road.

"So just as I'm wondering what *that's* all about," she continued, "this *maniac* comes swerving down the road. So I think he's totally buzzed, and I swerve out of the way, but we're talking a totally out-of-control vehicle here, so I have to swerve *again*. And we go off the road, and next thing I know, you're knocking at the door. Any luck?"

"It's ringing," I said. Now that the smoke had dissipated, I could see what I hadn't noticed earlier: another car, farther down the road, also up on the sidewalk. As the phone rang for the eighth or ninth time at the 911 control center, I started to wonder if maybe they were getting an unusually high number of calls today.

"Good." Sheila crossed back to the side of the bus and

peered up through the doors. "You tell 'em to come here when you get 'em on the line. I'm gonna boot up, see if I can't send a message to our sleeping beauties through the intercom."

For some reason, this plan set off alarm bells in my head. But before I could open my mouth and say something, Sheila reached up and pinched the bridge of her nose.

There was a moment in which she looked at me and smiled, rolling her eyes good-naturedly at the inevitable few seconds of lag as HIVE booted up.

And then Sheila's eyes kept rolling, all the way back into her head, until they were totally white. With a soft exhale, she fell forward onto the bus steps, as limp and motionless as all her passengers.

"Sheila!" I cried, rushing toward her and putting my free hand on her neck. She had a pulse, but it fluttered frantically—pounded, really, as if she was awake and agitated rather than totally unconscious.

This was when I realized the phone had been ringing for more than a minute.

More than a couple of minutes, come to think of it. And it wasn't a busy signal, as it would have been if my earlier theory had been correct. Just an endless, unanswered ringing.

In that moment, I had a chilling vision. Let's say you were an emergency dispatcher who got a call about a HIVE-related emergency, and then two calls, and then three. And let's say you finally said, "Okay, let's just boot into HIVE real quick and see what's going on."

And let's say you really shouldn't have done that. And now you were just lying there, unmoving, in an emergency call center where the phone would just keep ringing, and ringing, and ringing, as the emergencies piled up in the world outside.

Assuming, that is, that there was anyone else left out there to be getting into emergencies.

Slowly, hands shaking, I pressed the red icon on my phone screen and lowered it back into my pocket. I stepped gingerly out into the middle of the road, looking left and then right, and seeing nothing beyond the wrecked vehicles around me. In no time at all, that terrible silence had flooded back into the morning.

Had I finally become the only person in the world not inside HIVE?

The answer presented itself very quickly.

I heard the roar before I saw it, but only just barely: A car, old and battered and veering erratically, tore around the corner and sped down the road—toward me. *We're talking a totally out-of-control vehicle here*, Sheila had said, and now I understood what she'd meant. The driver, if there was one, seemed two steps past buzzed, maybe even *actually* buzzed (though that didn't seem likely—in a post-HIVE world, being addicted to an actual physical substance was pretty retro). Whatever it was, the car's path was totally unpredictable. I leaped to the right, but the car just swerved to match. I almost feinted left, but the car was already going left, so in a split-second decision I just froze, standing statue still and throwing my hands over my face as the car took one more hard turn, spun out, and whirled past me like a poorly skipped stone.

There was a crash, and then there was just blood rushing in my ears.

And then I turned around and realized that wasn't blood I was hearing but water, gushing from where the car had crashed right into a fire hydrant.

Ten minutes ago, I would have run toward the car, desperate to help the driver out. Now I just sighed and made my weary way over, preparing to be met with another headset zombie.

Then the door to the driver's seat flew open.

I came to a halt with a few yards to go. A hand emerged, grabbing at the top of the door, and then another hand. A foot stepped onto the street, wobbling like a newborn calf, and the driver's voice gasped and cracked with the strain of pulling themselves up and out of the car.

And I knew that sound.

"Jason?!" I cried as Jason Alcorn heaved himself up onto the door of the car. He was paler than ever, and blood trickled down his forehead as he looked from me to the bus and then back to me again.

"Kara?!" he said, which, all things considered, seemed understandable.

"What—what's happening?" I asked. "What's going on?"

Jason looked down, considering either my question or his wobbling legs or the water from the fire hydrant that was now flooding past his feet.

When he looked up again, a chill ran down my spine, and then all the way back up again, as if a pulse had boomeranged from my BrainSTIM Card.

"The world is collapsing," Jason said. "The Update is here."

And then he fell into the water.

LEVEL 7

Maneuvering an incapacitated teenage boy into the passenger seat of a smashed-up car should probably not have been as easy as it was just then, but two things worked in my favor. Thing one: years of helping Dad get upstairs after he'd spent a long weekend shift in HIVE. Thing two: Jason didn't weigh half as much as Dad, even soaking wet.

Which, to be clear, he was. His teeth were chattering as I buckled his seat belt for him. A combination of exhaustion, digitally induced wooziness, and gushing hydrant water had left him a shivering wreck.

"Do you have, like, a blanket back there?" I asked, peering over his shoulder. "We gotta get you warm. Or a— Oh, wow."

He had more than a blanket. There appeared to be a whole bedspread stretched across the back seat, and that wasn't all: Toothpaste. Wrinkled shirts. Multiple generations of HIVE headsets. And a bottle of dry shampoo, with the plastic seal still across the top.

"Jason . . ." Even after all the crazy things that had happened today, this sight robbed me of words. "Have you been . . ."

"I d-don't need you j-judging me," Jason shiver-snapped. I recoiled instinctively, like he was a dog who'd tried to bite me, but when I saw the look on his face, watching me, I felt instant guilt. Probably no one wants to be thought of like a rabid dog.

"Oh my God. I'm not judging you," I said truthfully. "I mean, my own car is a total— Well, that's not the point. The point is I'm trying to help you. *Again*." Before Jason could protest further, I reached past him and pulled a rumpled cotton blanket from the back seat, wiping at his hair a bit and then draping the rest around his shivering torso. He didn't say thank you or anything, but he didn't try to stop me, either, so I counted this as progress. Shutting the passenger door, I circled the car and got into the driver's seat.

"First things first," I said, turning the keys he had left in the ignition. "We're taking you to the hospital."

"Wrong," Jason said. Well, progress was fun while it lasted.

"Oh, pardon me," I said as the engine kicked and whined and eventually groaned to life. "I didn't realize there was already a game plan. Any chance you can show me a copy, or is *Step One: Dying of Hypothermia* secret advanced-level knowledge?"

"That's n-not the game plan." Jason looked pointedly out the window, away from me. "But the hospital is the wrong move. They can't help us anymore. Plus, I'm not dying, just buzzed. *Plus*, I can't afford it."

He spat this last part, like he was daring me to laugh about it. But it was his first point—*they can't help us anymore*—that really jumped out at me. Again I thought of the phones ringing endlessly at the call center, and again I shuddered.

"Okay," I said, pulling onto the road carefully; Jason's left-side mirror had been snapped clean off during his dramatic entrance. "Fair. But where *are* we going? And, Jason, what's *happening* right now?"

Finally, Jason turned to look at me again, and even with my eyes on the road I could feel him scanning me up and down, like he was sizing me up, deciding which difficulty level he thought I could play at.

"The Apiary," he said finally. "There's nowhere else to go."

I nodded. My knuckles whitened on the wheel as I realized: Before he'd even mentioned the Apiary, I'd already decided we were going there, too.

For a moment, there was just the ticking of the turn signal. Then, as if his personal server was processing at a delay, Jason finally seemed to hear my second question.

"Okay," he said. "You know I spend a lot of time in HIVE, right?"

"Duh," I said. "That's like your whole thing. Apparently. Though why I had to find that out from Markus Fawkes, when you and I used to—"

"Focus," Jason said. "So I'm in there today. I mean, I'm in there every day, but today I have an extra reason to be there, and so does everyone else. The Honeycomb is *packed*—you know, the main loading area with all the platforms?"

"I know what the Honeycomb is," I said, bristling. *My mom helped code it*, I almost added, but Jason *definitely* hadn't unlocked that secret advanced-level knowledge.

"All right, whatever, I don't know what terms Normals do and don't know," Jason said, and for the second day in a row he made the word sound like a slur. "Anyway, everyone's there. The Normals, the Casuals, the Moddies, the Trolls—I've never seen it this crowded. Everyone wanted to be there when the big Update dropped."

That was another thing Jason said differently—to him, the word *Update* had a pop to it, the way Digicast preachers said the word *Rapture* in their iSermons.

"Okay," I said. "So then what happened— *Augh!*"

I swerved suddenly to avoid a man's body. He was just lying in the road, staring into nothingness, much the same way Sheila had. And he wasn't alone; the farther we got into town, the more the creep vibe rose from abandoned ghost town to apocalyptic wreck. People were strewn across the sidewalks; we passed a car parked on the side of the road with two children in the back seat, each strapped into their headsets, neither moving.

"That happened. That was the Update," Jason said. He said it with astounding calm, and I realized then that he'd been driving from this direction, meaning he'd witnessed this entire spook show already.

"At first I noticed a few people in the Honeycomb getting kind of weird. I thought they were just annoyed because it was so crowded, but when I came down into the crowd, I realized it was different. Worse."

I frowned. "Came down from where?" I asked. The higher you went in the Honeycomb, the harder the games got—and frankly, weirder, littered with the cultish, intense games that appealed mostly to the true HIVE diehards. "What do you do in HIVE, anyway?"

Jason ignored me and pressed on. "There was this woman who was yelling, saying she'd tried to log off just for a second to let out her dog or something—but she couldn't. Log off. Like, at all. And other people were saying the same thing. Which was a little weird, but, y'know, whatever, I figured it just meant the Update was about to drop and things were buffering. I thought people were being totally Normal for freaking out, and I tried telling them to calm down, but there were too many of them, and a lot of them didn't speak English.

"So then this guy appears on a loading platform next to me looking totally stunned. He says he was just standing in his kitchen, trying to boot up to message his wife, because she wasn't responding—and now he's logged all the way in and can't log back out. That's when the numbers really start climbing—dozens, hundreds, thousands of new people, all doing the same thing, all having the same problem. They were all getting stuck in HIVE while trying to see why their friends were stuck in HIVE. That's when people *really* started to panic."

A memory came unbidden to me: how fast and hard Sheila's heart had been beating, even though she had seemed to be unconscious. No wonder; HIVE must have been an absolute madhouse right now. I thought of everyone who might have been in there this morning, just waiting for the Update: My brother. Sammi and Aaron. Gus, who— Oh no, Gus, whose last conversation with me had been a dumb fight about HIVE.

And Dad, who was working today.

And what had Jason just said? *Not all of them spoke English?* This wasn't just happening in Bullworth. This was the whole world.

I swallowed back the bile of fear. Worrying wouldn't help anyone.

"So the Update is glitching," I deduced. "Or it needs a repatch. That happens sometimes, right? For a few minutes?" I remembered Gus telling me once about a buggy Update that had, for a memorable moment, turned everyone bright blue until some genius coder had whipped up a quick fix.

I also remembered wondering if that genius had been Mom.

"It does happen," Jason admitted. "But like you said— for minutes at the most. If I'm estimating right, the Update dropped around nine fifteen Eastern Virtual Time this morning. It's been hours since then—and when I left, there hadn't been any announcement from the staff. No 'We apologize for the inconvenience' from Eric Alanick. Nothing. That's how I knew—"

"*Wait* a second." Finally, I realized the million-dollar question, and wondered how I hadn't gotten there earlier. "When you *left*? If everyone's stuck in HIVE, how did *you* get out?"

Jason looked away again, out the windshield.

"I spend a *lot* of time in HIVE. There's things I know about that not everyone knows." He darted his eyes sideways toward me. "Like a back door."

He fell silent after this. He seemed to think that he had given me a satisfying answer, and now that I had learned this deep and meaningful secret, I would have no further questions.

He also seemed to be insane.

"*What* back door?!" I asked. "Like a cheat code? Didn't you say there were no cheat codes in HIVE? Could other people use the door? Can we help them? Are you just screwing with me? Where the heck were you going when you were driving like a maniac? Where were you coming from? Where have you *been* lately? How—"

"We're here."

We were there. I'd gotten so caught up in Jason's story that I'd hardly noticed as I drove us into the Apiary parking lot.

It was, predictably, crowded. The Apiary was always the most popular spot in its little strip mall, but today cars stretched from one side of the lot all the way to the other, and somehow, I didn't think they were here for the deals at Ramy's Mediterranean Grill.

"People were *really* pumped for this Update, huh?" My gaze swiveled back and forth as we looped through the aisles. Was Gus's car here? Was my brother's? "I don't know how we're going to find a spot."

"I really, *really* don't think it matters," Jason said.

"Oh. Right." I gave up and double-parked in front of someone's truck. "I guess the apocalypse has perks. Now, about this back door— Hey!"

Jason's seat belt was unbuckled before the car had even come to a full stop, and as I scrambled to turn off the engine, he was already forcing his way out the door. I hopped out to chase after him, but he was clearly still a little buzzed because he was more or less limping his way toward the Apiary. This put me in the novel position of chasing someone by wrapping an arm around their shoulders and helping them hobble across the sidewalk.

"You still haven't answered any of my questions," I said. "So people are stuck in HIVE, but you know a way out? If that's true, shouldn't we tell someone? That could help a lot, right? Should we tell, like, the government?"

"No!" Jason gasped the word, and I didn't think it was just because he was winded. This line of questioning seemed to bring out a feral quality in him, something breathless and twitchy.

"No, it wouldn't help?" I asked. "Or no, we shouldn't tell the government?"

"Both," he said, turning to face me. "The back door is . . . compromised. I went through it, yes, but it wasn't like when I've used it before. It was like something popped. And now I can't get back in."

"You tried to go back in?" I couldn't believe it.

"I *need* to go back in." And with the way Jason looked at me as he said it, I found that this, I *could* believe.

"And as for the government," he continued, "half of them are in HIVE at any given time. More, if you count the ones who . . . actually matter."

"I wasn't about to speed-dial the CIA," I said, trying not to visibly roll my eyes, which was difficult, as Jason's face was *very* close to mine. This was a crackpot conspiracy that just wouldn't die—the idea of HIVE as a shadowy spy's paradise, where you could conduct top-secret international meetings instantaneously, with no risk of getting poisoned or bugged, and no need to look like your real self.

Jason, for the record, had no qualms about rolling his eyes right in front of me.

"Those aren't the people I was talking about," he said. "But they wouldn't help, either."

But before I could ask who in the world he *could* be talking about, he turned forward again and said, "Help me push."

Together, we opened the heavy double doors and stepped into the Bullworth Apiary.

Well, into the lobby, anyway. I'd been here just last night to pick up Gus and Co., and as far as I could tell, nothing was different; it was still a cross between a dentist's waiting room and a laser tag holding pen (back from before HIVE had come along and made laser tag redundant). Leather banquette couches stretched around a small semicircular den, where patient parents or very cool, understanding significant others (like yours truly) could wait to pick up their beloved gamers. The lighting was dim, swathing us in darkness with flashes of yellow and black-cherry red. It was all meant to inspire a sense of excitement and anticipation, aided by screens that flashed little slogans like EVERYONE BELONGS IN HIVE or GAME ON, AND ON, AND ON, which someone who had a problem with HIVE (like *not* yours truly) might have found slightly creepy.

What was undeniably creepy, though, was that the screens were currently *still* flashing those slogans—as opposed to, for instance, something like SORRY FOR ACCIDENTALLY ABDUCTING EVERYONE YOU KNOW; WE'LL FIX THAT ASAP. On top of that, despite all the cars and bodies we had seen outside, these screens were flashing for a totally empty waiting room. I'd expected to see kids splayed over the couches, or even an employee slumped across the counter, like Hiro at the sushi place, but it seemed like absolutely everyone had been in the actual gaming chambers when the Update went down.

Well, no matter. We'd get them out soon, and then we'd—well,

I wasn't sure what we'd do next, but we'd do *something*. The only thing keeping me from going nuts right now was my determination to help.

"They must have them packed two to a chamber in there," Jason mused, limping away from me toward the left side of the lobby. "There's no way this place could normally fit everyone parked out there, even with all those extra units we shipped in."

"Hey, the chambers are through this door over here," I said. "You're going the wrong— Wait, *we?*"

Jason fixed me with that same look from yesterday in Mr. Teigen's classroom—that *you poor fool, you are so far from understanding* look—and then pushed his way through a door marked EMPLOYEES ONLY.

As I hurried after Jason, following him into a disheveled break room, everything finally began to fall into place. No wonder Jason knew so much about HIVE: He *worked* here.

"Jason, this is great!" I said. "I didn't realize this was your job! Have you gotten in touch with anyone else in the company? Maybe they can tell us what's going on, and we can—"

"They can't help us."

He said it offhandedly, not even looking at me as he made his way through the clutter of the break room toward some filing cabinets. But despite that—or maybe precisely because of that—I finally ran out of patience. I couldn't just keep following Jason like some confused puppy; I planted my feet in the middle of the room and crossed my arms.

"Okay, Jason," I said. "So according to you, the hospital can't help us. The government can't help us. And the people behind HIVE can't help us fix—let me remind you—*the thing that is wrong with HIVE*. Why did we even come back here, then? Why don't I just go home?"

This got Jason to turn around just long enough to look at me.

"I thought *you* wanted to help," he said.

"Of course I do!" I threw my hands in the air. "But according to you, that's not going to be possible!"

"Oh, it's possible." Jason turned back around and started fiddling with something between the filing cabinets. "It's just that I'm the only person who can tell you how to do it."

"And why should I believe you, Jason? I've saved your butt *twice* now. In two days! So you work at HIVE—big whoop. I know a lot more about HIVE than you think I do, not that you ever bothered to ask. What makes you think you're so special? What plan could you possibly have that no other HIVE employee could come up with already themselves? And what . . . is that?"

I'd wound up following him after all—albeit only so I could harangue him from up close—and as I approached, I'd seen what was sandwiched between the two filing cabinets: another door, smaller and unmarked, which Jason had just now unlocked.

He swung it open and flipped a light switch on the other side of the door.

"Now do you believe me?" he asked. "That I'm your best shot?"

And in that moment, I couldn't help it—my jaw dropped.

And I believed.

LEVEL 8

If the break room had been disheveled, this room looked like it had never even been heveled to begin with. Comic books and old HIVE instruction manuals were strewn across the floor in equal measure. Someone had pushed a cracked mirror up against the far corner of the room, which wasn't actually that far—the walls were close and the ceiling was low, and from the middle of the ceiling dangled a single unguarded light bulb, which flickered on and off like a firefly having a fit. As I took a step into the room, I accidentally kicked an empty Big Slurp cup. It was like someone had taken the back of Jason's car and turned it into an entire room.

When I saw the mattress on the floor, rising up out of lone socks and cheeseburger wrappers, the truth finally hit me. This room wasn't a bigger version of Jason's car; Jason's car was a smaller version of this room. It was a satellite, something sent out to orbit the mother ship when Jason couldn't be near his home.

Because this *was* his home.

"You don't just work for HIVE," I said slowly. "You live here. In the Apiary. How did I not know about this?"

Jason had been watching me carefully, and even in the

flickering light I could see the mix of emotions in his eyes: the vulnerability; the fear of showing someone something he'd never showed before; and at the same time, the fierce, defensive pride.

"Mr. Wamengatch isn't so hot on people knowing about the arrangement," he said, bending down to pick up what looked to be a state-of-the-art headset. "He runs this franchise. Well, he *owns* this franchise—I run it, really." And there was the pride, the swell of the painfully skinny chest. "I stay here overnight. I make sure the cooling vents are always running. And I know all the little tricks for each chamber that the seasonal employees never remember, and the secrets inside HIVE that they never even find out. And in return Mr. Wamengatch lets me live here, rent free, and I get to spend as much time in HIVE as I want."

He paused, and one of his hands brushed, almost unconsciously, against the back of his neck—the spot where everyone's BrainSTIM Card was buried.

"Until now," he said.

He fell quiet. The only sound was the buzz of the light bulb. I realized he was waiting for me to say something. And not just something—the right thing. This was a very important moment. Once again, Jason was looking at me like a jittery animal, but now, seeing the depth of his relationship with HIVE, I finally believed he was the only person who might have some idea what to do in this situation. I couldn't afford to scare him away.

"It's a pretty good setup," I said, looking around the room. "But, I mean . . . not perfect."

Jason cocked his head at me. His grip on the headset tightened just a little.

"It needs one of those beanbag chairs," I continued. "You know, from the library reading room? *That* would pull this place together."

Success. Jason's grip relaxed. He didn't smile, but he didn't do that condescending scowl thing, either.

"Well, thanks for not being totally Normal about it," he said. "Now come on—let's get started."

"Right, okay, so about that," I said, looking around the chaos of Jason's room. "Get started doing *what*, exactly? How are we going to help get people out of HIVE?"

I turned back just in time to see Jason's skinny arms jerk, and before I knew what was happening, I'd caught the headset he'd just thrown at me.

"By going into HIVE." In an unexpected flurry of motion, he plucked certain items up from the piles of mess as easily as if they'd been waiting for him on a well-labeled bookshelf— some charging cords, a six-pack of energy drinks, a laptop of the kind I hadn't seen used in half a decade—and then hurried past me back out into the break room.

So much for not following him like a puppy.

"We're going into HIVE?" I asked, following Jason like a puppy (who could talk). "The place where no one can get out and everyone's panicking?"

"*You're* going in," Jason corrected me, using a bony hip to open the door into the lobby. "But I'm going to help you. I still have messaging capabilities within the game. Whatever made it so I can't go back in, it made it so I'm also the only person who can talk to players without getting sucked in myself."

"Then why do you need me?" I asked. "Why not just talk to your friends in the game?"

For just a moment, Jason stopped. I could only see a sliver of his face, and the lighting in the lobby was as dim as ever, but somehow, I knew what he was going to say right before he said it:

"I don't really . . . have any friends."

We stood there. A cable slowly unwound from around Jason's fingers until it was dragging on the carpet, as cables do.

"Jason, I—"

And then he started up again, as if he'd never stopped moving, continuing to talk to me even as he led us out of the lobby and into the gaming chambers . . . chamber.

"But *you* do," he said. "Have friends. I've seen you with them. And you said your boyfriend played. Is he in there now? Are they all in there?"

I nodded, and then remembered that he was walking in front of me, and said, "Yes."

"So I bet you want to see them again, right?" Jason was briefly scanning each chamber as we passed them by—big curved pods, packed together tighter than I'd ever seen them before, like an overabundant crop of some bizarre harvest stretching from floor to ceiling, each with a little red indicator on the side: IN SERVICE. IN SERVICE. IN SERVICE. We kept moving.

"Here's my deal," Jason continued as I tried not to trip over his dragging cable. "You go back into HIVE. You find whoever it is you care about. I'll guide you all where I need you to go, and then I'll get you where *you* need to go."

"You mean the back door?" I watched Jason's shoulder blades shrug begrudgingly through the back of his T-shirt. "You *do*. So you think you can help me fix this?"

Jason stopped abruptly, and at first I thought I'd struck a nerve again, but then I realized he'd found what he was looking for. Here, amid a sea of occupied chambers, he'd found a single pod with a little green legend: AVAILABLE FOR USE.

Suddenly, the reality of what I was about to do hit me— the image, the locked-up-tight *feeling* of me crawling into that chamber and sealing myself off from the outside world—and I staggered under a wave of second thoughts. Which, since the plan had seemed crazy from the moment I'd heard it, were really more like first thoughts, back with a vengeance. Jason, to his credit, seemed to sense this and turned to face me for the first time in several minutes.

"I think we have a darn sight better chance of making something happen in there"—Jason gestured with his neck at the chamber—"than we do out here. What are we going to do, fix it in the real world? Everyone and their mother was in HIVE when it went down, Kara. That includes the HIVE programmers themselves."

I couldn't help but stiffen at those words, thinking of my own mother, but Jason either didn't notice or—possibly, since this was Jason—didn't care.

"Everyone in the world who I trust to fix things is standing in this room," he went on. "For example, I'm the only person in the world who knows HIVE inside and out who isn't missing, or hiding, or trapped in HIVE."

"And me?"

For the first time all day, Jason smiled.

"You're the only person in the world who has the good fortune of being in the same room as me."

I scoffed and began to turn around, but Jason quickly backtracked or, at the very least, zigzagged.

"*And* I know you've got a reason to care about what's going on," he added. "And I know you, and how you act when you see a problem you care about. And I . . . I trust you."

He paused.

"More than I trust most Normals."

Seemingly out of words, he turned his face from mine, pretending to inspect the conditions of the gaming chamber. Or maybe he actually was inspecting them, who knew. Certainly not me.

I only knew one thing.

"Beats any plan I've got," I said, sighing and beginning to

unwind the straps of the headset. "And I never really trust anyone but myself to solve a problem anyway, so, like, I get it."

As I snugged the headset around my forehead and stepped toward the chamber, Jason smiled again—but it was a different smile this time, broader, the kind that came from letting your guard down rather than from having it up. *Maybe having him guide you through HIVE isn't the craziest idea in the world*, I thought as he pushed a button and the chamber door slowly hissed open.

Obviously, this thought should have set off major alarm bells, but for the past few hours absolutely everything had been setting off major alarm bells, so in my defense, all the bells were sort of starting to sound the same.

The chamber door slid open like a slab being pulled from a tomb (again: bells), gradually revealing a plush, Kara-sized seat and an array of tubes. Meanwhile, Jason had plopped down onto the floor, where he'd opened up his old-fashioned laptop—and the first of his energy drinks—and was hooking the laptop up to the chamber, plugging a cable into a port that I would never even have known was there.

"What's that for?" I asked, trying to distract myself as I clambered into the chamber.

"Little bug in this specific generation of headset I found." Jason took a swig of something bright blue in between furious bouts of typing. "Gives me videofeed on my—our—your headset. I'll be able to see what you're seeing and guide you where I need you to go."

"Right, speaking of, where do you need me to go?" I turned and twisted, trying to find a comfortable sitting position. Nothing was worse than emerging from a multi-hour HIVE session where you'd been sitting funny. Well, I mean, clearly several things were worse than that, but at least this was a problem I could be proactive about.

"Obviously, you'll be dropped into the Honeycomb," Jason said while I began hooking myself into the chamber. "The first thing I'll want you to do is to go up."

"The first thing I'll be *doing* is finding my people," I reminded him.

"Oh. Right. Yeah. Suit yourself. But once you've done that, or while you're doing that, or whatever, I'm gonna need you to go all the way up to—could you hook that cord into the left side of your headset, I need to load into your neural grid—all the way up to the top of the Honeycomb. There's some stuff up there I think might solve my problem—and yours. Then you'll have the people you care about back in your world again, and I'll—your other left—be back on my way to the real world."

"Great," I said, finally hooking the cord into my headset. "Perfect. Wait. *What?*"

"Okay!" Jason clapped his hands and leaned back from the laptop. "I'm loading into your neural grid! No going back now—now, we just wait."

"No. Jason. Hold on." I leaned as far forward out of the chamber as I could without snapping any cords or tubes. "What do you mean, *the real world?*"

"Oh. Huh. Did I say that?" Jason gave me that sizing-up look again, and then sighed and threw his hands up. "I suppose if you're going to really be helpful to me, you were going to have to find out at some time."

He gestured around at . . . the air? The Apiary? All of it, as it turned out.

"None of this is real," he said matter-of-factly. "This building, Bullworth, our Earth—I mean, it is, but only in the sense that it's as real as any other game in HIVE. It's real code, but it's virtual reality. What's *really* real is the Honeycomb, and the people who made it, and wherever they're from."

I stared at him, looking for the slightest hint he was joking. Terrifyingly, I found none.

"Okay, that's enough," I said, reaching up to yank the cord out of my headset. In a second, Jason was on his feet, hands shooting out in panic.

"No!" he yelled. "If you stop the upload now, you'll fry your neural grid!"

"*What?!*" I froze.

Even in his panic, Jason found time to roll his eyes. "Look, can you pick one thing to be incredulous about and stick with it? We'll be here all day."

"No. Wait. Hold on." My hands danced around my head, not daring to pull the cord, but suddenly unable to move forward with this boy as my guide. "So you think the real world is—is in HIVE? You think it's . . . dragons, and race cars, and talking birds, and . . . and *games*?"

"Of course not." Jason scoffed, like I was being impossibly thick. "Those are all simulations. Everything behind one of those HIVE hexagons is a simulation."

"Yes," I said, grateful for this shred of shared reality.

"Including us."

"No!"

"Why not?"

I shouldn't have had to struggle to answer, but I did. Where did you even start?

"This world is so . . . so . . ."

I looked around at the strip mall walls, the low-level fluorescent lighting, the carpet that hadn't been cleaned in who knew how long.

"Boring," I said. "Who would want to play this game?"

"Don't you play *The Skims*?" Jason pointed out. "That's just a reality simulator. You make fake people do real-people things."

I saw his point and searched for a different counterattack.

"Okay, so we're a really dull reality simulator," I said. "But we can . . . go into the other games? How would that be possible? None of the other NPCs can do that."

I realized as soon as I said it that it wasn't true, and Jason dug in before I could backtrack. "Yeah, except for Sidekicks," he said as I silently cursed myself. "They follow you everywhere if you want. And that's why we're different. That's what makes our game unique from *The Skims*. What if there were a world full of NPCs who thought they could play with you? Wouldn't that be adorable? We're like Sidekicks you can kiss."

This was the problem with people who lived in fantasy worlds: There was so much wrong with what he was saying, I couldn't figure out the first thing to set right.

"So we're the NPCs." I tried, anyway. "Who are the PCs? Who's coming to our world from HIVE?"

"Oh, there's plenty of players from the real world, if you know how to spot them," Jason said, and his voice shifted in a way I couldn't nail down. "People you see sometimes who go away. Kids from elementary school you remember that no one else does. People who are here one day and gone the next."

He looked into my eyes with no emotion.

"People like my parents."

I opened my mouth to speak, but nothing came out.

Ding!

"Oh, phew." Jason returned to the laptop on the floor. "The upload's done. Okay, time to really get this LAN party started."

My thoughts were racing around in circles. I thought of Jason's messy room in the back of the Apiary, of the way he'd practically vanished from school and the library, and of the way parents could be here one day and gone the next. Several things became clear all at once: Jason had been through more than I'd ever imagined. Jason was possibly just a little bit insane.

And Jason was the only person who had any idea how to get me and the people I loved out of this terrible day.

"You think *you're* real," I said carefully, trying to keep my voice neutral. "That you were born to real parents. And you think if you get back into HIVE, you can find your way to—to the 'real world.' And you think you're helping me to . . ."

"To find the other NPCs you've been programmed to care about and return them to your game, yes," Jason said. "I can't promise you'll make it through the back door okay, or that you'll ever be able to reenter the rest of HIVE, but I promise I'll bring you all back to your world."

I noticed that it didn't even *occur* to him to say *our* world.

"Why?" I asked.

Jason shrugged. "I've always been a sentimentalist."

Before I could bark out a bitter laugh, he added quietly: "And you've always been nice to me."

There was silence. My mind was still racing, but no longer in circles. I could feel, with a rising sense of dismay, that all my thoughts were headed in one direction.

Toward what I had to do.

"Kara?" Jason asked. "Did you short-circuit? Ha ha. I'm joking. But did you?"

I shook my head wearily and sighed, pulling the headset down over my eyes and shrouding my world in darkness.

"Seal the chamber," I said. "Let's play some HIVE."

Jason didn't say anything, but he must have pressed the button because there was a pneumatic hiss as the door slid closed. I hooked up my last tubes and felt a shadow slide over me, somehow turning my dark world even darker. The familiar buzzing feeling stole over my body, but ten times more intense than before because of the immersive tech of the chamber.

This was insane. I was trusting a boy I categorically could not trust to guide me through a world that had stopped working to find people whose whereabouts I did not know and return them to a world that was . . .

Real. Of course it was. My world was not a game.

But if it *wasn't* a game, then why did I just think of it as *my* world, instead of *the* world?

And if it *was* a game . . . what would happen if I lost?

With that thought, the world flashed white, and the game began.

PART TWO

LEVEL 9

The four thousand and ninth time you entered HIVE, everything was on fire.

Well, not literally. Probably nothing in the Honeycomb was flammable—*was* programmed *to be flammable*, I corrected myself. *The Honeycomb isn't real.*

But the fear and frustration of the people inside the Honeycomb was very, very real—and things were getting very, very heated.

Before this moment, I'd never imagined how many people it might take to fill up a space the size of a moon, or what it would look like when it happened. Now, standing on my trusty floating platform, surrounded by a sea of others just like it, I knew: It took millions, and it looked like a mess. Each catwalk and walkway along the edge of the Honeycomb was packed with people, just as Jason had described. Here were the Moddies with their insanely tricked-out avatars, sticking out from the default sleek uniform of the Honeycomb in more ways than one—as I watched, a player with a pair of flaring leathery wings turned at the edge of a parapet and accidentally gave a face full of wing to a cyborg with a mullet. There were the Anons, hooded brown cloaks and painted masks hiding their faces as they hurried up stairways and striations, desperate not to be noticed. And everywhere, squeezed onto every surface, were the—the Normals? The Casuals? *The players*, I decided. Regular, run-of-the-mill gamers, turned desperate by a situation with no clear cause and no hope of a solution. Everyone was arguing, yelling, or pushing past one another in an effort to get . . . somewhere. Anywhere.

But somehow, in the biggest room coders could ever invent, there was nowhere left to go. The only escape was ducking into one of the games, which I saw more than a few gamers doing—not even checking which world they were entering, just hopping through the first hexagon that would get them away from the crowd.

Well, I say crowd, but as it turned out, the line between a crowd and a mob was frighteningly thin. As I craned my neck up and around, taking it all in, a flash of silver caught my eye. Two players stood nose to nose on a skinny walkway, each unable to move past the other, each refusing to back down. The flash of silver had been caused by one of the players pulling a sword from its sheath.

I gasped. Drawing a weapon was a *huge* no-no in the Honeycomb. It didn't matter how big your in-game grudge was, or how many cool pieces of gear you'd gathered during your years in HIVE—the Honeycomb was neutral territory. But now I watched as, unnoticed in all the bedlam, Sword

Guy's opponent quickly produced her own plasma blaster. The sword swung up; the blaster hummed to life.

"Harassment is a violation of HIVE policies."

It seemed they weren't unnoticed by *everyone*. That was the unmistakable voice of a worker Drone, the faceless gray droids that patrolled HIVE looking for gamers who were either in trouble or causing it. These two hotheads were both, and within moments a hovering droid had cut through the chaos of the Honeycomb to reach them.

Glimpsed from afar, Drones mostly looked like sleek cylinders whose corners had been rounded off. Up close, they were . . . well, they were *bigger* than you'd have thought they'd be, for one thing. But although they were the height of a tall human being, Drones had no legs or limbs to speak of. Instead, they had screens, gleaming at roughly face level, that rotated toward you to indicate you were under their watchful eye (they also did not have eyes). So all things considered, the Drone bearing down upon the two players now was a sight to behold.

Then it was a sight very much *not* to behold, as the pair turned to face the Drone just in time for its signature security measure: the blinding flash of light that temporarily stunned any player it was directed at, freezing the rule breakers long enough for a stern talking-to or a swift removal from HIVE.

"Harassment is a violation of HIVE policies. Your weapons will be confiscated and your avatars—"

Since a swift removal was no longer an option, I assumed that the stern talking-to was imminent.

I was terribly wrong, but I wouldn't find that out until much later, when it was already too late.

In the meantime, though, I'd seen enough. Law and order was hanging on in HIVE, but just by a thread, and I wanted to be out of here before that thread snapped. And while I couldn't know where all the people I cared about were, I could make a pretty safe guess for at least one.

"All right," I said, looking down at my platform. "Take me to the offices of Takumi & Wright, LLP."

Obligingly, the platform began to lower me toward my destination. Most virtual offices in HIVE were tucked away near the bottom of the Honeycomb, below the really popular mid-level games, but above the really easy games for babies (and stressed-out non-babies who wanted to be a little less stressed. I happened to know Sammi liked to play *Manny the Manatee's Mix-n-Match* the closer we got to finals every year). Whereas game hexagons advertised themselves in yellow and gold, workplaces—like restaurants or any other HIVE business— were marked by powder blue, and if I leaned out and squinted, I could see the trademark ozone-colored halo far below me.

Too far. My father and I were currently separated by a sea of platforms, people, and Sidekicks, and my platform juddered as it slowly weaved its way around and down through the first-ever HIVE equivalent of a traffic jam.

Speaking of Sidekicks—and sidekicks—now was as good a time as any to check in with:

"Jason? Are you there?" I spoke the words out loud, not sure how messaging worked in a post-Update HIVE. A woman floating by had just enough time to look at me funny before I was at eye level with her feet.

"Yeah, I'm here." I nearly jumped off the platform—I was used to having my messages announced by a pleasant Drone voice, but whatever hack Jason had figured out made it sound like he was just chilling in my head, waiting for the right time to pipe up.

"And I'm seeing all of this," he continued. "It's—"

"Scary, yeah," I said, right as Jason said, "Totally cringe."

What a fun voice to have in my head.

"Like, I'll admit that I panicked when I was in there," Jason said, "but I'm *real*. I have a home to get back to. The rest of these people, they were always stuck in the simulation anyway, so all this panicking is pointless. Like, did you see that guy with the big leathery wings? How does he not know that he's fake?"

That last part almost wiggled its way past my rational brain and into my doubts, but I shut that down fast. Now that Jason wasn't sitting in front of me with those pleading, wounded-animal eyes, I felt more emboldened to establish some boundaries.

"Look, if we're going to work together, I need you to not be a jerk," I said. "I'd *like* you to not be crazy, but I'll settle for you not being a jerk."

"Calling me crazy doesn't make *you* a jerk?" Jason shot back.

"Sorry. You're right. I can tell you've been through some hard stuff. And I've also had problems with my parent . . . s," I conceded carefully. "But I didn't decide everyone I know is a hologram because of it!"

I expected this to get a big reaction from Jason, but I could *hear* the shrug as he said, "Agree to disagree."

"You can't agree to disagree on reality!"

"Agree to—"

"Oh, *come on.*"

"And *anyway*," Jason pivoted, "if we're going to work together, I need *you* to be going up to the top of the Honeycomb rather than in the *exact opposite direction*."

"I told you," I said. "I'm finding my people first. Starting with my dad. And if you want that to go quickly, tell me a faster way to get down there." I pointed down and then, after an awkward moment, moved my hand out in front of my eyeline so Jason could see.

There was a pause in which Jason appeared to actually consider the question. Then:

"You could jump," he said.

I looked down and gulped. Unlike drawing a weapon, there was technically no rule against leaving your platform in the Honeycomb. But unless you had (say, just for example) big leathery wings, it wasn't the smartest thing to do. I'd become a bit numb to it over the years, but it was a dizzying fall from here to the bottom of—well, I wasn't even sure the Honeycomb *had* a bottom. It was just you, a vast abyss, and maybe a scattering of platforms to break your fall. And normally, the platforms were so far apart that it just didn't seem worth it—like how you might imagine jumping from one rooftop to the next but never actually do it.

Now, though . . .

"Here goes nothing," I said, and leaped.

"Whoa!" said Jason, who clearly hadn't expected me to do that.

"Whoa!" said the girl whose platform I'd fallen onto, who *really* hadn't expected me to do that. But before she could react, I'd already jumped off again. The place was so thick with players that it was like hopping from one moving lily pad to another—like a three-dimensional version of a certain highly beloved early-generation HIVE game. Except the lily pads weren't extraordinarily big, and they *were* extraordinarily occupied, meaning I left a column of disgruntled gamers in my wake.

"Knock it off!" yelled a player as I thudded onto the lip of his platform, and "Rrrrr" growled someone's miniature wolf-shaped Sidekick as I fell just past their snout, and "Ouch!" roared someone who—okay, this was my bad—got their toes squashed by my thick black boots. But no one was fast enough to stop me, and pretty soon the blue lights of the business district were rising up to meet me. And as Jason whooped and clapped with excitement, I couldn't help but smile. Because, okay, giant world-shaking catastrophes aside, this was *fun*. And now here, coming into view, was a curved wrought-iron catwalk I knew well—ever since my first visit to Takumi & Wright, LLP. That ornate metalwork marked the entrance to my father's office, and it meant I was almost there.

"Not gonna lie," I said to Jason, "this is almost as good as *Mind Your Manors*, which is—"

And then someone was fast enough to stop me.

"Ow!" I hissed as a hand shot out from behind me and wrapped around my wrist. A *big* hand. Whoever'd grabbed me wasn't just fast—they were huge, and they were strong.

And their hand was covered in red, curly hair.

"Hey, nerd."

Oh no.

"Oh no," said Jason.

Maneuvering around my captured wrist, I turned to see Markus Fawkes sneering down at me.

"I told you you wouldn't want to meet me in HIVE."

"Markus," I said, trying to keep calm. "What are the odds?"

"Of you finding me?" He smirked. "Real low. But of *me* noticing *you*? When someone was causing all that commotion on the way down here? I'd say one to"—he squinted into space as if even a brief attempt at doing math had overheated his CPU, and then shrugged—"not as much. All I had to do was look up, and then get myself into position. And now here we are."

He grinned. It was a bad grin. For someone who was so big in real life, you'd think Markus would be confident in his size in the game, but no—he'd pushed his avatar's bulk up by a few feet and a few dozen pounds, and strapped on a medieval armory's worth of equipment to boot. Same red hair, though.

"And now," he said, noticing me noticing his gear, "I'm fully equipped. So what do you say to a rematch?"

"We can't," I pointed out. "This is the Honeycomb. You pull a weapon and the Drones will be on us in seconds."

I didn't think it was possible, but Markus's grip on my wrist tightened.

"You know," he said, "right now, my strength could be all the weapon I need."

I took a deep breath—but before I could shout for help, a flash of light swallowed us up. It seemed a Drone had already come to my rescue.

Then, as I slowly regained my vision, I realized it wasn't just me and Markus blinking our eyes, but everyone around us as well—and above us, and below us. That light wasn't a Drone at all.

It was HIVE transforming itself.

In the last sixty seconds, every single hexagon in the Honeycomb—blue, yellow, gold, whatever—had flashed bright white. When that light dimmed, the hexagons returned not to their original patchwork of colors but to one unified glow, becoming panels in the largest telescreen I'd ever seen. And now, stepping onto that screen, were hundreds of men in black suits.

No, wait—it was one man, repeated over and over again, up and down the walls of the Honeycomb in hundred-foot-tall units so that absolutely everyone could see him. The effect was dizzying, like watching a presidential address through the eyes of some monstrous insect.

Except it wasn't the president of the country addressing us.

"Valued HIVE users," said the thousand towering faces of Eric Alanick, founder and CEO of HIVE. "We here at HIVE headquarters owe you an apology."

He paused, and I heard something for the first time: silence in the Honeycomb. Everyone's eyes were glued to whichever Eric was in front of them, and I could just about feel us all thinking the same thing: *This better be good.*

"We know you are dissatisfied with the rollout of today's Update," Eric continued, "and we deeply regret any inconvenience it may have caused."

Based on the groans that immediately went up around us, this did not qualify as good.

"'May have'?!" yelled a girl with a pixie cut and pixie wings. "Try *did*!"

Whatever system Alanick was using to talk to us, he sure didn't seem able to hear us, or I like to think he might have blushed, or raised his hands appeasingly. Then again, maybe he wouldn't have.

"He can't even pretend to be sincere," I said. "He looks like he's being forced to say all this at gunpoint."

"Heh," Markus chuckled, even though I hadn't been talking to him. "Maybe he is."

"Oh no," Jason said, but I didn't have time to follow up on that because Alanick was barging on.

"This is an upsetting event to all of us here at HIVE. Our team is moving with a sense of urgency to address and resolve this situation, and conduct our own detailed assessment of what occurred. We know this represents a significant breach of trust, and we're taking steps to make sure it doesn't happen again."

"Happen *again*?" someone roared. "It's still happening *now*!"

"Our top priority has always been our mission of connecting people, building gaming communities, and bringing the world closer together," Eric said, apparently oblivious to the growing unrest. "I know we will learn from this experience to secure our platform further and make our community better for everyone. As I speak, our best architects are working to expand HIVE's features and policies so we can better address these things moving forward, and we hope to have those changes in place shortly."

"How shortly?!"

"I thought he was going to apologize! Did anyone hear an apology?!" The Anon who shouted this had a point—Alanick had used a whole bunch of words, but it was hard to tell if he'd actually *said* anything.

But if I was being honest, the only thing I had heard was *our best architects*. That had to include Mom. I wondered if she was working frantically somewhere right now, her hair pulled up into the messy topknot that meant she was about to kick some piece of code's butt. Was she thinking about us—me, Dad, Kyle? Was she worried? I hoped she was. No, I didn't care if she was. No, I—

"Kara," Jason said, cutting off my thought spiral. "What if he *is*? Being held at gunpoint, I mean? Maybe he's been taken hostage. Maybe this whole disaster wasn't some coding issue—maybe this was planned."

"This is not the time to add an additional conspiracy theory to your conspiracy," I hissed.

"What?" Markus frowned.

"Believe me," Eric said, and I had to admit that if he wasn't being held hostage, he was doing a *terrible* job at seeming relaxed—his strained smile barely registered as a human emotion. "We here at HIVE are just as concerned by these events as you are. We hope you will join us in taking this opportunity not to fall apart, but to pull together until a solution has been found. To all of you who are here in the game with us, we say: Game on!"

And just like that, the Eric Alanicks were gone and the hexagons were back, leaving a stunned community of gamers—and one eavesdropper.

"Wait," Jason said. "Did he just say—"

"He did," I confirmed.

"He did what?" Markus asked, but I barely heard him. My stomach was too busy twisting up in knots.

Nobody was coming to help.

The zookeeper was locked inside the zoo.

Hostage or not, Eric Alanick was somewhere in the game *with us*.

LEVEL 10

By this point we had already established that Jason and I lived in different worlds in at least a couple of ways, but now he really proved it:

"We *have* to find him!" he insisted. "If you can find Eric Alanick, maybe we can find out what's gone wrong and—and stop it! And get me back into HIVE!"

"First we need to get through what's about to happen," I said.

"What do you mean?" Jason asked, at the same time as Markus yanked on my wrist and said, "Hey, nerd. Who are you talking to?"

I froze up, but luckily—sort of—I didn't get a chance to answer.

"Eric Alanick's stuck here in HIVE with us?" someone yelled two feet from our platform, causing Markus to jump and turn. But it didn't stop there.

"I thought he was gonna be the one to get us out of here!"

"If he can't fix this, who *can*?"

"We should find him and give him a piece of our mind!"

"You wanna threaten the man who's in charge of all this? Are you insane?"

"Yeah? Are you gonna stop me?"

"What, you think I can't?"

And then we were right back to the drawing of weapons. I'd been watching nervously as Markus darted his gaze back and forth, trying to keep up with all the arguments breaking out, but both he and I turned sharply at the *shhnk* of metal on metal. The same Anon who had shouted earlier had now pulled a scimitar from a sheath, and was bearing down on a player who was defending themselves with—okay, wow, points for style—a pair of whirling nunchucks.

"Harassment is a violation of HIVE policies."

A Drone descended quickly, but before it could get within flashing distance, another cry went up from the far wall, where one more conversation had just gone from heated to armed. The Drone froze, torn between two targets—and even as a second Drone hovered up to help, another fight was breaking out, and another, until it seemed like no number of Drones could possibly hope to contain the madness. If HIVE was a zoo, then the fur was seriously about to fly.

Case in point: Someone must have been a terrible shot with a blaster because a stray bolt of burning plasma flew right over our heads. Well, right over Markus's head, anyway; I, with my afore-mentioned height, was safe to the tune of something like fourteen inches. So there was one thing to thank Mom for, I guess.

And another: As Markus cursed and ducked to avoid being given a sudden reverse Mohawk, his iron grip on my wrist loosened. Not much—from iron to bronze, basically—but just enough that I could twist my hand around, grab, and pull on the first thing I could reach. Which in this case was all that curly, red forearm hair.

"*Yow!*" Markus's fingers spasmed open. Before he could regain his senses, I yanked my hand away, bent my knees, and jumped backward off his platform.

Those paying close attention may notice that I skipped a famously important step there, i.e., looking before I leaped. Luckily, I fell only a few feet before landing on another platform. Even more luckily, this one was somehow empty of any gamers, affording me plenty of space to tumble backward onto my butt.

Then a throwing star ricocheted two inches from my hand, and I realized this platform was empty because the prior occupant had just gone off to attack someone a yard to my right.

Okay, so, not a good place to remain on one's butt. I clambered to my feet, looking around for—there! The Takumi & Wright catwalk beckoned, and I obeyed. There was a split second when I worried, as I jumped to a new platform, that I might be leading Markus Fawkes right to my father. Then I heard the *thud* of a very heavy redheaded bully landing on the platform I'd just left, and then the roar of pain one might hear if a very heavy redheaded bully had, in fact, been struck by another stray throwing star. I looked back long enough to see him turn and explain to my recent neighbors exactly how he felt about this development—employing helpful visual aids in the form of his fists—and then, having seen enough, I turned forward again just in time to avoid running head-on into a Moddie. I apologized and kept jumping.

After just a few more leaps—and a few more dodges to avoid projectiles, players, and pitifully overworked Drones—I landed on the catwalk. Before I stepped through the powder-blue door, I took one last look behind me to make sure Markus wasn't right on my heels. Already, the air was so thick with Drones and disgruntled players that I could see neither hide nor hair of him, which I assumed meant he could see neither hide nor hair of me. Satisfied I'd lost him, and relieved that I'd finally be in a safe, mundane office instead of a dangerous, weapon-filled war zone, I turned back around and stepped forward into the offices of Takumi & Wright, LLP.

I was greeted by a dozen lawyers pointing laser pistols directly at my face.

And, noted some small point of my brain that hadn't just frozen up entirely, one threateningly brandished clipboard, courtesy of a paralegal in the back.

"Whoa," I said, holding my hands out in front of me. "Hello. Sorry. I'm—"

"Kara?!"

"Dad!"

As various legal professionals lowered their weapons sheepishly and mumbled vague apologies, a bushy brown mustache with a man attached pushed through the front line and wrapped me in a hug. Just like me, Dad had never felt the need to make his HIVE avatar look any different from his regular self, even though most virtual businesses allowed for a certain amount of, shall we say, self-expression in their employees. Before I'd been trapped in the world's tightest hug, for example, I was pretty sure I'd seen an attorney with gills.

But as he pulled back to get a better look at me, I remembered the one thing that made HIVE Dad look just a little less real than Real Dad: In HIVE, Dad's eyes never looked tired.

"Are you okay?" he asked, squeezing my shoulders and looking me up and down. "What are you doing here? I didn't think you'd be in the game today. Have you seen Kyle?"

"I'm okay, Dad. I just . . ."

As my eyes flickered over Dad's shoulder at the front offices of Takumi & Wright, I couldn't help but notice several lawyers milling around their desks, very clearly eavesdropping and holstering their laser pistols while trying to look like they were doing neither of those things.

"Actually, is there somewhere private we can talk?" I asked.

"Of course," he said, putting his hand on my back and leading me away from the crowd. "Let's go to my office."

In real life, private offices would probably have been reserved for partners, but that was one benefit of virtual real estate—here there were rooms for everyone who wanted them. Dad ushered me down a hallway and to the right, leading me into a spacious office decorated with pictures of me and Kyle.

He closed the door behind him while I collapsed onto a couch in the corner of the room.

"You'll have to forgive my colleagues," he said, in a tone that made it absolutely clear neither he nor I had to forgive his colleagues. "They'd been getting antsy just watching what was happening through the doorscreen, and then of course when there was that message from . . ."

He trailed off, gesturing at nothing as he joined me on the couch. I knew at once what he was saying, or rather, not saying: Dad hadn't spoken Eric Alanick's name out loud since the day Mom had left her note, even as Alanick shot past household-name status to cover-of-*TIME*-magazine-every-few-months status. ("Magazines" were these things they stopped making right after that, which people used to— Oh, we don't have time, we'd be here all day.)

So it wasn't just the people in the Honeycomb who knew that something was up, or who'd seen Eric Alanick's message. And if Dad had seen that, then it wasn't just me who he was thinking about . . .

"Don't worry," he said as if he'd read my mind. "If she's on the case, we'll all be out of here in an hour. Two hours, max."

He smiled thinly, and I wanted to hug him all over again. That was something about my dad that amazed me. Some days it filled me with pride, others with anger, but every day it was fair to say it amazed me: He'd never once, ever, said a harsh word about Mom since she'd left.

"Who is he talking about?" asked a voice in my ear, and I

almost fell off the couch. I'd been so happy to see Dad, I'd completely forgotten that Jason Alcorn was chugging energy drinks somewhere, hearing everything I heard and seeing everything I saw. For the first time, I realized just how invasive this setup was, and wondered if he and I shouldn't have a stern talk about it. But of course, if everything went according to plan, I wouldn't be in HIVE long enough for it to really matter.

Obviously, you and I both know that everything was not going to go according to plan, but I was working with the info I had, so.

"Kara?" My dad frowned. "Is everything okay?"

That brought me back to reality. Or, I guess, virtual reality.

"That's actually why I'm here," I said to Dad, ignoring Jason for the time being. "I'm not sure that Mo—that anyone at HIVE *is* going to be able to get us out of here. You heard what Alanick said: He's as stuck in the game as we are. We're on our own."

So much for ignoring Jason. Now I sounded like him.

"So when you got trapped in HIVE, you came to find me." Dad nodded. "Smart thinking. I hope your brother does the same. In an emergency, it's best to hunker down."

"No. I mean, yes, you're probably right, but that's not why I came here." I took a deep breath and looked him in the eyes. "I'm here to get us all out."

Dad's mustache would have bristled, if that was a thing mustaches actually did.

"Everyone?" he asked. "Kara, that's a very admirable thought, but . . . how?"

"Not—not *everyone* everyone. Not yet, anyway." I looked guiltily in the direction of the front office and all its inhabitants, and then turned back to him. "But you. Me. Kyle, wherever he is. And Gus and my friends. I know something about a . . . a back door."

Over the decades—and especially the last few years—Dad had become so good at keeping his face neutral that only the foremost experts in the field of Dad studies (hello) could determine his true thoughts, and even then only by reading the tiniest flickerings in his eyes. Right now, based on a squint in the left and then a twitch in the right, he appeared to be searching for that elusive balance between "supporting my daughter" and "politely telling her she's lost it." I would have laughed if it wasn't so serious. Was this how Jason had felt explaining himself to me?

"Kara, this . . . back door . . . is this something she told you about before she . . ." Dad once again gestured, carrying on half a conversation with all the words he didn't say.

"Who's *she*?" Jason asked again, and I rolled my eyes, which Dad must have seen because his bewildered squinting only increased. All right, then, time to rip off this medpatch.

"It's not— Okay. You remember Jason Alcorn?" I asked.

"Your friend from the library?" Dad's eyebrows scrunched up, which was always a dramatic process since they were almost as bushy as his mustache.

"Right. So. It turns out he's a computer genius, or at least a HIVE genius, and he's maybe the only person in the world who's managed to escape HIVE since the Update began, and he thinks he can help us get out but he can't get back in himself, so *I* went in, and now he's helping me, and also he can see and hear you right now through me."

"Hi," Jason said.

"He says hi."

There was a pause as Dad studied my face carefully.

"Oh, Kara," he sighed eventually.

"You don't believe me?" I wouldn't have blamed him, but he just shook his head.

"No," he said. "I believe you. There's a giant problem and you've decided it's your job to fix it. It's the most believable thing in the world."

The thin smile returned.

"It's just what your mother would have done."

All right, that was my cue to stand up. If Dad was unfazed enough to be saying sentimental junk like that, he was unfazed enough to get moving.

"So you'll come with me? We'll find Kyle and everyone else and get out of here?"

Dad stood up as well and dusted off his slacks, which must have been a force of habit—unless someone had programmed HIVE offices to have digital dust.

"It's as good a plan as sitting around here," he said. "Well, it might not be, but I'd really like to find your brother. We actually messaged this morning after he reached the Apiary, but I think HIVE's servers must be overwhelmed because I haven't been able to reach him since everything went . . ." Gesture.

"Did he say where he was?" I asked.

"Last I heard from him, he was about to go into *Brawl of Duty*."

"Oh, perfect," Jason said. "That's on the way up to where you need to go."

"Great," I said, moving toward the door. "We'll swing by that game, see if we can find him, and then we'll get both of you out of here before it gets any crazier."

"Wait," Dad said. "You won't be leaving HIVE with us?"

"No." My hand rested on the knob. "If it works, I'll have to . . ."

"Tell everyone else how to get out. Of course." Dad gave me that proud look again, and again, it just made me want to leave the room. "Always thinking of how to help."

"Actually, I don't think you should tell anyone about the door," Jason piped up. "I'm still worried about this whole Alanick thing. I don't trust anyone but you right now. And I barely trust you. And also it's not really worth it because none of you are, you know, real."

"Gee, thanks," I muttered, but not softly enough for Dad not to hear.

"What did Jason say?" he asked.

"If it's all right with you," I said, neglecting to specify which of them was *you*, "I think I'll try to get the word out. After I've made sure the people I care about are safe."

From the silence that ensued, it was clear this answer had satisfied neither Jason nor my father. To be honest, it didn't really satisfy me. But I'd read somewhere that this was the nature of a good compromise—when nobody wins, everyone wins.

Like one of Gus's favorite games. The thought came and went before I could stop it.

"All right," Dad said, breaking the silence at last. "Stay close to me and don't say anything. I'm not letting you back out in the Honeycomb until we see what it looks like on the doorscreen. But we also need to act normal—we don't want my coworkers getting all excited about some escape route we can't guarantee works."

I nodded and held the door open for him.

In the front office, things had returned to a semblance of normality—emphasis on semblance. People were shuffling papers intently, but they couldn't keep their eyes from darting our way as we approached the doorscreen. And this may have been me projecting, but the typing sounds filling the office were exactly the kind you got when someone was typing something like, *Look at me, I am typing something productive, but secretly I am eavesdropping.* Is it just me who does that? I don't think it's just me who does that.

Evidence: "You guys headed back out there?" asked an attorney with a calculated lack of interest, barely looking up from his computer in a way that made it *so clear* he wanted to look up from his computer. His throat was what really gave him away, though. While the rest of him remained still, he couldn't stop the high-velocity fluttering of what was, indeed, an impressive set of gills.

"Just checking to see if the coast is clear," Dad said, serving up an all-time classic Casually Emotionless Dad Voice. What a star. "Thought we might go see how my son is doing."

"Mm." Gills still didn't look up, choosing instead to staple a printout like it had personally wronged him. "And how is the coast?"

Actually, I wanted to know that, too. Looking at the doorscreen, I expected to see the same mayhem I'd left behind, or worse. But the Honeycomb appeared to be empty. Or, no, wait: The Honeycomb was still packed, but not with rioting players. The streaks of gray flickering across the frame weren't video static, liked I'd assumed; they were Drones. Scores of them.

"Seems like they got the situation under control," Dad said. "Shall we?"

I nodded. "Bye, everyone," I said, in case that was a thing a normal-acting person might have said. It seemed to work because a few lawyers just muttered sounds of acknowledgment, and then we were able to step peacefully back out into the Honeycomb.

Very peacefully.

A few minutes ago, the din of combat had been deafening.

Now there was only the soft almost-sound of Drones moving through virtual air. Some of them slowly circled the perimeter while others rotated in place, scanning for any new outbreaks of disorder. In most cases, though, they just hovered, still and silent, stacked up in wide, all-seeing rings.

After the riot, it should have been a relief. In practice, though, it was sort of just . . . creepy.

And the handful of players left in the Honeycomb seemed to agree. They hurried across the catwalks quietly—an Anon here, a Troll there—but they were sparse and uniformly silent, like they were afraid to make any more noise than the sound of their footfalls.

"Where'd everyone go?" Dad asked. "Did people find a way out after all?"

"Jason?" I figured if anyone in the Apiary had woken up, he would have noticed.

"No idea," Jason said. "No activity out here."

I bit my lip, watching a Drone slide by. "Maybe they all went into the games," I said. "I saw a few people doing that earlier."

A bitter laugh rang out, causing us to turn. A player in a wheelchair had been hurrying past us on a catwalk one story up, but stopped now to look at us incredulously. She seemed like a real prepared-for-anything type, dressed in a functional jumpsuit and a heavily stocked utility belt.

"You mean you don't know?" she said. "They're not in the *games*. And the ones who are are even worse off. Only go in there if you know you can get out."

"What are you talking about?" Dad asked.

"Oh, no." Jumpsuit shook her head. "I'm not sticking around long enough to help you two level up. Ask *that* guy to explain it to you."

This was when things started happening really fast.

Jumpsuit jabbed her finger over our heads. Dad and I turned to find out who she was pointing at. Markus Fawkes, previously hiding where neither we nor the doorscreen could see him, froze in his attempt to creep up on us, looking for all the world like a stunned ginger mountain cat. Then he shook it off and redoubled his approach. Dad stepped in front of me. From behind us came the whooshing sound of someone stepping out of Dad's office to join us in the Honeycomb. Markus froze again, and from above me I heard Jumpsuit say, "Wait, *what*?"

And a moment later, I understood why.

Because whoever had just left Dad's office was pressing a laser pistol into my back.

LEVEL 11

"Don't move," someone hissed in my ear, and upon hearing his voice—and the whispering of air that accompanied his every syllable—I realized it was Gills. I guess we hadn't been as convincing as I'd thought.

"*None* of you move!" he spat, driving the muzzle of his pistol farther into the small of my back. Markus, who had just started to inch away, froze once more. Dad was barely breathing.

"Are you crazy?" yelled Jumpsuit from somewhere above me. "Don't you know what's going on?"

"Oh, I know *exactly* what's going on," Gills said, with relish. "These two are trying to use their family connections to escape to safety and leave the rest of us in the lurch. You big-tech types are all the same."

"What is he *talking* about?" Jason said as my heart plunged through my boots. Dad didn't say anything, his hands up and behind his head, staring hollowly at the middle of my stomach like he hoped he could remove Gills's hand from behind it through sheer force of will.

"You know I'm on the hiring board, right, Tilden?" Gills

continued. "I've kept quiet about this for years, but not any-more. I know you're married to Kimi Swift. That puts you in the innermost circles of HIVE—and instead of using that power to help, you're sneaking away. This is just like you elites—only looking out for yourselves, even while you make life so much harder for everyone else. Well, not anymore. You're going to tell me what you know."

There was a horrible silence, punctuated only by a low whistle from Jumpsuit above us.

I felt awful. Gills was wrong about where our intel was coming from, but not how I'd chosen to use it. By trying to keep the back door a secret, I'd been acting like this whole nightmare was some game only a select few could win—and in doing so, I'd made it an even more dangerous game than before.

But look how people respond the moment they find out, said an aggrieved voice in my head. *That's not your fault—you* have *to be playing this game to win.*

Speaking of voices in my head:

"Your dad is married to *who*?!"

Obviously, I couldn't respond, but I had to admit: Under different circumstances, it would have been gratifying beyond belief to hear Jason Alcorn so totally stunned. For several rea-sons, I hoped I'd get a chance to circle back to that later.

Meanwhile, outside my head:

"It's not like that, Bret," Dad was saying slowly, through clenched teeth, as if even one overly twitched jaw muscle might make the pistol go off. "If you'd let my daughter go, she can explain—"

"Oh, no," said Gills (Bret? Nope, sorry, he was Gills to me forever). "I don't need a Swift to defend a Swift. The power's not in the hands of the few now. Now it's in the hands of *me*."

I wanted to tell him that I was more of a Tilden than a Swift. And that we had been just as hurt by the "few" he was talking about as everyone else—more, arguably. *And* that, mathematically speaking, one "him" was an even smaller population than one "few," and so this was not, *morally* speaking, much of an improvement in power distribution. But, you know, laser pistol, back, et cetera.

And even as I was thinking all that, I was quickly becoming fixated on a new thought entirely: I had no idea what happened when you got wounded in the Honeycomb. If you died in a game, obviously, you popped out here, fine as could be. But that was only in the games, and only when HIVE was working normally. Now we were out in the open, and nothing in HIVE was working normally.

Well, almost nothing.

"Harassment is a violation of HIVE policies."

"Oh, crud, here we go," said Jumpsuit as a Drone hovered down from above us.

Based on Jumpsuit's whole vibe, that wasn't such a weird reaction. What *was* weird was the way Markus's eyes had just gone wide with fear behind my dad.

"Please drop your weapon," the Drone said, stopping above our heads.

"Yeah, yeah, what are you going to do to me?" Gills sneered at the Drone. "You can't kick me out of the game—you can't kick *anyone* out. That's another thing about you startup goons: You always want to disrupt things, but if you keep disrupting yourself, sooner or later it's just chaos. And—"

"Look away before the flash!" yelled Jumpsuit, interrupting wherever that monologue was going. "Close your eyes and look away!"

Again, I might not have put much stock in what Jumpsuit was saying, except Markus was doing exactly that, moving for the first time since the laser pistol had entered the scene to shield his eyes from whatever was coming. If *he* was doing it . . .

I made eye contact with Dad. He nodded. We each scrunched up our faces, closing our eyes as tight as we could, and I buried my face into my shoulder for good measure. Startled at this unexpected movement, Gills raised the laser pistol up from the small of my back, and even through my shut eyes and the sleeve of my shirt, I felt the flash.

There was the clattering of pistol against metal as the laser dropped from Gills's hand and, luckily, did not accidentally shoot hot plasma through my ankles.

And then there was another sound, one that shot chills up my spine, not least of all because it was coming from two inches behind me.

Gills was screaming.

I knew I should have been moving, getting out of there, but I couldn't help myself—I had to turn and look. And when I did, I understood the scream and bit down one of my own. Even Jason said "Whoa" in my ear, though this time, it was much less fun to hear him caught off guard.

Because Gills was transforming.

It started with his skin, and at first I just assumed the flash must have whammied my vision more than I thought, but no: Gills was turning—had already turned—a silvery gray. Gray like dull spray paint. Gray like a crawling mold. His arms were lifting up with no apparent input from his brain, and then— oh, please, no—*shortening*, and thickening, until they were more like fins than arms, smooth curves pushing out from his sides. His legs did something similar, sealing to each other and pulling up into his torso—which somehow stayed at the same elevation even as his feet disappeared.

Which meant Gills was now hovering.

This was when I realized what was happening, and I think it's when he realized it, too, because his scream became something too hoarse to hear.

Somehow, Gills was becoming a Drone.

His neck swiveled as he tried to take in what was happening to him, but the swiveling slowed as his spine appeared to freeze up, until he could only look dead ahead—directly at me. There had been rage in his eyes when this started. Now there was just confusion and fear.

And then the color of his skin leached into his eyes, and there was just gray.

The second-to-last thing to vanish were his gills, smoothed over into stainless steel.

The last thing to vanish was his mouth.

And then there was a new Drone. With a dreadful, quiet calm, it floated up to join the Drone that had transformed it, and together they drifted off back into the void. As I backed up toward Dad, I looked around that void with a dawning horror.

This was why there were so many Drones all around us. This was where all those rioters from just half an hour ago had gone. This was the latest, most horrifying result of the Update, the glitch you got when you were programmed to remove players from a world they could no longer be removed from.

Or worse still: Maybe this wasn't a glitch. Maybe Jason had been right, and HIVE had been hacked, and all this was happening on purpose.

"Well, don't say I didn't warn you guys," Jumpsuit said in the jaded tone of someone who had already seen this happen dozens of times. "Now you know. Don't do anything stupid. And don't go into the games—that'll just be worse."

I wanted to ask her how that was possible, but she was already wheeling away, and I couldn't blame her. She'd never wanted to stop in the first place, and now I understood why.

She wasn't the only one who'd made a hasty exit. Markus had gone to ground again, vanishing while we were distracted.

I doubted he'd gone far, though. I'd seen the look in his eyes when the Drone had first arrived. Markus had known what was about to happen, had seen it already, and somehow escaped having it happen to himself. That was why he'd been lying in wait for me just outside Dad's office—he'd been planning to push me back through that door, banking on being able to take his revenge where the Drones couldn't get him. Could they not get him in there? I wasn't sure. I was willing to bet he wasn't certain, either, but that he'd sure be prepared to try. Markus was only crafty up to a certain point; after that it was just instinct and want. Which was why . . .

"Dad," I said, looking around. "We have to split up."

"What? No."

"There's no time to argue. That boy who was coming for me? He's not going to stop coming for me. But not for you. You don't have that problem. Get on a platform." I snapped my fingers to summon one and it appeared, pulling up to our feet. While looking down I noticed the laser pistol, still on the catwalk, and I bent to pick it up. The safety had been on the whole time, so that was nice, I guess.

"Go up," I said, shoving the weapon into Dad's hands. "Go to—"

"Terms and Conditions," Jason leaped in helpfully.

"Terms and Conditions," I repeated, and then, "Wait, what? What game is that?"

"Just go there! Go to the back!"

"Just go there!" I relayed, throwing my hands up. "Go to the back! And find Jason when you're out."

"No. I'm going to find your brother," Dad said. "*We're* going to—"

"Hey, nerd!" And there he was. Striding from behind a support beam, not running so as to avoid Drone concern, but bearing down on us purposefully nevertheless. Markus had decided to target me the exact way he had never targeted, say, graduating from high school.

I pushed Dad forward onto the platform. "I'll find you at Terms and Conditions!" I hissed, so that no one could hear. And then I kicked the platform off the catwalk with my foot, and before he could protest, Dad was going up, up, and away, ascending heavenward and out of the reach of danger.

Well, this particular danger, anyway.

"Should have gotten a platform for yourself." Markus grinned as I turned back to him. He was almost upon me now.

"You're right," I said. "I probably should have." And as I said it, I realized I was no longer faking that devil-may-care tone in my voice. Markus was still bad news, sure, but after everything I'd been through this morning, he was more like a page-six paragraph than a front-page headline.

When I looked him in the eye, I was no longer just playing at the game of being brave.

But I was still winning.

"Guess I'll have to improvise," I said.

And then, just as Markus reached out to grab me yet again, I repeated a move of my own: I threw myself backward off the catwalk, plunging into the Honeycomb.

The dumbfounded look on Markus's face as I fell away was almost worth it. It was an expression that stated very clearly he would *not* be following me into the abyss. But it didn't stay in my vision very long.

Because, you know. Abyss.

This time around, there wasn't an endless sea of platforms to catch my fall. There was just empty space, and a body dropping through it, and row after row of those chillingly still Drones, lining the walls of the Honeycomb, watching me fall. For a millisecond, a panicked thought blew through my head, rushing up with the wind in my ears, asking what I'd do if one of those Drones decided this was a violation of HIVE policies and came to me now, prepared to make me one of their own. But I guess a girl hurtling unimpeded toward terminal velocity wasn't technically harassing anyone because nothing stopped me as I fell ever farther and ever faster. The only thing that was going to break my fall was a very, very hard landing—or falling right into a game.

Guess it was time to play a game.

My eyes watered as I accelerated downward, but even through my tears I could see the blue of the business district give way back into gold and yellow, narrowing in around me as the sphere of the Honeycomb bottomed out below. Was it a sphere? An egg? I was always better at language arts than geometry, and now I was about to become an object lesson in physics.

But then I saw what lined the bottom of the Honeycomb. Not yellow hexagons or hard steel, but a sea of warm, welcoming pink. Of course—the kids' games, the ones that took up the lowest level of the HIVE world. Well, that didn't sound so bad, no matter what Jumpsuit had said. And it certainly beat going *splat* against a catwalk.

Time to aim. I straightened my neck. I clasped my hands together over my head. I tilted my toes upward. I'd tried one terrible season of diving freshman year, and now I found myself thinking that if it had been anything like this, I might have been much better at it. For one thing, you had a *lot* more time to get the technique right.

"Kara!" Jason cried as I plummeted. "Kara, what are you doing?"

I tried to answer, but the wind just flapped at my gums.

"And *why didn't you tell me your mom is Kimi Swift*?!"

And I couldn't help it—whether out of the absurdity, or the exhilaration, or just out of sheer adrenaline-laced panic, I laughed.

And then, with a golden-pink sigh, I fell smack-dab through a hexagon and into the game.

LEVEL 12

I was still falling.

No, wait. After a moment of panic, my brain caught up to its surroundings, making sense of the lack of ground beneath my feet—feet that, suddenly, were pointing the right way down.

I wasn't falling—I was floating. I mean, floating *down*, so still technically falling, but at a much slower rate than before. No body-exploding impact for me. Not just this moment, anyway.

That said: For some reason, my shoulders hurt. I looked down and saw I was wearing a brown leather shoulder harness that definitely hadn't been there before I entered the game. The straps dug tightly into my chest and were adorned at the top by a set of strings. I turned my gaze up to follow the strings and found myself under a parachute, bright and colorful and wide, lowering me gently from a beautiful blue sky.

Well, that made as much sense as anything else.

Then I looked back down, and what I saw made *more* sense than anything else—certainly anything that had happened today. After a morning of careening from one high-stress situation to the next, I could finally breathe a sigh of relief because I knew exactly where I was, and I was going to be just fine.

I was in *Animal Flossing*.

Now, fad games come and go, so I don't know if this will be a timeless classic to you or a long-forgotten novelty. But for the uninitiated, or those who were initiated so long ago they have since forgotten: *Animal Flossing* was perhaps the purest available virtual expression of *fun*. It was the ultimate game of HIVE birthday parties, or of little kids cutting class. Heck, even I had a soft spot for it.

Which I guess wasn't saying much because of how totally fine I was with HIVE, as you know. But still. Whatever.

The gist was this. Cute bipedal animals—and you!—were dropped onto a cozy woodland island with very few resources beyond a parachute, pluck, and the occasional plunger gun. Or bubble blaster, or some such. Your goal was to be the last one remaining on the island, taking out your fellow players and NPCs with gumdrop gauntlets, or bismuth-plated butterfly nets, or such some. If you tried to hide and wait them out, you'd be eliminated anyway, inevitably getting caught and thrown into debtors' prison by Tom A. Toehead, an adorable red mole who appeared to run the island with the firm capitalist paw of a nineteenth-century industrial baron. And if you won? You got to do the most *delightful* little victory dances.

It was cute. It was innocent. It was exactly the kind of game Sammi convinced us all to play whenever she was stressed out from taking six AP classes and helping with one of her older sisters' weddings. And more to the point, it was the perfect place to hide from Markus Fawkes, and the first stroke of good luck I'd had all day.

"You have to get out of here."

Rather than respond, I closed my eyes and enjoyed the last few seconds of peaceful descent before I breached the forest canopy. I would not let Jason spoil my moment of Zen.

"We've really gotten off track," Jason persisted, un-Zen-ly. "We're farther from the top of the game than we were before. I don't know where the rest of your friends are or how to help your dad when he gets there. And I'm no closer to getting back to where I belong. Except maybe I am because apparently, your mom is the *second-most famous HIVE architect who ever lived*."

Okay, that, I would respond to.

"Second-most?" I frowned, eyes still closed.

"Well, Eric."

"Oh, you two are on a first-name basis now?"

"I don't know, are *you*? Because apparently you *could* be, and you haven't been *telling* me!"

"I don't see how this is my—*aak*—fault."

My eyes popped open at the feeling of something snagging on my feet. I had reached the tree line now, and my slow descent became even slower as I found myself having to knock branches away from my face.

"You definitely saw her when she picked me up from

the—*pfftaak*—library. A few times she—*blegh*—asked if you—*arh!*—wanted a ride home. *Oof.*"

I'd made it through the branches, but my parachute had not, having quickly become entangled in limbs and leaves. I hung there helplessly in the air, swinging in circles six feet above the forest floor.

"Okay, but she never mentioned she was the great VR genius of our time," Jason said, taking full advantage of his captive audience. "And neither did you! That information could not be *more* relevant to the problem at hand! She could be our connection to Eric—heck, she and Eric could be in the same place right now! And here I am, trapped outside of my true home—do you know what that's like? And you just let me dangle like—like—"

"Like me?" I asked, dangling.

"Well."

"Look," I said. "My mom is a genius, yes. But she's not that great. And it's not that relevant. I haven't heard from her in years, Jason. None of us have. I honestly have no clue where she'd be right now. Do you know what *that's* like?"

At long last, a thoughtful pause from my inner critic.

"Yes," Jason admitted finally. "I do."

"Great," I said, reaching up to unbutton my left shoulder strap. "So you understand. Nothing's changed."

"Well, I wouldn't say that," Jason said, and something about his tone made my hand freeze. "Kara, don't you know what this means? You're real, too."

"Yes," I said slowly. "I am real. We're all real."

"No," Jason said, like somehow *I* was the one who was off base here. "Real like *me*. If Eric Alanick is from the real world, and my parents are from the real world, then Kimi Swift is *definitely* from the real world. And so are her kids. Those other players? They're just code. No wonder they were easy to turn into Drones—it's just HIVE converting its NPCs from one type to another. But you . . . you may not even be able to become a Drone. And— Oh, of course. How didn't I *see* it?"

I wasn't going to ask. I *couldn't* ask.

"See what?" I asked.

"Kara, what are the odds we would find each other today in the street? Me, the person in Bullworth with the most knowledge of HIVE, and you, the daughter of a HIVE architect and the only person not to be in there for the Update? What are the chances we would have known each other in the first place? None. Because it wasn't chance. It was the simulation. It brought us together. It knew we could help each other."

For a minute now, my hand had been frozen in front of my shoulder harness. Now it wasn't frozen—because it was shaking.

"You're sick, Jason," I said. "You need help." And before I could think anymore about the points he was making— and how they were almost, maybe, possibly, actual points—I unstrapped myself from my parachute and fell the last few feet to the forest floor.

"My only sickness is that I'm trapped outside of the world

I'm actually from," Jason said. "I can feel it, and it's awful. You're lucky. You're in there. You know I'm right. I do need help—I need your help."

My fall to the ground had a bracing effect, sending shock waves up through my knees and freeing me from the fog of Jason's words. Some games played tricks with their physics engines, making you lighter so you felt like you could do anything—Aaron *loved* those games—but even in *Animal Flossing*, gravity still ruled. I stood up tall with renewed intent.

"I'll help you," I said. "But only *after* I help my friends. And I'll only do *that* after I've spent a few more minutes in here to make sure Markus doesn't follow me. And since I'm here . . ."

I picked up something I had spotted while hanging in the air—a plunger gun hidden between two bushes. Classic *Animal Flossing*.

"I might as well have some fun."

Jason groaned so loudly I almost didn't hear the rustling in the trees behind me. I turned, smirking as I held up my wacky weapon.

I froze when I saw the girl who had emerged from the undergrowth. She was not smirking. Like, at all.

"Please," she said, her voice cracking. "We don't have to do this."

She was holding what appeared to be some sort of a weaponized waffle iron, but it was pointed at the air, her hands raised high above her head in surrender. She had outfitted herself in an adorable sundress and cat ears. I realized the cat ears were actually a Mod when I saw them quivering with fear. Did I really look that threatening?

"We can get through this together. You don't have to shoot me. We can form an Alliance."

I was unnerved by her serious tone, but I still found myself laughing—partly to put her at ease, and partly because I couldn't help myself. The contrast of the absurd handheld waffle iron with her deadly serious expression was just too great for words.

"Hey, listen, I think you have the wrong game," I said. "I'm not trying to harsh your mellow. I'm not even sure how this thing wor—*ohp!*"

I had tried to gesture at my plunger gun to indicate how little I knew about it, but since I was holding it, it was more like gesturing *with* my plunger gun. And apparently one of the many things I didn't know about gesturing with plunger guns was: It caused them to fire.

The girl screamed and threw herself to the ground, narrowly dodging a plunger to the stomach and firing off her own weapon in return. Her panic made her a poor shot, and I easily sidestepped as three waffles flew up past me like spinning discs. They were things of beauty to behold: perfectly golden brown, and whipping syrup and butter off them in spiraling arcs as they whirled through the air.

And collided with another girl who had just emerged from the trees.

This girl was taller than either of us, and as such, she caught two of the waffles right in the face, each landing with a syrupy *splat*. The third bounced off her forehead, causing the first two to detach and fall to the ground, revealing a face slathered with maple, butter, and seething rage.

"You *jerk*!" she spat, pulling out a slingshot and loading it up with a rainbow-colored jawbreaker. "I was going to help you ambush her!"

"Please," begged the first girl, pushing herself up from the ground. "It was an accident! I would never—"

But it was too late; I heard the *snap* of the slingshot's release, and then the rainbow jawbreaker was whizzing right past me and conking the girl directly between her cat ears. I'll admit I winced—I could *hear* the bruise forming already—but I still didn't understand the girl's wail of abject misery upon being struck.

Then I heard the hoarsening of the tall girl's voice as she croaked, "I hope you're happy now, Lexi. You've doomed us both."

I knew that croak. I'd heard it just a few minutes ago.

I turned around and, sure enough, the tall girl was frozen in place, her knuckles clenching white around her slingshot. No, not white—gray.

I whipped around again, like following a terrible tennis match. Lexi's cat ears were sinking into her head, and her body was beginning to float off the ground.

They were both becoming Drones.

"No," I breathed, though I wasn't sure who I was addressing. "I didn't—I didn't know."

But Jumpsuit's words echoed in my head: *Don't go into the games—that'll just be worse.* I may not have known, but that didn't mean I hadn't been warned.

And now I was getting another warning:

"Look out!" Jason cried. Instinctually, I threw myself to the ground, and for the third time in as many minutes, something flew past my head—a gumdrop that embedded itself with a *thunk* in the tree behind me. Looking up, I saw a player in a glistening gauntlet striding out of the trees, drawn to our little clearing by all the commotion and here now to see if there were any survivors he could pick off.

"Shoot him!" Jason urged, and sure enough, another plunger had magically appeared in my gun. Talk about instant reload. But I couldn't bring myself to use it. I already felt bad enough about accidentally contributing to Lexi's and her friend's horrific transformations; I couldn't imagine how awful I'd feel being the direct cause.

The new player didn't have any such qualms. He was already aiming his gauntlet down at me. I popped to my feet and—oh no, I was *taller* than him, he was a *child*, a blond little boy with a flyaway cowlick. I was racked by a wave of conflicting emotions until he fired his gauntlet again and missed me by a mile, at which point I just felt grateful. Children: not fantastic with hand-eye coordination.

Also: not extraordinarily fast runners. I took off into the undergrowth, grateful to have encountered, for once, someone with legs even shorter than my own. Twigs snapped and cracked under my boots as I ran, but all I could hear in my head were the other words Jumpsuit had said: *Only go in there if you know you can get out.*

My thoughts flashed to my friends. What if they were in these games? What about Kyle if he really had gone into *Brawl of Duty*—and what about Dad if he had decided to go find him?

And what about me, trapped, absurdly, in *Animal Flossing*?

Winning a HIVE game—even a fun, family-friendly game like this—was no longer just a way to score points or bragging rights. Now it was the only way to get back to the Honeycomb with your body and soul intact.

And if you lost a HIVE game . . .

Well.

I just couldn't afford to lose.

LEVEL 13

I couldn't run forever—both because that was a surefire way to get thrown into debtors' prison by Tom A. Toehead and because, well, I just couldn't run forever. After only a few minutes I had to stop and put my hands on my knees, gasping for air. I was currently being granted the slightest bit of cover by a shaded thatch of close-grown trees, festooned with what appeared to be licorice vines. I listened for the pitter-patter of murderous children's feet, but I couldn't hear anything coming from behind me.

I could, however, hear a rustling from some tall grass in front of me.

I took one last gasp of air and then held it, trying to stay silent. Without really wanting to, I wrapped a finger around the trigger of my plunger gun. Could I use it if it came down to it? Could I turn another player into a Drone to save myself, or to save my friends? Was it worth visiting that horrific fate on a stranger if it meant saving Gus, or Aaron, or—

"Laddu!"

No *way*.

My jaw dropped, releasing the gasp I'd been holding, as

a small orange butterball launched itself out of the shadows toward me—and then straight over my shoulder. I turned, bewildered, and saw that one of the licorice vines was in fact a snake, wearing a bow tie and horn-rimmed glasses (*How did they stay on?* wondered a very dazed part of my brain). It had been descending from the trees, ready to wrap around my throat. Now, though, Laddu distracted it, just like he had distracted the dragon yesterday—holy cow, was that *yesterday?*—and just long enough for a colorfully bedazzled boomerang to slice through the air like a jeweled fang, lopping the adorable cartoon snake in half and then returning over my other shoulder with a hiss.

And then a *slap* as it was caught in the gloved fist of one Sammi Khanna.

"We have to stop meeting like this," Sammi said sternly, stepping out of the grass. "If I keep saving you, you will owe me *so* many rides to school."

And then she grinned, her violet eyes twinkling, and then we were hugging, as a bow-tied snake head flopped and died at our feet.

"It is *so* good to see you," I said, pulling back.

"Same, sort of." Sammi holstered her boomerang. "I thought you weren't in here today! I couldn't believe it when I saw your name on the player board—I came to help you as fast as I could. It's the Update—it made it so that the only way to get back out of a game once you enter is to win. Otherwise, you become . . ."

I nodded. I knew what you became.

"I heard people talking about it before I came in here," Sammi said, "but I thought they were being insane because when I came here to escape the Honeycomb, *everyone* out there was being insane."

"Wait, yeah." I stopped and looked around. "Why *did* you come here?"

"Because the simulation is helping us," Jason hissed in my ear. I swatted at the air like I was swatting at a fly and then felt silly. Sammi just raised an eyebrow.

"Um, duh-doy?" she said. "I always come here when I'm stressed. And right now, it's like . . . stress city. Stress *world*."

"And now this is Stress Island." I sighed. Laddu hopped onto my shoulder to give me a comforting nuzzle. It was not unappreciated, but the problem remained:

"What are we going to do?"

"Oh, duh," Sammi said offhandedly. "We're going to win."

I smiled at the trademark Khanna confidence, but a terrible thought nagged at me.

"Wait—can we win?"

"Of course. This game had already been running for a while before you got here, so a lot of the competition is gone. And do you have any idea how many hours I've logged in here, Kara? You know how they say you need ten thousand hours to become a genius at something, or something? I'm . . . pretty genius."

"No, I mean"—I gestured at the two of us—"can *we* win? As a pair? If the only way to get out of here is to be the victor, wouldn't one of us have to . . ."

"Oh, that's right," Sammi said. "You haven't played in a while. You can do Alliances now—means you can win as a team. Here, give me your hand."

She put her metal glove out in front of me and we clasped hands. The moment we did, a blue glow lit up the air between us, hovering over the spot where our hands met and then racing up our forearms and enveloping our bodies. Laddu flew right into the blue zone, putting his little wing on our hands, which was, if not strictly necessary, then certainly very cute.

"Now we should get moving," Sammi said, "because that's going to trigger—"

"Alliance formed!" boomed an omnipresent voice, as perky as it was loud, and the blue light spiraled up through the trees and into the sky like a beacon.

Sammi grimaced. "That."

Within seconds, two opponents came creeping out of the darkness. Luckily for my conscience, they were both NPCs—unless some players had Modded themselves so thoroughly that they were now a fluffy bunny in plaid and a moose with a ukulele, respectively. The moose reached behind its back to grab its uke, but I didn't intend to find out what would happen if he got a chance to play it. I fired off my plunger gun as Sammi released her boomerang.

Sammi's aim was true, and the boomerang knocked the bunny to its feet before returning to sender. I was less skilled, and my plunger shot up over the moose's head.

Luckily, the thing about moose was that the space over their heads contained even more moose. With a sound I could only describe as *fwap-ap-ap*, my plunger just barely snagged on the tippy-top of my opponent's antlers, suctioning on nevertheless and causing him to stumble backward once, twice—and then he tripped over the bunny, and down he went.

I froze, waiting for the two animals to either get back up or turn into Drones. They did neither, remaining on the ground like the snake before them.

"There's one knock against your theory," I muttered. "*These* NPCs don't turn into Drones. Because they're the only ones who *are* NPCs."

"Hrmph," Jason said.

"What are you talking about?" Sammi asked.

I was almost grateful when she was distracted by the ground beginning to shake under us.

Key word: almost.

"No!" Sammi cried. "This can't be happening! It's not fair!"

But already, the ground was breaking apart, uprooting trees diagonally left and right. Out of a widening hole in the earth popped an inquisitive red snout.

"Has someone been hiding from the game?" asked Tom A. Toehead, crawling out of the dirt with a smile. Which, for the record, even when not in a nightmarish post-Update world, it is pretty unnerving to watch a mole mouth attempt to smile.

"We haven't been hiding!" Sammi protested. "We were fighting! We're—"

But Tom wasn't even listening to her. He moved past her to a tree, snuffling and sniffling.

"Oh dear!" he said. "This Camouflage Cardigan must have cost you a pretty penny at our store, but it won't help you here!"

The mole took a big snort with his star nose, and suddenly a mottled cardigan was pulled from thin air, revealing a player who'd been hiding against the tree this whole time. She was two or three years younger than us, pressed up against the bark and looking at us with wide eyes.

"You know the rules—you need to work for a Victory Bell to stay on Toehead Island!" Tom chirped. "Looks like you get the No-Bell Prize!"

"Wait—" I said, but it was too late. Tom had clapped the Shackles of Debt over the player's wrists, and where the metal touched her skin, she had begun to turn gray.

"Get out of here!" she said, while she could still talk. "Save yourselves!"

I felt something on my wrist and cried out in fright, thinking it was another set of handcuffs. But it was just Sammi, looking at me gravely.

"She's right," she said. "We have to get to the cabin in the middle of the island. That's where these games always end."

And *she* was right.

So we ran, racing past Tom as he waved us a cheery goodbye, leaping over burbling island springs and kid-sized booby traps, past flaming patches of farmland and grain silos swirling with candy cane stripes, and—increasingly, as we got closer to the center of the island—past Drones, floating around aimlessly, keeping watch over the whole macabre mess, surveying the players who'd lasted just that much longer than they had.

Then we burst into a gigantic clearing, a wide ring of open terrain that sloped gently upward to a grassy knoll. There, perched atop the knoll, was the structure at the center of every game of *Animal Flossing*: a candy cabin, made out of gingerbread and packed full of loot, weapons, and carbohydrates.

This was where we would make our stand.

Leaving the trees meant exposing ourselves to assailants, but Laddu kept watch as we climbed the hill, twisting his neck this way and that with the kind of 360-degree ease that makes you very happy to have a bird on your team.

"So do you know where Gus and Aaron are?" I asked. Sammi waved an armored hand in a sort-of-yes, sort-of-no gesture.

"Last I heard, Gus was trying to convince Aaron to go into *The Elder's Scrawls*."

We had just reached the front door of the cabin, but I would have frozen even if we'd been right out in the open. *The Elder's Scrawls* was one of those games Gus loved, the kind that you could never technically win—just die in and come back to later. If they had gone in there before the Update . . .

"But Aaron was pushing for *AATG*," Sammi said, instantly spotting my concern and speaking in a tone that said: *Breathe.* I breathed, and Sammi pushed the door to the cabin open slowly, her boomerang up and at the ready.

AATG—short for *Ain't Auto Theft Grand*—wasn't a frolic in the park, with its mean streets and car chases, but it was survivable. Anyway, *Animal Flossing* literally *was* supposed to be a frolic in the park, and yet here we were, creeping into a cabin, my hand hovering above my ridiculous sidearm and my thoughts flurrying around our odds of survival. The room was hushed and still, but I scanned each open doorway intently, not knowing which would be worse: a player getting the drop on us, or us getting the drop on them.

"It might not be killing them," Sammi said, but she couldn't look at me as she said it. Instead, she placed one foot slowly on the bottom step of a sugarcane stairwell, making sure it wasn't booby-trapped. "You know, when the players . . . turn. Maybe when the Update is fixed, they'll come back."

I didn't know about that. Seeing a man's mouth disappear into his face had felt pretty unfixable to me.

"Couldn't we expand our Alliance?" I asked softly, following Sammi as she crept up the stairs. "That way, more people could win. Or—or there could be a tie."

"Game doesn't work like that," she said, looking both ways

down the second-story hallway. "They cap it at two. We have to make sure we're that two. And I've never heard of anyone tying—you'd have to die at the *exact same time*, and I don't see how that's possible. Plus then you'd be, you know, dead."

"There *has* to be a way." I sounded like a kid having a tantrum, but I didn't care. "I mean, I want to get out of here, but I hate that winning means someone else . . ."

"Losing," Sammi said, lining herself up against a door (made, for the record, out of a giant chocolate bar). "That's how games work, Kara. For you to win, someone has—"

She kicked the door in. We held our breaths. No one inside, just a dingy gingerbread room with one small window and a busted-up peanut brittle bookshelf.

"To lose," she finished. "Here, keep a lookout. I'm going to check the player board."

She positioned herself behind the bookshelf, pinched the bridge of her nose, and froze in place. Like many games, *Animal Flossing* allowed you to check out the map and who was on it, but you had to make yourself vulnerable to do so, entering a temporary trance. That left it up to me to stand guard.

Well, me and Laddu, who perched on my shoulder while I stationed myself by the window. The good news: From here, I had an unimpeded view of half the clearing. If anyone stepped out of the woods from this direction, I would see it in an instant.

The bad news: I had an unimpeded view of *half* the clearing.

At least it was all quiet on the this-half front. The only

sounds were leaves rustling in a digital breeze, and somewhere in the distance—because this was, after all, *Animal Flossing*—the soft, sick strumming of soothing music.

"She's right, you know," Jason said. "You have to win, no matter what."

"Easy for you to say," I muttered, causing Laddu to cock his head. "You don't even think the people we're playing against are real."

There was a pause.

"I'm not sure," Jason said softly.

I froze, and not just because of what Jason had just said. Had a shadow at the edge of the tree line just . . . grown?

"I mean, I'm sure I'm *right*," Jason continued. "But remember—some of the players in HIVE have to be from the real world, or else, what's the point of HIVE? *Someone* has to be playing it. So, yeah, maybe some of them got stuck in there during the Update, too. Maybe some of them are real. But wouldn't it be easier if we just decided they weren't?"

It was a sad thing to say. It was a *scary* thing to say.

And it was true. It would be so much easier.

(The new shadow, if I wasn't imagining it, looked small—like that of a young boy.)

"But there has to be a way out we haven't thought of yet," I insisted, to myself as much as to Jason. "We have to be smarter than *Animal Flossing*. And being smart is just noticing things. What haven't we noticed?"

You'd have to die at the exact same time, Sammi had said.

What did that make me think of? Why did I feel like I'd already noticed something I hadn't even *noticed* I'd noticed? (Yeesh.) I'd gotten myself in and out of more HIVE hijinks in the last twenty-four hours than I had in the last few years, but how had I done all that, *really*? Mostly just by jumping off things. Was that a sustainable strategy for success?

Wait. Was it?

(If that shadow turned into a boy, if that boy came toward us, I would have no choice but to—)

That's when I remembered exactly what I'd noticed.

That's when I made my plan to get everyone out of the game safely—or no one at all.

And that's when a scream rang out across the island, and everything spun out of control.

LEVEL 14

The scream was shrill, coming from somewhere deep inside the forest. It grew in volume, pitch, and terror—and then abruptly, it cut off.

"Someone just vanished off the player board." Sammi's voice behind me made me jump. "I think Tom got them."

I nodded but didn't turn, refusing to take my eyes off the clearing for even a moment. "Who's left?"

"Just us and two players now—and I don't think they're NPCs."

"Was one of them Markus Fawkes, by any chance?"

"What?" Sammi laughed. "No. Their usernames were TrollKid3000 and Ender_Of_Games. Why?"

"Long story. Sammi, I think we should go to the— *There! There he goes!*"

The blond boy exploded from the tree line, making a mad dash for the cabin. In a moment Sammi was at my side, boomerang in hand, but I reached out and grabbed her wrist. Laddu burst from my shoulder, fluttering between us and squawking in distress.

"Sammi, we don't have to— Oh, come *on*—"

The kid wasn't making it easy for us. Or rather, he was: He had seen our skirmish in the window and stopped mid-dash to *do a taunting little dance at us.* That had to be TrollKid3000. Young gamers, I swear. A different breed entirely.

"It's a perfect shot!" Sammi protested.

"We don't have to take it!" I said. "If you'd listen to me—"

"If we *don't* take it, someone else will!"

And then someone else did.

From somewhere outside our line of view, a pie came streaking through the air. It hit the boy right as he was doing a particularly involved dance move, catching him off guard and sending him flying. He landed in the grass in a scattering of (if I had to guess) banana cream.

I turned away from the window. I couldn't look, and I didn't have time to. With Sammi's wrist still in my hand, I pulled us toward the door.

"We have to get to the roof," I said as we stumbled out into the hallway, an ungainly tangle of four legs and two wings. "I have an idea. No one else has to die."

"They *might not be dying!*" Sammi reminded me. "But if they are, whoever you're trying to save, he just showed us he's very comfortable *killing a kid!*"

"You were about to do the same thing!" I said, looking around frantically. "Where's—ah, there!"

Blending in with the brown gingerbread walls was a pretzel stick ladder leading up to a hatch in the ceiling. The hatch, which was made of rock candy, looked heavy. Remembering the unexpected force my plunger gun had showed earlier, I pulled it out and shot it straight upward. Sure enough, the plunger knocked the hatch off its hinges, sending it clattering up into a dimly lit gloom.

"You climb first," I said. "Quickly."

"Kara," Sammi said. "Sooner or later we're going to have to—"

"You climb first," I repeated, pointing the plunger gun straight at her heart.

Sammi's jaw dropped open for a moment, but one thing about Sammi: She never had nothing to say for long.

"I don't think that would even work on me. We're in an Alliance. And look, if we run, Tom's just going to get us. I'm trying to *help* you, Kara."

"So am I!" I insisted.

And then a cabin-shaking boom rose up from the ground floor, followed by a sound like the scattering of a thousand little pebbles. Or crumbs.

Sort of like the sound you'd get if someone kicked down a giant, perhaps overly baked, gingerbread door.

Sammi and I stared at each other for just one more moment, and then:

"After I save your life, I'm going to kill you," Sammi grumbled, and began to climb, Laddu flying up ahead of her.

As I waited my turn, I looked down the hallway toward the stairs. I heard a lot of clomping around on the ground floor, but nothing that sounded like someone climbing a stairwell. If we were quiet, we'd have a couple of minutes more to ourselves.

"Hey!" I yelled. "We're upstairs!"

As Sammi's feet disappeared into the attic, I heard her curse the way only someone fluent in eight languages can, but I didn't have time to explain. "Look for a way onto the roof!" I called up to her as I started my own climb up the ladder, trying not to cut myself on any particularly large salt crystals.

By the time I pulled myself into the attic, I could definitely hear heavy footsteps approaching from below. Sammi stood by a window, round and uncovered like a ship's porthole, that provided the attic's only light. She gestured at it brusquely as if to say, *Here it is. Are you happy?*

I was. The porthole was just big enough to clamber through, and I did, pulling Sammi after me, with Laddu popping out afterward. The island spread out from us in all directions, bright and green and dotted with Drones. Before Sammi could ask what my plan was, I made my way over to the edge of the roof. We were actually pretty high up; just peering at the ground below made my stomach flop.

Perfect.

"Be ready to attack whoever comes out of that window," I said. "But please—*don't actually do it.*"

Sammi grumbled but raised her boomerang. To show she wasn't in this alone, I also aimed a plunger at the porthole. We stood and stared, waiting for Ender_Of_Games to arrive.

When they did, they were so big they couldn't fit through

the window. A beefy arm reached out, and then a foot attached to a thick calf—and then, frustrated, Ender_Of_Games just punched out the edges, stepping through the gingerbread wreckage to join us on the roof.

He wasn't Markus Fawkes, but he was a fine entry into that particular genre of human being. He towered over both Sammi and me, his long black hair somehow managing to be stringy and greasy in, I hasten to remind you, a world where you could *customize your appearance.* At some point since landing on the island he'd acquired what appeared to be a pie bandolier, with three tins strapped on a sash across his chest. One, where the banana cream had presumably been, was empty; the other two were decidedly not, and even as he emerged, he was reaching for the chocolate pecan.

Then he saw us.

"You throw, we shoot," I said. "And there's two of us and one of you, so: Don't throw."

The man's fingers stopped just above the pie, locking us in a standoff.

"Look, ladies," he sneered. "I've got two pies, so I'd say it's still an even match. And it's nothing personal. I don't *want* to obliterate you."

"Neither do we," I said.

"I mean, I'm fine," Sammi muttered.

"Ignore her," I said. "I'm dead serious: I think I know how to get us all out of here without anyone else getting Droned."

"Yeah?" said Ender. "How's that?"

"We're all going to jump off the roof," I said.

For a brief moment, no one spoke. It was a very brief moment.

"Why is that your answer to *everything*?" Jason groaned.

"I can't believe we're friends," Sammi said.

"All right, pies it is," said Ender, moving his other hand up to the bandolier.

"Wait!" I pleaded. "It's the gravity. I noticed it when I first detached from my parachute—the game is a cartoon, but the physics engine is real."

"Physics engine?" Ender frowned. His fingers were still too close to the pies for my liking, but he was intrigued.

"It's what my mo—what video game designers call the rules of the worlds they design," I said. "And it means that if we all jump at the exact same time, we'll all hit the ground at—"

"The exact same time," Sammi breathed, finally realizing where I was going.

"No, we wouldn't!" Ender looked back and forth at us, trying to figure out if we were joking. "I'm way bigger than either of you! I'd hit the ground first! You'd both win!"

"That's not how gravity works," Sammi and I said together.

"All objects fall at the same rate of acceleration no matter their mass," I added. "We learned that in physics, uh . . . last year."

That last sentence was probably not the way to make us sound cool and convincing. But it was the first part that seemed to have stuck with Ender_Of_Games. Slowly but surely, his hands were lowering to his sides. He was really thinking it over.

Obviously, that's when the roof exploded.

"Uh-oh!" said Tom A. Toehead, popping out of the roof of the cabin like that was a perfectly normal place for moles to pop out of. "It's been a while since anything happened. Is everyone here trying their hardest to get that Bell, or do I need to do a Welfare Check?"

"Come on!" I yelled at Ender over Tom's head. Gingerbread was crumbling into the hole Tom had made, and if it kept up long enough, the whole roof would cave in. "We have to do this now!"

"This is crazy!" he yelled back. "What if you're wrong about the gravity? Or what if you're right, and instead of us all winning, we all just become . . . you know?"

"I have no idea," I said honestly. "But if you don't try, we'll all be 'you know,' anyway!"

As if to prove my point, Tom was now pulling himself onto the remainder of the roof, sniffing between the three of us to decide who he would take first.

He chose Sammi.

"Kara!" Sammi shrieked. At the same time, Laddu cried *Laddu!* and threw himself at Tom, but he bounced off the mole as harmlessly as a fly off—well, off an invulnerable, oversized mole. Tom just kept approaching as Sammi backed herself toward the edge of the roof. I wanted to help, but in the world of *Animal Flossing*, Tom was unstoppable—and I couldn't take my eyes off Ender.

"If she becomes a Drone, I'll make sure you do, too!" I

yelled. Ender opened his mouth to protest, but looking into my eyes, I think he realized something at the same moment that I did: I actually meant it.

"On three," I said. "Let yourself free-fall straight down. One . . ."

"Kara, this is insane!" Jason said.

"Two . . ."

"By the way, have you visited our museum?" asked Tom.

"Three!" I yelled, looking between Sammi and Ender to make sure we were all watching one another. *"Now!"*

In what was starting to become a routine, I threw myself out into the air. It was a much shorter fall than the last time I'd done this, but it left me with just enough time to wonder: Had we timed it just right? Was my theory correct? Was Jason's ongoing stream of panicked commentary a sign that he cared about what happened to me, or just a sign that he cared about his best chance at getting back into HIVE? And most pressingly, would it hurt when I hit the ground?

And then I found out.

LEVEL 15

Okay, I won't leave you hanging. The answers were, respectively: We had; it was; who knew; and, blessedly, no.

Where there should have been a bone-shattering impact, there was just the world freezing, and that same booming voice from earlier proclaiming: "Congratulations! You've won the Victory Bell Royale! Come back soon!"

And then me, Sammi, Laddu, and a bewildered man with (not to harp on this, but) some seriously greasy hair were all staring at one another, stunned, sitting on our butts on a trio of platforms floating just above the very bottom of the entire Honeycomb. It was as quiet in the massive chamber as it had been when I'd left it, and it was hard to know who would break the silence first.

Just kidding. Obviously, it was Sammi.

"I can't believe that worked," she said.

"I can't believe you helped me," said Ender_Of_Games. "You totally had the drop on me. You could have just taken me out. Why didn't you?"

"That was sort of the whole point," I said. "We *didn't* want to do that."

"I mean, we might have—"

"We wouldn't," I said over Sammi. "Keep that in mind if you have to go into another game, okay? Not everything is win-lose. There may be a way out you haven't thought of yet."

"Wow." As Ender stood up, he unconsciously scratched at the spot on his chest where the pie bandolier had vanished. "I don't know about all that, but thanks. And they say there are no cheat codes in HIVE—maybe there are. I didn't have you pegged for such an experienced gamer."

I heard a snort, looked around, and realized it was Jason. I shrugged.

"I'm really more of a casual player," I said.

Ender just shook his head. "I dunno," he said as his platform began to float up and away from us. "I think we're in here for a while. There's no such thing as a casual player anymore. You girls stay safe."

And then Ender_Of_Games was gone.

Which was our cue to get going, too. The last time I'd emerged into the Honeycomb, I'd been ambushed six ways from Sunday; I didn't intend for it to happen again. I hopped onto Sammi's platform faster than she could say something about it—so, very fast—and said: "Take us to the top of the Honeycomb, to—"

"Terms and Conditions," Jason reminded me.

"Terms and Conditions," I finished. And as the platform began its ascent, Sammi leaped up, grabbed my face with both armored gloves, and tilted it sharply this way and that.

"Ah!" I winced as she squinted into each of my ears. "What are you—"

"Where's the earpiece?" Sammi grunted, her teeth between her tongue as she got up close and personal with my earwax (did I have earwax in HIVE? Ugh, next question). "I *knew* you were talking to someone, it's so obvious. How did you get messaging to work? Is it Gus? If you and Gus are holding out on me, I swear—"

"It's not Gus!" I said, finally smacking her hands away. "It's—it's a long story."

Sammi gestured around at the sea of silence and steel through which we rose. "It's a long way to the top of the Honeycomb," she said. "Try me."

I hesitated.

"I'm not sure you should tell her," Jason said, which settled it.

"Okay," I said. "I'll tell you. So this morning . . ."

And so the long, eerie ride up through the Drone-infested void was spent telling Sammi exactly how I'd ended up here. To her credit, Sammi was as good a listener as she was a talker, and she nodded and exclaimed appropriately as I told her everything, or almost everything: That I'd been in the real world when the Update happened. That I'd met someone who'd escaped the Update, and that they knew a way they could guide me in, and then maybe help me guide people (e.g., Sammi and my father) back out. Also, I'd saved that person from Markus Fawkes just yesterday, and now Markus was on some kind of bloodthirsty revenge quest. Also *also*, that person I'd saved was—

"Jason?"

"I bet she doesn't even remember me," Jason muttered.

"Jason *Alcorn*?" Sammi said, earning a begrudging grunt from Jason. "I remember him. Only kid who did better than me in our ninth-grade coding unit. He sure wasn't humble about it, either."

"Sammi, you're not humble about anything."

"I didn't say it was a bad thing, did I?" Sammi shrugged. "But *Jason*? Wow. That's so random. Or, like, the opposite of random—I mean, the biggest Hivehead in town? What are the odds?"

"Fascinating," Jason said. "The AI allows her to tiptoe right up to the precipice of realizing this must be a simulation, but it doesn't let her break through."

"Shut up," I hissed.

"What?"

"Hmm?"

"I thought you said—oh. Jason. I see." Sammi tilted her head at us—I mean, at me. "So, uh . . . how is that going for you, then?"

Acutely aware that Jason could hear us, and not wanting to open the whole can of worms that was *He's had a total break from reality and thinks you don't exist*, I searched carefully for the right words to avoid suspicion.

"He's got . . . a perspective on HIVE that I wouldn't have had otherwise."

"There's something you're not telling me," Sammi said instantly.

"What? No, there's not."

"No, this is good." Sammi peered at me intently. "Don't tell me. I'll totally guess what it is."

"Believe me," I muttered wearily, "you will never guess."

"So there *is* something!" Sammi pumped her fist triumphantly.

"Dang," I said, and Jason whistled.

"She's good," he admitted. "You know. For an NPC."

I would have pushed back on that, but I had neither the energy nor the time. We were nearing the top of the Honeycomb, as evidenced by the slowly sloping curve of the walls above us—and the weirdness of the games now lining those walls. As mentioned earlier, the games at the top of the Honeycomb were intense and odd, meant for HIVE's true believers and novelty seekers. If I let my gaze settle on any one game long enough, holographic titles would appear, offering tantalizing or unsettling hints of what lay behind each hexagon: *Nightmarathon. Undead Undemption 2.* And one that just said *Frisbee, but Bad.* Gone were the comforting pink glows and cute catwalks of the world below; here there were only the barest of steel beams connecting one game to the next, and the occasional abandoned platform. This far up, there weren't even any Drones hanging around—just Sammi, Laddu, and me. Yesterday, that would have been normal; today, it just felt like one more thing to be creeped out by.

At this point it occurred to me: This was where I'd sent Dad. And that had been at least an hour ago.

"Jason?" I said, causing Sammi to perk up with interest. "Have you heard anything from my dad? Or my brother?"

"No, sorry," Jason said. "If your dad's been trying to get in touch with me, he hasn't found me. And if your brother got out, I assume I'd know."

I frowned. "How would you know if Kyle got out?"

"Well, your dad said he was at the Apiary, right? So if he went through the back door, I'd notice him doing the same thing I did when I made it out."

"Which was?"

"Falling gasping out of a pod and then pulling myself across the carpet with my shaking, useless limbs," Jason said flatly.

"Oh." I winced. "Right."

Sammi read the look on my face and said, "Didn't your dad say he was going to get Kyle? Maybe they just haven't made it here yet."

She was trying to be comforting, but when I imagined my dad stepping into *Brawl of Duty*, totally unaware of the new stakes of entering a HIVE game, my breaths got short and tight.

"You're here," Jason cut in. "Time to get moving."

Of all the moments for Jason to be an impatient jerk, why did he have to choose now? I drew myself up, ready to reprimand him.

"Trust me," Jason added, more quietly this time. "Doing something is easier than worrying about where they are."

Oh.

"Oh," Sammi said as the platform came to a smooth halt. "We're here."

Looking around, I couldn't see what either of them was talking about. None of the games around us were titled *Terms and Conditions*. When I turned to ask Sammi where it was, I found the answer by following her gaze—straight up.

We were hovering a couple feet under the very tip-top of the Honeycomb, which was exactly one hexagon wide. The hexagon wasn't gold, pink, blue, or any other color—it was an aggressively unremarkable pale gray. And if you looked at it long enough, three words appeared in an ever so slightly whiter shade of pale:

TERMS AND CONDITIONS.

"Huh," Sammi said. "Funny how I never thought to see what was up here."

"You still haven't," Jason said, and *there* was his impatient voice. "Let's go!"

"Oh. Right." I began to stand up, with Sammi following my lead. "Come on, let's"—I straightened up, and the Honeycomb vanished—"go."

The lights in Terms and Conditions were dim, a series of long, low strips on the walls, like the kind you'd find running off the backup generator of a bunker somewhere. But this place wasn't a bunker—or not *just* a bunker, anyway. We stood at the entrance of a massive library, strip lights stretching away into unending aisles of shelves. The first few aisles were marked like they would be in a real library (A–J, K–S, and so on), but they quickly devolved into numbers and characters from a coding language I'd never seen. Under those signs were glowing touchscreens, each one hexagonal and displaying equally incomprehensible prompts like BACK-END ARCHIVES—ACCESS? or HIVE SIMULATOR—ENTER? And instead of books, each shelf was lined with—

"Scrolls?" Sammi said, stepping forward to pick one up. Jason had just enough time to say "Don't touch the—" in my ear before Sammi reached out and touched a scroll. With a sound like a printer tray exploding, the scroll shot out into the aisle, an endless sheet of paper whizzing past a startled Sammi, colliding with the shelf across the way, and then continuing to unwind until it was piling up on the ground around her feet. It was like watching a frog's tongue leap out, if frog tongues were made out of parchment and also half a mile long. After a full minute of frenzied rustling, the scroll finally slowed to a creep, then a crawl, and then stopped altogether in a mountain of coils that came up to our shins.

Sammi reached into the pile of paper and picked up a

random section. "'BrainSTIM Card removal must always be supervised by a licensed biotechnician,'" she read aloud. "'Unlicensed BrainSTIM Card removal is illegal, an improper use of trademarked technology, and constitutes an act of copyright theft. It may also be detrimental to the Player's continued life. For guidance on how to acquire a removal license, see Shelf . . .'" She paused for a moment, confused. "Okay, I don't know how to pronounce that, and I'm *me*."

"It's the rules," I said, looking around. "It's a whole library of how HIVE works."

"Not just the rules," Jason said in my ear, while Sammi continued to read. "You know every time you've ever downloaded something new and been asked to agree to a set of regulations, and stipulations, and privacy violations? Have you ever once read any of them?"

"No," I admitted. "And I love to read."

"Exactly," Jason said. "You just scroll past all those words and click yes. Everyone does. Pages and pages of words, and more for every new Update, and longer every time. They add up. And they're all here. It's the perfect hiding spot for everything someone doesn't want you to know—because nobody *wants* to know anything in Terms and Conditions. Nobody wants to care."

Credit where it was due: Jason was making new strides in creeping me out.

"Thanks for the color commentary," I said, signaling to

Sammi that it was time to get moving. "Speaking of hiding spots: Which way are we going?"

"Straight ahead," Jason said. "I'll tell you when to turn."

I stepped carefully over the pile, and Sammi dropped her reading material and followed me as we moved forward into the dim light of the library. I'd walked through a lot of library aisles in my life, and normally I liked to drag my fingers along the spines of the books as I passed through, feeling the accumulated ridges of all those words waiting to be read. Now, though, I took care not to touch any of the scrolls, fearing I'd set off another paperslide. Sammi had either had the same thought, or she was just as creeped out by this place as I was because she held Laddu close to her chest as we walked.

"Okay, turn left here," Jason said. "And then in two aisles, turn right."

This guided library tour went on for a while—certainly for much longer than I'd expected. As the twists and turns piled up, Jason's little speech really began to sink in: This library was *huge*. You could hide anything in here, easily. And even more easily than that, you could get lost.

"Maybe my dad did make it here," I whispered. (Just because we were seemingly the only people in a spooky magical virtual shelf maze didn't mean I was going to be *loud* in a *library*.) "Maybe he just got turned around."

"Maybe," Jason said. "But speaking from experience, if he made his way to the back like you told him, he'd find the door eventually. I'm just showing you a shortcut. You know, like how you can get to the kids' reading room faster if you go through the Romance aisle."

Sammi raised her eyebrows at my sudden smile, but I couldn't help it. Jason's acknowledgment of our shared childhood was as unexpected as it was dead-on. I couldn't count the number of times one or both of us had run our latest pile of books back to the Bullworth Library reading room, giggling as we passed by scandalously illustrated paperbacks with names like *In Love with a Hologram* or *Kidnapped by a Bitcoin Billionaire.* Somehow I'd forgotten all about it; how had Jason, of all people, remembered?

Jason must have realized I was about to follow up on this because he quickly sputtered, "Okay, uh, you're almost there. Take two more lefts and a right and then *wait for my instructions.*"

This attempt at regaining his tough-kid clout was both unsuccessful and hilarious, but I let it go as I led Sammi and Laddu around one more corner and then another. My heart started to beat faster as we approached the final corner. I'd spent so much time rushing from one crisis to another that I'd barely given myself a second to imagine what this mysterious back door was, or how it would work when we found it. Who'd put it in Terms and Conditions, and why? Would Sammi really be able to pass through it? Would Dad be waiting for us there? Was it even, like, an actual door?

But as I turned the final corner, I froze in place, and as

Sammi came up behind me and started to say "What," I clapped my hand over her mouth.

None of our questions were getting answered anytime soon. However the back door worked, whatever it looked like, our view of it was blocked. Because we weren't the first people here.

Between us and where I assumed the door would be, there was a swarm of Drones. And when I say a swarm, I mean it—not just the neat, still rows of watchers we'd seen out in the Honeycomb, but a cluster of Drones, a mess, crammed in from floor to ceiling, sliding over one another like insects, a living wall of nonliving guardians. And they were doing something I'd never known Drones to do before: They were all producing a wordless, agitated buzz.

And between us and the Drones were still more figures: not more NPCs, but real, genuine, flesh-and-blood, not-actually-flesh-and-blood digital actual people. Sammi and I whipped back around into the aisle before any of them could notice us, but they were all too concerned with the Drones and one another to see us, anyway. Not just concerned, come to think of it—they were upset. From the brief glimpse I'd gotten, they were all people who weren't used to wanting for anything; they were men and women in expensive, important-looking outfits, interspersed among giant men in dark suits with ear-pieces and weapons.

And standing between two of the biggest men, looking away from the Drone wall just long enough to frown at something, was a face I had never expected to see in person—even, or especially, in HIVE. And as Sammi and I stared at each other and held our breaths, that person spoke.

"Did any of you hear something?" asked the president of the United States.

LEVEL 16

What. *What?* Our shock was matched only by our fear of get-ting caught. My hand was still over Sammi's mouth. Sammi's hand was over Laddu's beak. We stayed frozen like that until the deep voice of one of those giant guards—a Secret Service member, I now realized—said, "All I hear is the Drones, sir."

"Hmm." This answer seemed less than satisfying to the presi-dent (what?) of the United States *(what?)*. "Why are they doing that, anyway? Buzzing? They don't normally do that, do they?"

"No, sir. It seems to be one more glitch resulting from—"

"Phase One, right," the president sighed. "I hope it's not like this going forward."

"It shouldn't be like this *now*," snapped a woman's voice, clipped thin with irritation and an austere English accent. "We were told we'd be granted immunity before Phase Two began. I'm supposed to be on my way to a bunker under Buckingham right now. Why have we been blocked in here with the rest of the . . . commoners?"

The disdain dripped from her voice, but I was too shocked to be offended on behalf of us commoners. Phase One? Phase Two? *Buckingham?*

At that point I remembered what Jason had said: *Half the government is in HIVE at any given time.* I didn't know if I was more annoyed or terrified to realize that Jason had been right. We'd stumbled onto one of those top-secret international meetings I'd dismissed out of hand. And it sounded like they were discussing some truly *top* top secrets.

Because apparently, Jason had been right about something else: The Update hadn't been an accident at all.

"Someone get Alanick on ze telephone," another voice snapped, in another thick accent. "Vhat good is having him at our beck and call if ve cannot actually call him?"

"Yeah," said an American. "Or . . . or beck him."

"With all due respect, all messaging systems are down," said a deeper voice, another guard. "And I think we're all aware that Alanick is a little . . . tied up right now."

"Yes! I *called* it!" Jason cried, and I flinched before remembering only I could hear him. Then he added, much less excitedly: "Oh no. I called it."

And he had. Eric Alanick was being held hostage somewhere by people who had managed to crash all of HIVE—people who controlled the highest levels of real-world government. And while I couldn't begin to imagine why they'd done it, it was clear they didn't care how many innocent players got trapped, or Droned, or worse—just so long as they got what they wanted.

But whoever had made the plan hadn't known everything. Clearly they had never anticipated this wall of malfunctioning

Drones between them and their way out. And they *definitely* hadn't anticipated us.

Which also meant we were the only ones who could do something about it.

I straightened my spine, getting ready to move, and instantly, Sammi's eyes bulged. *No*, she mouthed. *No, no, no.* She pointed her thumb over her shoulder, back toward the way we'd come: *We have to go.* I didn't budge, but now Jason had seen how Sammi was responding to me, and guessed what was going on.

"Kara, now's not the time to make a stand," he said. "I know you want to help, but that's not the smart way to play the game."

"Why does everyone keep telling me this is a *game*?!" I snapped.

Sammi gasped.

Jason groaned.

The president of the United States said, "Okay, we *all* heard that, right?"

And no amount of breath or beak holding could prevent our good friend in the Secret Service from lumbering over to the aisle, regarding us coolly from behind his sunglasses, and calling out, "Over here, sir."

"*What's* over there?" the British woman snapped.

"Couple of teenage girls and a . . . bird," he said. "Not a problem, we'll just— *Aah!*"

In the moments he took to reach for his sidearm, I used

the first line of defense I could think of: an entire shelf full of exploding scrolls. I ran my hands over every one I could touch, and *whoosh!* They all erupted at once as the guard cried out and vanished in a blizzard of fine print. Sammi, seeing what I was doing, quickly deployed the opposite shelf, providing double the cover and double the fun.

"Go!" I yelled as the aisle began to fill up. "Go, go, go!"

Sammi bolted and I followed her, running my hand along more scrolls as we went. Confetti cannons of rules and regulations shot off behind me, making sure no one could chase us up the aisle.

"I've got 'em!" yelled a voice to our left.

Oh, right. Libraries had multiple aisles.

"Take a right!" I cried as we neared an opening in the shelves.

"But we came from the left!" Sammi said.

"Freeze!" yelled a guard, barreling into view on our left.

"Never mind!" Sammi said, and as Laddu flew directly into the guard's forehead, we went right. While the guard roared and flailed, I looked back to make sure Laddu was okay, but Sammi herself pulled me into a new row, pushing me onward.

"He'll be fine!" Sammi said. "Does Jason know a way we can get out of here?"

"Just keep going forward!" Jason said.

But already there was another set of footsteps thudding up the aisle to our right. If we just kept going forward, they'd have us surrounded in no time.

"What'd he say?" Sammi asked as we reached a new intersection.

"He said left!" I said, and we bore left. Then a shape burst forth from a shelf in front of us, and we screamed and dodged right into a new aisle—only to have that shape fly ahead of us, shaking its tail feathers in our faces.

"Oh. Hey, Laddu," Sammi panted. "Knew you'd be fine— oh, there he goes again."

Again, the first guard had entered the aisle behind us, and again, Laddu circled and dove. I was too busy running forward into a new aisle to look back, but based on the shriek that resulted, this time Laddu had aimed lower than the forehead.

"I love him so much," Sammi said.

Blinking touchscreens and mysterious aisle markings raced by: ADA–UNIX; 101010–EVERYTHING; ???–!!!!. I was running out of breath, and at this point so many people were yelling from all over the library that it was impossible to tell where any of our pursuers were—or where we were, for that matter.

Then I saw it, coming up on our right: K–S, one of the aisles we'd first seen upon entering Terms and Conditions. We'd made it back to the front.

"This way!" I hissed, not wanting to give away our location. Sammi nodded and we darted up K–S, ready to make a quiet escape.

Then we reached the end of the aisle and froze.

"Was that there when we came in?" Sammi asked.

"That was definitely not there when we came in," I said.

Nevertheless, it was there now: another swarm of Drones, smaller than the one at the back door but still big enough to look seriously tough to pass through, thrumming and humming around the door that would lead us out to the Honeycomb.

"Do you think they'll attack us if we try to get out?" I asked.

"Do you really want to find out?" Sammi responded, which, fair. But we had to do something quick—all those shouts and footfalls, while still scattered across the library, were definitely getting closer.

"Laddu?" Laddu asked, appearing behind Sammi and perching on her shoulder, feathers ruffled but none the worse for wear.

"You're asking me," Sammi sighed.

"You could let them catch you," Jason suggested. "Maybe they'd take you to wherever they're keeping Eric Alanick. Then you could find out what's happening and I could—I mean, *we* could do something about it."

"That's *really* your best idea?"

"No," Jason sighed. "But I didn't want to tell you about the other one."

I could feel my blood pressure rising, which was really impressive because, again, not my real body. *"Why would you not want to tell us?!"*

But I knew the answer without him even responding: He cared more about us finding Eric Alanick than he did about us actually escaping.

"Jason knows a way out?" Sammi asked, catching on.

"Sort of," Jason said. "Do you see the touchscreen next to you?"

I did. Glowing on the edge of the shelf was one of the mini-hexagons I'd spotted upon entering the library. It was the one that read HIVE SIMULATOR—ENTER?

"I see it," I said. "What's a HIVE Simulator, anyway? That seems redundant. We're already in HIVE."

"That's not—just touch it," Jason said. "Both of you. Or just you, obviously. I don't really care about Sammi."

"You little—"

"I hear them!" yelled a voice that was much closer than any of the others had been so far.

"Touch the screen!" I hissed, and without even questioning it, Sammi joined me in slamming a hand down on the console. Over Sammi's shoulder, I saw a goon emerge from the stacks, looking the wrong way, but the moment he turned he would see . . .

Nothing, apparently, because at that moment the goon vanished, along with Sammi and the rest of the library. In a sharp contrast from the library's strip lights and steel, I suddenly found myself standing in a beam of warm sunshine.

And in another sharp contrast, I suddenly found myself inches away from a wrinkled, pale beast with no face, lumbering closer to me with every second, ready to tear me apart.

LEVEL 17

"Aah!" I cried.

"Aaah!" yelled the beast, rearing away.

"Laddu!" cried Laddu, popping up from behind the beast's shoulder.

"Kara?" asked the beast.

"Sammi?" I asked, and that was when I realized my hands, which I'd thrown up in fear, were currently the same shade of pale as the creature in front of me. Not only that—they were twice as big as they'd been a moment ago.

Because Sammi and I were both wearing beekeeping suits. The suits were white and baggy, and they obscured everything from our forms to our faces with mesh nets just thick enough that we could see out of them but not, apparently, see into them. Even Laddu, I now noticed, was covered in a fine netting, much to his clear displeasure.

As one, Sammi and I turned out from each other to gaze at the open-air greenhouse in which we now stood. Late-afternoon sunlight slid over boxes of white pine, stacked on top of one another in towers, each one emanating a familiar buzz.

"Oh," I breathed, putting it together.

"Yeah," Jason said. "Trippy, right?"

We hadn't entered a HIVE Simulator.

We'd entered a *hive* simulator.

In HIVE.

"Who put this here?" I asked as Sammi and I moved forward to walk among the hives. A few bees danced around the outside of each tower, but the moment I got close to one, a dozen more emerged in a defensive cloud, and the soft humming from inside the hive became a buzz-saw whine as countless unseen bees sent up a would-be battle cry. I pulled my hand back and stood stock-still as the bees calmed down and darted back into their box. Suit or no suit, I did not intend to get on any of their bad sides.

"I think it's a private joke for the HIVE architects," Jason said. "I found it by accident during one of my reading sessions. It's amazingly realistic—like, weirdly so. It's just straight-up beehives. Not much of a game—but I figured it'd be a good place to hide."

I'd been relaying his words to Sammi as he spoke, and she nodded.

"Good thinking," she said. "Whoever those guys are out there, I don't think they know to look for us here, or we'd have seen them by—wait." She frowned. "One of your *reading sessions?*"

I'd noticed that, too, and it had reminded me of the things Jason had mentioned back in the real world. The secrets he knew that other HIVE employees knew nothing about; the time he spent hanging around the top of the Honeycomb; gradually, a portrait of Jason's past few years was beginning to come together.

"Jason," I said, "how much of Terms and Conditions have you read?"

After a moment's hesitation, Jason said, "Most."

"Most," I began, "or all?"

Another hesitation, and then:

"There were some parts I didn't understand," Jason admitted, his voice soft, as if this was a shameful secret.

Crack! Sammi and I whirled around, and the hives sent up an indignant buzz as a sharp sound rang out from the front of the wheelhouse. But it was just Laddu, squawking in distress as his attempts to remove his protective netting led him to knock over a bizarre device that looked like a metal fan.

"Okay, look," Sammi said, heading over to clean up Laddu's mess. "I would *love* to know more about whatever PhD in weirdness Jason has slowly been earning. But we still have to find a way out of here—past those Drones and past those guys in the library. And by 'those guys' I of course mean—because I feel we really have not stressed this enough—the *British prime minister* and the *president*."

"Oh, was that the prime minister?" I asked.

"Honestly, Kara," Sammi said, picking up the fan and turning to fix me with a look I could feel through two layers of mesh. "I've seen you read *Jane Eyre* three times. How do you never read the news."

Jason snorted, and I tried to get things back on track.

"Well, you're right," I said, looking around the greenhouse. "We need an escape plan. Let's think. What do we know? Is there something here that can help us?"

"Something in a beehive simulator?" Sammi asked skeptically.

"Sure, why not? You're the puzzle-game queen, Sammi— solve this puzzle."

"Maybe," Jason said, still enjoying himself, "you could try jumping off a beehive."

I ignored him.

"I've never heard of portals from one game to another," I said. "Let's start there. That's not normal, right? Is that new?"

"It's not normal, no," Jason said while Sammi mulled it over. "Game developers want to keep you in their games once you're there, not send you away. That way you keep making in-game purchases and they keep making profits."

"Why would developers need our money for their games if we're not real?" I muttered, softly enough that Sammi couldn't hear over the buzzing of the bees. "Your theory is flawed. Checkmate."

"Oh, please," Jason said. "Companies use bots to drive up revenue all the time. Your friends are just the bots. Next question."

"What about mini-games?" Sammi spoke up, unknowingly interrupting a biting retort from me (that I had not actually thought of yet). "Some games have those, like the bocce ball courts in *Super Plumber's Backyard Barbecue Enjoyment.* Maybe this is one of those."

"That makes sense," I said. "Except Terms and Conditions isn't really a game—it's a library. So these breakout rooms must be like . . ."

"Mini-libraries." Sammi snapped her fingers. "Those touchscreens—the Hive Simulator, the Back-End Archives— they're not games, they're holding cells for specific types of information. Like some sort of—"

"Reading room," Jason and I said at the same time, and I was glad that my bulky beekeeping suit kept anyone from seeing the shiver that ran down my back.

"But I don't see any books," Jason said as I looked around.

"Well, there weren't books in Terms and Conditions, either," I said. "There were scrolls. Different information gets stored in different ways."

"So the information in a hive simulator," Sammi said excitedly, "would be stored in . . ."

Two pairs of eyes, and three people, turned to look at the greenhouse's main attraction: stack after stack of pine boxes, each one literally overflowing with swarms of stinging insects, each insect ready to fight and die to protect their home.

"The hives," I finished, and for a moment there was only buzzing in the greenhouse.

"You could always just go back and make a run for it," Jason said at last.

"You're just saying that because you want us to get caught."

"Excuse me for thinking outside the box!"

"Look, this'll be fine," Sammi said, hoisting up the metal fan Laddu had knocked over. "I heard this story about bee-keeping on that Digicast program *Several Things Discussed*. What I'm holding is a smoker. We'll use it to blow smoke in the hives, and then the smoke puts all the bees to sleep, so we can open up the hive and look at whatever we want."

"*All* the bees go to sleep?" I asked.

"Well, it was on the Digicast, so I couldn't actually see how it happened," Sammi admitted. "But the buzzing sounds definitely got *softer*. Look, do you have a better idea?"

I didn't (Jason's didn't count). And Sammi was already creeping toward the first hive, arms outstretched to hold the smoker as far from herself as possible. When she was just out of arm's reach, a handful of bees rose from the hive to dance inquisitively around the tip of the smoker. But Sammi was already pulling the handles of the fan apart—and then squeezing them tight together. With a creak and a wheeze, a plume of smoke enveloped the bees before rolling its way past them and into the hive. The effect was immediate: The bees we could see tumbled right out of the air, and the buzzing from inside the tower did, indeed, get notably softer.

"All right, Kara," Sammi said. "Now's your chance. Open the lid."

Though I wasn't exactly overjoyed to be leaving my safe position behind her, I couldn't help but feel a small thrill of anticipation as I stepped forward and wrapped my gloved hands around the top of the hive.

And pulled.

The top of the structure came clean off in my hands, feeling remarkably light as I bent down to set it on the ground. When I straightened back up and looked into the hive, I saw what had been hiding underneath: row after row of thin wooden slats, lined up vertically next to one another, like those record collections you saw sometimes in old media museums. Except, you know, covered in bees. The bees clung to a sticky brown-and-yellow substance on the sides of each slat. A few of them rose up sluggishly, displeased by the intrusion, but after Sammi gave the smoker a second squeeze, even the biggest bees fell back down like someone had turned up their own personal gravity knobs.

"Those must be the frames," Sammi said. "The sticky stuff is the honeycomb—like, *actual* honeycomb. That's what bees make in hives, and what humans harvest."

"Like I said," Jason sighed. "It's just regular beehives. No secret messages, just some weird inside joke."

But something had caught my eye, even through the mesh and smoke and walls of sleeping bees. It was hard to get a good look at the honeycomb, but it almost seemed like . . .

"Give me more smoke," I said, and Sammi obeyed. I reached out again and set to work loosening the first frame on the far left of the hive. This was much harder than just opening the hive; even half asleep, the bees clung and crawled grumpily across my gloves, and the honey was like glue, keeping the frame stuck to the box unless I pulled extra hard. But I wiggled the wood back and forth, and soon, with a sound somewhere between a *squish* and a *smack*, the frame finally came free, popping up into the air and shedding bees like fuzzy yellow glitter into the hive below.

Shedding so many bees, in fact, that for the first time, it was possible to fully see the patterns formed by the swirling brown and yellow of the honeycomb.

Not just the patterns—the words.

"No way," Jason gasped.

"*What?*" Sammi breathed.

"Are you happy now?" I asked. And although Jason was too stunned to answer, I had to admit, *I* was sort of happy, even if I had no idea what came next. Sue me—I liked being right.

Because the first frame of the hive said, in huge letters spelled out of dried brown honey:

LET'S PLAY:
SAVE THE HEAD OF HIVE.

"This is why this is here," I said. "This is how we find Eric Alanick."

LEVEL 18

If you've ever played a particular kind of video game—the kind where you crawl around dungeons, say, or sneak onto pirate ships to steal back your treasure, or live on a pirate ship as a pirate who is going to steal someone else's treasure—if you have played any of those, then you know exactly how great it feels to open up a chest and find that secret thing you were looking for. Sometimes it's gems. Sometimes it's a map. Sometimes it comes with a cute little trumpet fanfare as you raise your prize to the sky, pumping your cute little digital fist.

And sometimes, instead of trumpets, all you hear is bees, fighting against the special bee drugs you have coated them in so that they might not wake up and sting you, as you stare at a secret message either for or from the man who created the giant inescapable video game reality from which you are determined, somehow, to escape.

Truly, it felt great. Just a new joy every minute over here.

"He must have suspected ahead of time that he would need to be rescued," Sammi said. "Or did he find a way to send this message from wherever he's being held? Or did another architect do all that for him? And is it the same person who got all those Drones to block the exits in Terms and Conditions? Maybe they knew they'd be under siege. Maybe someone's fighting back."

I hadn't even considered that, and beneath the beekeeping suit, my heart began to race. What was it Dad had said?

There's a giant problem and you've decided it's your job to fix it. It's just what your mother would have done.

"Kara," Jason said, "maybe this is—"

"I think I saw something on the back," I said abruptly, and flipped the frame over to reveal more words, in coder jargon:

```
EMERGENCY PROTOCOLS
If(HIVEAttacked=true)
Run("SaveMe")
```

"There must be more on each of these things," I said. "Come on, Sammi, help me out."

With each of us wiggling a different side of the second frame, it came out in no time. But when we held it up to the light, I could only frown at the mysterious message.

THERE ARE NO CHEAT CODES IN HIVE.

"Well, I could have told you *that*," Jason huffed.

"Look at the back," Sammi said, and I turned it around.

BUT THIS HIVE HAS BUGS.

"I'll say it does," I grumbled as a half-dozen bees ambled irritably over my boots.

"Bees aren't bugs," Sammi said.

"I think," Jason said, "they mean bugs like—"

"*Computer* bugs." I slapped my forehead, accidentally squashing two bees. "Of course. Like the kind that cause the Updates—or that this Update caused."

"This is incredible," Sammi said. "Somehow, it's all connected."

"Sure," I grunted as we worked a third frame loose. "But why do all these messages have to be so cryptic? It's not the most helpful form of communication."

The front of the next frame just said:

36 CHARACTER LIMIT.

"Oh," I said, feeling sheepish. Then we turned it over:

ALSO, TALKING 2 U = SUPER DANGEROUS.

"*Oh,*" I repeated. Not for the first time that day, I felt a crawling sensation up my neck.

Then I felt the crawling sensation several other places, and realized we were in another kind of danger.

"Uh, Sammi? The bees are getting, uh, antsy."

"Oh, shoot." Sammi dropped her end of the frame and grabbed the smoker again, giving a rapid one-two squeeze to first my suit and then the hive. But the first puff of smoke came out weak and wispy, and the second puff was smaller still. A few bees fell to the floor, but not that many.

"We're running out of smoke," she said as a bee threw itself at my foot stinger-first. As we watched, the bee lodged its stinger into the suit before tumbling to the ground to die. I hadn't felt the sting through the thick fabric, but I didn't want to find out if that would hold for the third or fourth time I got stung—or the thirtieth or four hundredth.

"Let's hurry," I said, moving quickly to the next frame. In my haste, I yanked the frame right out of the hive, which was good, but woke up many more bees in the process, which was bad.

"What does it say?" Sammi asked as she squirted the smoker furiously, and I read aloud:

BUGS ARE SCATTERED ACROSS THE HIVE.

Sammi looked around the greenhouse, but I shook my head.
"I think they mean *HIVE* HIVE," I said, and as three bees stung at my wrist, I turned to the back of the frame.

YOU MUST RACE TO FIND THEM.

"Well, obviously we're going to *hurry*," Jason said. "Why would he waste frames like this?"
"Talk about a slow *frame* rate," Sammi said.

I stared at her. I had to believe Jason did, too.

"Sorry," Sammi said. "Pull the next one."

But I was still looking at RACE TO FIND THEM, even as the buzzing grew harsher around me.

"I don't think he—I don't think they *did* waste a frame," I said. "I think it's a clue. For where to find the next one. *Race.*"

"That could be any number of— *Aah!*" A bee had gone to sting Sammi right in the mesh of her mask, and instinctively she had tried to swat it away. This only served to anger it, and now she was just as much of a target for the bees as I was—and there were enough bees awake now to easily attack both of us. Laddu now looked very glad to still be in his netting as he waddled nervously away from where we stood.

There was just one frame left in the hive, and it was honey-stuck but good. As I pulled and pried at it, I was swallowed up in a cloud of furious yellow and black, making me wince as the bees moved to defend the last of their home. I couldn't blame them—we were stealing their life's work, after all—but the collective effect of all of them throwing themselves against my suit was like being buffeted by a very small hailstorm with a grudge. The fear that one of them would break through my suit was growing stronger by the second—and, somehow, I suspected their stings would have a worse effect than some light swelling.

"Why would Eric do this?" Jason asked. "If he wanted anyone to find the messages, why would he guard it like this?"

"Because he didn't want just *anyone* to find the messages," I said. I spoke through gritted teeth, both because I was pulling as hard as I could and because I already regretted what I was about to say. "He only wanted it found by a true Hivehead—by someone—like—*you*!"

I had to yell the last word as the final frame came loose with an enormous crack and a roaring of enraged bees. They were so thick around me now that I could barely read the message, but I could still make it out:

NOW MOVE LIKE YOU STOLE IT.

And just like that, I knew where we had to go.

"Move!" I yelled. "Move, go, now!"

I tucked the frame under my arm and turned to run. Sammi brandished the smoker into the cloud of bees, but they just feinted and then re-formed, bearing down on us as we dashed back to the front of the greenhouse.

"How are we getting out of here?!" Sammi asked.

"I don't know," I said. "I just hoped we might leave the same way we—"

Flash.

"Came," I said, and then the two of us were standing in Terms and Conditions.

Facing a bunch of guards.

"Hey!" said a guard. "Who are you?"

Which was strange because, from the claw marks on his forehead, I could definitely tell this was the same guard who'd been chasing us before. Why wouldn't he recognize us?

Maybe because we were still wearing our beekeeping suits was why.

"What?" Sammi asked. "How did these come through with us? Things stay in the game they're from."

"Put the—put your things down!" said one of the guards. They were steadily advancing on us.

Which was how I found out I still had the final frame tucked under my arm, and Sammi still had her smoker.

"It's not really a game, remember?" I asked. "Maybe anything can come in and out."

"Which means . . ." Sammi began, and luckily, we both knew the end of the sentence before she said it.

Which was why we both threw ourselves to the ground as a swarm of seriously ticked-off bees came spewing out of the mini-hexagon behind us, descending upon the legion of guards in a cacophony of buzzing and screaming.

"The door!" I hissed.

"What about it?" Sammi asked.

It was now unblocked by humans, as they ran from the bees—but still blocked by Drones.

"I have an idea," I said. "Come on!"

As I got back up off the ground, I snatched the smoker from Sammi, pointed it at the door, and squeezed as hard as I could with just the one free hand. The smoker released one last pitiful puff of smoke, but it was exactly enough for the Drones, which scuttled away from it like cockroaches from sunlight. It made no sense; it made perfect sense; and most important, it made a perfect opening for us to leap through, escaping from Terms and Conditions with a flash of light and a sudden, bee-blocking silence.

In a gut-churning moment, we lurched from jumping forward to falling straight down, as we were spat back out into the very top of the Honeycomb. But our platform was waiting for us right where we'd left it, and I twisted around just in time to slam into it on my back, holding the frame up safe in the air. Sammi landed with a grunt next to me, and then Laddu came to a hovering halt just above her.

"*Ain't Auto Theft Grand!*" I yelled to the platform. "And *hit it*!"

Laddu squawked and wrapped his talons around the platform edge just in time to get brought along as we plummeted out of the Honeycomb heights.

"You want to go find Gus and Aaron right now?" Sammi asked, stunned.

"I want to go find the first of these bugs," I said. "And I think we might just happen to find it in the same place that we'll find Gus and Aaron."

"Why in the world would you think that?"

"The clues," I said, brandishing the frame. "*Race* to find them. Move like you *stole* it. What game famously features stealing things and then racing them?"

"*Ain't Auto Theft Grand*," Sammi gasped. "Of course. Wow, what *are* the odds?"

"It's the simulation," Jason gloated. "It's working *perfectly*."

Then he paused.

"Or it's glitching," he said. "I think it happens sometimes. I think that's how we got platypuses."

At some point, we were going to have a very serious talk about Jason's views on reality. We were also going to have to figure out what the governments of the world wanted with HIVE, who was trying to help us stop them, and where the people I loved were now.

And if those last two questions were related.

One problem at a time, Tilden, I told myself.

"That was fast," Sammi said, cutting off my internal dialogue as the platform slowed down. "We're here. You ready?"

"Let's go," I said, getting up. "Or, wait, hold on—we should probably take these beekeeper suits off first."

Luckily, outfits in the HIVE world worked on video game logic—even, it turned out, those found in mysterious mini-libraries. With a pinch of our noses, we were able to file our suits away to our invisible Inventories, returning us to our standard clothing. Finally, I could see Sammi's face again—and it was troubled.

"Kara," she said, "*AATG* is a *huge* game. It takes place across an entire sprawling old-timey megacity. How are we supposed to find Gus and Aaron in all that? Let alone a bug whose shape, identity, nature, or even existence we can't be sure of?"

I did my best to look calm and confident.

"A wise person once told me: One problem at a time," I said.

Sammi frowned.

"I never said that," she said.

"I wasn't saying—never mind," I said, stepping to the edge of the platform. "Come on. We'll figure out how to find our friends once we're inside the game. If they're even inside the game at all."

We stepped inside the game.

We stood in the middle of a screaming highway, perched precariously on the thin strip of grass that served as a median. Roadsters raced by us at illegal speeds, scraping the paint off one another as they tried to push their opponents' cars off the road—which unfortunately had a fifty-fifty chance of pushing that car straight toward us. Sammi cried out in horror as one bright yellow Rolls-Royce in particular flew into a hard spin, spiraling across four lanes of traffic and coming to a screeching halt straddled atop the median mere feet from where we stood. When you got right down to it, the odds of that car landing there were incredible—they really couldn't have done better if the driver had been aiming for it.

The driver's seat opened.

"Hey, girls—looks like you need a ride."

Aaron grinned at us with bright eyes.

On the passenger side, someone leaned their seat back until their face could be seen over Aaron's shoulder.

Their stupid, handsome face.

"Guess it's a good thing we found you," said Gus.

LEVEL 19

A tip for any emotional reunions you may plan on having in the future: Don't hold them on blazingly dangerous highway medians.

Or do. It makes everything *very* efficient.

"Kara," Gus began.

"Gus," I said.

"Get in the car!" yelled Sammi and Aaron.

Sammi had already hopped into the back seat of the canary-yellow-colored convertible Rolls-Royce, and she now pushed the back door open as an eighteen-wheeler roared by, its side-view mirror narrowly missing an opportunity to take off my head. I leaped into the back seat next to Sammi and was still pulling the door shut behind me when Aaron floored it. With a grinding thump, the Rolls-Royce careened over the median and into the opposite lane from which Aaron and Gus had arrived, completing the world's most daring—and dumb—U-turn.

"Hold on tight!" Aaron shouted over the wind as he accelerated down the highway. We were racing down the edge of Neversleep City, the open-world metropolis that sprawled across an entire seaboard and gave *Ain't Auto Theft Grand* its setting. On our right, skyscrapers flickered past like so much background data; to our left was the kind of warehouse-festooned waterfront found in a thousand old gangster movies. Aaron's showy driving was only made showier by the fact that he was steering one-handed, using the other hand to keep a fedora from flying off his head. Gus was similarly dressed in the nattiest three-piece suit this side of 1929. It looked, I had to say, *very* good on him—albeit slightly rumpled by high-velocity winds. A sequin smacked me in the face as Aaron changed lanes, and that was how I realized I was wearing a vintage flapper dress. Not the most practical outfit for adventuring, but classic *AATG* couture. At least a quick glance downward confirmed I still had my trusty boots.

"How did you *find* us?" Sammi asked. Her turban and gloves remained unchanged, but the rest of her armor had been converted to brown leather and furs—the outfit of a daring aviatrix.

"Isn't it obvious?" Aaron asked, weaving across three lanes without so much as glancing at his turn signal.

"The simulation!" Jason said.

"The save function," Aaron said. "The last time any of us played this game, the four of us were doing a mission as a crew. The game always reunites crews with each other."

"Oh, duh," Sammi said.

"Ugh," Jason said.

Gus turned around in his seat, hugging the headrest with one arm to stay balanced while he reached out for my hand.

"What are you doing in HIVE?!" he asked. "I mean, not that I'm not happy to see you! I just never thought you'd voluntarily get trapped in here!"

"I'm here to save you!" I said, yelling over the blaring horn of the Studebaker Aaron had just cut off.

I'd thought it was a nice line, but Gus just squeezed my hand, tilted his head, and asked:

"What?!"

"And me," Sammi said. "And her dad and brother, and—and everyone, really."

"*What?!*" said Gus and Aaron.

"Long story," I said, and then gasped as we swerved onto an on-ramp at the last second, nearly smashing head-on into a concrete divider.

"*C-c-c-combo! Ten trick driving points!*"

"Also," I yelled over the in-game announcement, "why are we driving like this?"

"Because Aaron always drives like this," Sammi pointed out correctly, rolling her eyes as she pulled the middle seat belt as tight as it would go across Laddu's body.

"Well, pardon me for being awesome!" Aaron protested. "And for enjoying the one time in life when my hands definitely won't shake!" But as his eyes flickered to his rearview mirror, he added, "Real talk, though, it's because we're being chased."

Now it was our turn to say, *"What?!"*

"By *who*?" Sammi added, just in time for a sleek black roadster to speed onto the on-ramp behind us as—oh boy—a mobster holding a tommy gun leaned out from the passenger side.

"By them," Aaron said. "Hold on!"

He switched lanes so fast that Gus fell forward and I slammed into the left side of the car, which I might have toppled out of if I hadn't dug my fingers into Gus's wrist. From the clanking sounds behind me, something heavy in the trunk had just taken the same hit. Now we were heading off the highway we'd been on—and up onto a bridge that curved high over a wide, dark river. I heard the distinct sound of bullets firing, but our pursuers must not have made the exit in time because the gunfire quickly dopplered out of earshot. Nevertheless, Aaron only sped up as we rose over the river, leaving behind the island hub at the center of Neversleep City. The bridge was dizzyingly high and impossibly long, and there were several miles at least between us and the desolate plain of smokestacks on the river's far shore. Below us, the drop from the bridge to the water became greater and more fatal with every second.

And I couldn't be sure, but here and there on the face of the river, I thought I saw a scatter of gray—a dotting of doomed and wandering Drones, from players who had fallen before us.

"We're still playing that mission from last time," Gus explained. "Remember? We had to steal the hooch from that speakeasy and deliver it to the drop-off spot under the bridge without getting caught by the speakeasy's, uh, employees."

Well, that explained the gunshots, and the heavy clanking that was still coming from the trunk.

"We didn't finish it at the time because Sammi had to go to her tutoring job," Gus continued, "and also you all agreed that it was . . . well, it was . . ."

Sheepishly, Gus dropped my hand and adjusted his tie.

"Too hard," Sammi filled in for him. "We said you'd picked a game that was too hard. Like you always do."

"Well, that's not quite how I remember it," Gus said, in a tone that suggested it was exactly how he remembered it. "But yes, something like that. And that's bad news. I don't know if you guys have noticed, but if you lose a game right now—"

"We know," Sammi and I chorused.

Gus looked like he wanted to follow up on that, but at that moment, Aaron cut in—both to the conversation, and to the carpool lane.

"Good, then you're all caught up," he said. "I've managed to lose them a few times today—like when we found you and switched directions on the highway back there—but they keep catching up to us. We've been driving around the city all day, but we can't do this forever. I mean . . ."

He abruptly pulled us ahead of the ambulance he'd been tailgating.

"*I* could do this forever. This is like the one thing I *could* do forever. But sooner or later we'll run out of gas. But now that we have you guys, maybe we can win this!"

"We can't win this," I said.

"What?!"

This time, everyone said it. Except for me, of course, and for Laddu, who said, "Laddu!"

Because a hail of bullets had just passed over our heads.

The black roadster was back. Sammi, Gus, and I all threw ourselves down out of sight; Aaron, unable to do so, dropped his seat back as low as it would go, bashing the back of my head but saving him at the last second from a follow-up round of gunfire.

"Why are we in a convertible?!" I cried. "This is a car chase game!"

"You chose this!" Aaron said. "Remember? You said it was like the car from that book you loved!"

"Oh yeah," I said, blushing and remembering how I'd mainly agreed to play this game because I was going through a *Great Gatsby* phase at the time.

"Don't listen to Aaron," Gus said. "But, Kara—why don't you think we can win? If it's because you think it's too hard, I swear, together, we can do it! And by the way, all day I've been wishing I could talk to you—I need to apologize for the way that I—"

As enticing as that line of thought sounded, the growing roar of the roadster behind us told me that we didn't have time for any of it.

"We can't win because we need to stay in the game," I yelled, even as the staccato pinging of bullets ricocheting off bridge supports made it feel like we very much did not. "Because of what we found on *this*."

I held up the honey-covered frame so Gus could see it. Of course, Gus's mystified expression reminded me that this would mean nothing to him, so I continued:

"A bug. There's a bug somewhere in *Ain't Auto Theft Grand*—"

"Probably," Sammi said.

"And finding it could be the key to finding out what's been done to HIVE—and putting a stop to it."

"What kind of bug?" Aaron asked.

"We don't know."

"'Done to'?" Gus frowned. "This was on *purpose*? By who? Why? *How?*"

"We don't know that, either," I admitted. "Right now we just need to solve the problem in front of us."

"I'll say," said Aaron. "Hang on to something!"

For all Aaron's fast and fancy driving, the roadster was gaining on us with the single-minded focus that was so often the delightful hallmark of NPC personalities. Just as it was about to pull abreast of us, Aaron broke two lanes to the right and dropped his speed, managing to put a white stretch limousine between the mobsters and us.

"C-c-c-combo!"

"Guys," Aaron crowed, "I *rock* in HIVE."

"You rock all the time, buddy," Gus said.

"Well, duh," Aaron said. "But that part goes without saying."

"How *do* you find a bug in a video game?" Sammi asked, not wasting a moment of our temporary reprieve.

"Some people—debuggers—that's all they do," Gus said. "It's their job. I read about it."

"What did you learn?" I asked. "How do they find the bugs?"

"They just . . . play the game. I remember because it sounded like a dream job."

"Great," Aaron said as a bullet pierced one of the windows of the limo, missing our car but bringing with it the scream of someone in the limo and what sounded like the faint tinkling of a shattered champagne glass. "Very *helpful!*"

"Okay, right, okay," Gus said, pulling at his tie nervously again, "but to speed it up, they . . . they play the game . . . wrong. They do things you wouldn't expect. They go to weird places on the map. Which exposes weird glitches and, and edge cases, things that programmers couldn't have anticipated their players would find."

"We can't afford to play the game wrong!" Sammi said, and then gasped as the Rolls-Royce shuddered and jerked. Whoever was driving the limousine had had enough of being caught between us, and was now trying to push us out of our lane; unfortunately, the only thing to the right of our lane was a deadly drop to the banks of the Neversleep River.

"Why don't you pick on the guys *shooting at you* with a

gun!" Aaron roared at the limo driver, begrudgingly dropping the car back and surrendering our cover.

"Probably because of the gun," Sammi pointed out.

Aaron looked for another car to hide behind, but everyone else on the road had noticed something bad was going down and had begun to give us a wide berth—or as wide a berth as they could within the confines of the bridge. Slowly but surely, the black roadster was revealed to us, two lanes over but just a few yards behind—and closing in by the second.

"Wait," Aaron said. "So you're saying that to find the bug, we should play the game wrong?"

"I—sure," I said, watching as the roadster drew level with us once more. "It's the best plan we have."

"Which means doing things you wouldn't expect?"

"Sure!" I said, increasingly frantic. The mobster, a man in a dark suit and glasses, was rising from his seat.

"Okay." Aaron looked into the rearview mirror. "Just checking. Unbuckle your bird, Sammi."

"Okay," Sammi said, hurrying to free Laddu, "but why—"

The man in the roadster took aim.

And then—in the middle of a busy bridge, hundreds of feet above a vast and inky river, surrounded by high-speed traffic and right in the crosshairs of a gun-toting gangster—Aaron hit the brakes.

LEVEL 20

I screamed, as did the gears of the Rolls-Royce and every vehicle around us, completely unprepared for Aaron's sudden death wish. But as I closed my eyes and braced for impact, I felt no pain—just the soft unsensation of my feet pulling up from the ground.

It's happening, I thought. *I'm becoming a Drone.*

Then I felt something odd. It was a lurching sensation, as if the ground had vanished from under my feet . . . again.

Which was impossible.

Unless someone was using some sort of—

"Double jumps, baby!"

I opened my eyes. Aaron was grinning wickedly as he pulled us through the air in a physics-defying leap, holding Sammi in one hand, me in the other, and wedging a bewildered if amused Gus under his left armpit. Laddu fluttered up beside us, looking just as nonplussed as anyone else.

"All right, everyone," Aaron said. "Prepare to grab on in three . . . two . . ."

And then he let go of my hand. If I'd had more time, I might have panicked—or, I suppose, panicked *more*—but there was only enough time for the great iron curve of the bridge's arch to rush up at me, at which point instinct took over. I threw my arms out and wrapped them around a conveniently placed railing, the frame slipping out of my grasp and clattering onto the iron below. Sammi, daringly but deftly, snatched the far railing just in time to avoid a plunge into the murky depths; and Gus tumbled onto the thin walkway sandwiched between the railings, much the same way he'd tumbled from the wings of a dragon not so much as twenty-four hours ago. Aaron, showboat that he was, landed next to Gus, beaming and on his feet.

Don't look down, I thought, clambering over the railing and trying not to register the drop from here to the bridge below—or from the bridge to the water. *Don't look down, don't look—*

"Oof!" I fell onto the walkway, or more accurately, onto Gus.

"Are you okay?" I asked, hopping off him and helping to pull him up. "I—"

Instead of answering, Gus pulled me into a kiss as soon as we were both on our feet. Actually, a little sooner; I staggered back toward the railing, but Gus just wrapped his arms around my waist and held me steady. Now that I saw his smiling face up close, I realized it matched his suit: a little rumpled, a little beaten up by the bridge, but roguishly, undeniably charming.

"Don't worry," Gus said. "You know me. I like playing at the tough level."

I smiled, but somewhere inside me, a rebellious voice whispered, *Really?*

"Really?"

Oh my *God.*

"Jason," I hissed. "Shut *up.*"

Gus's roguish smile turned down two watts.

"'Jason'?" he asked, uncircling his arms from my waist.

Blessedly, Sammi chose that moment to yank off an armored glove and smack Aaron over and over with it. Laddu, ever the loyal ally, hovered nearby and got in a few pecks in solidarity.

"How—in—the—world—could—you—know—that—would—*work*?" Sammi exhorted between slaps. "I didn't think you even *could* do double jumps in *AATG!*"

"You normally can't," Aaron said, all smiles despite the verbal and physical onslaught. "Unless you save up a *bunch* of points. Which you could only do if you'd, say, been driving for almost an entire day executing a seemingly endless and *certainly* flawless series of trick driving stunts. I bought the power-up just before you guys entered the game, but I didn't know when the right time to use it would be."

"I'm still not sure it was the right time," I said, finally summoning the courage to look down as I bent to pick up the frame. Far below us, the Rolls-Royce and the roadster sat crumpled up and smoking in a ten-car pileup, all twisted metal and broken glass. The motorists who had managed to escape the wrecks of their cars were standing around shaking their fists ineffectually at one another—or, in the case of the few who'd seen the cause of the crash, looking up and shaking their fists ineffectually at us.

And then there were the ones who *hadn't* escaped their cars in time. And I didn't think they were all NPCs. Because now, out of driver's seats and debris heaps, a couple of players had begun to rise . . .

"Oh, come on," Aaron said, oblivious to the scene below. "You have to admit that was *amazing.*"

"He does have a point," Jason said.

I pointed down at what were now, undoubtedly, a pair of Drones.

"Do *they* have to admit that was amazing?" I asked, unable to keep the frustration out of my voice. "We're not the only people stuck in this game, guys. I know you said you could do this *forever*, Aaron, but thanks to you, some of those players down there don't have a choice. We're trying to *save* everyone, not sacrifice them!"

"Oh." Aaron's whole body deflated, and I wondered if maybe I had gone too far. "I didn't mean to—it wasn't—I was *trying* to help! Like you guys said! I just wanted to try a crazy idea, so we could save our skin and maybe find this so-called bug. That is, if it even exists—"

"I think it does," Sammi interrupted. "And I think . . . maybe . . . your idea worked."

We all turned to her, but she wasn't looking at any of us.

"Look," she said, pointing up.

As far up as we were on the bridge's arch, there was farther still to go. The bridge peaked about fifty yards beyond and above us, at which point it began, finally, to descend back down to the distant shore. But up there at the peak, unfathomably high above a fathoms-deep river, sunlight danced and sparkled off the top of the arch, and also off—

"What is *that*?" Gus asked, shielding his eyes and squinting. The sun wasn't just bouncing into our eyes; it appeared, somehow, to be bouncing *twice*. Like there was something hovering in midair, catching the light and refracting it in a way that our brains registered as wrong.

Like a bug.

"No way," Gus breathed. "It couldn't be that easy. Is that a loot box? Or a secret *AATG* thing, like Aaron's power-up?"

"Can't be," Aaron said. "They don't shine like that. Maybe it's— Hey!"

I knew from experience that Gus and Aaron could bicker for hours. I didn't think we had that kind of time, so I set off up the walkway, leaving the others to catch up behind me.

Down on the highway, the people who'd noticed us earlier were now pointing and gesticulating urgently, and as traffic backed up, more and more people were getting out of their cars to watch the weirdos high up on the walkway. For a moment as I looked down, it seemed like even the Drones were rising up to check us out—but I couldn't be sure, and anyway, I had bigger things to worry about. The climb got steeper and more precarious the closer we got to the top, and the winds grew stronger, threatening to topple us off the side. Soon I was pulling myself up the handrail one step at a time, clutching the honeycomb frame to my body and digging my boots in for as much traction as I could get.

And then I reached the peak.

As I stepped forward, the light that had been so blinding a moment ago slanted and shifted, and finally I could see what we'd come for.

The Bug.

It floated impossibly, four feet above the walkway, frozen in the air despite looking as large and heavy as a gold brick. What was really odd was that it had four gossamer wings, but used none of them to keep itself in the air. In fact, it didn't move at all: not the wings, nor the bulbous black-striped abdomen, nor the honeyrod thorax, all of which marked the object out as . . .

"A bee," Jason said. "Another bee."

"It's an *actual bug*," Gus said. "The Bug is a *bug*."

"Bees aren't bugs," Sammi said.

"*Bugs* aren't bugs," Aaron said, and before anyone could question that, he added, "Like, computer bugs aren't literally insects. I think some license is being taken here."

"Actually," I heard myself say, "one of the first recorded bugs in computer history was a moth that flew into a gigantic navy supercomputer. They had to remove it from the room before they could get things working again. It's part of why we call glitches bugs."

Three faces turned to stare at me, open-mouthed. I knew how they were feeling. I hadn't thought about that fact in years.

"Whoa, book girl," Sammi said. "Where'd you learn *that*?"

"My mom told me," I said softly.

Sammi closed her mouth again as Gus's eyes popped open.

"Wait, Kara," he said. "Do you think your mom—"

"All right," I said, shooting my hand out toward the Bug. "We've wasted enough time here. Let's see what this thing is—"

"Freeze."

I froze.

The two Drones flanked the walkway, hemming us in on either side.

"This anomaly is in violation of HIVE policies," said one of the Drones. "Thank you for detecting it; it will be handled by authorities from here. Please step away from the anomaly."

"Wait, whaaaat," Aaron breathed.

"Please step away from the anomaly," said the other Drone— I think. Honestly, it was hard to tell where their voices came from. "Step away or your avatars will be expelled."

"Kara," Gus cautioned, moving forward and placing a hand lightly on my shoulder, "maybe you should—"

"Freeze," the first Drone repeated, whirling toward Gus. "Do not step closer to the anomaly."

Gus obliged, his hand still on my shoulder, my hand still

stretched out toward the Bug. Without moving my head, I flickered my eyes downward. By now, half of Neversleep City appeared to be clustered on the bridge, staring up at us, waiting for something to happen.

And then something happened.

Out of the very corner of my vision, I saw Sammi's hand fly to the belt of her aviation suit. The Drones turned to face her, but she had already pulled out the smoker, clipped at her waist since we'd left Terms and Conditions. With a pair of quick puffs, she aimed at first the one Drone, then the other. Again, barely any smoke came out; and yet again, the Drones recoiled as if they'd been attacked with a flamethrower.

I shot my hand forward, seizing the moment and seizing the Bug. As soon as my fingers wrapped around it, the golden light of the Bug slid up my arm and enveloped my body. I noted dimly that the light continued to flow up Gus's arm and around his body as well, but I didn't really get a chance to process that because suddenly I could hear and taste and sense everything ten times more acutely than I could just a second before. It was as if touching the Bug had jacked me into the inner workings of HIVE itself. I smelled each plume of smoke that had been programmed to rise across Neversleep City. I felt the panicked whirring of every Drone in the game. I heard Gus crying, "Aaron, grab my hand! Sammi, grab on to—"

And I heard a cheery, disembodied voice say, "Bug found! Override initiated for game-winning protocol. You may now return to the Honeycomb."

And the people on the bridge must have heard that, too, because someone yelled, "Wait, *override?*" prompting a similar chorus of bewildered and outraged voices.

And then I heard none of them at all.

Because we had returned to the Honeycomb.

LEVEL 21

Gus held my shoulder. Aaron held Gus's hand. Sammi held on to the back of Aaron's neck. I held the Bug.

And for a moment, balanced across four platforms in the middle of the Honeycomb, we all held perfectly still.

Then a flash of gray from far above us snapped us back into action. No Drone had noticed us yet, but they continued to circle lazily around the Honeycomb, like sharks in a tank.

"Kara," Gus said. "The Bug. What if the Drones see . . ."

But the Bug solved that problem for me. For the first time since we'd found it, the Bug moved, fluttering its wings and jerking up out of my hand. I bit back a scream—I'd had my fill of bees by now, and *especially* mysterious reality-warping bees the size of my face—but instead of attacking any of us, the Bug just swiveled in midair, angled itself downward, and flew directly into—

"The frame!" Sammi gasped.

We watched in wonder as an object the size of a football flew into a surface no thicker than a flat-screen TV, and disappeared. Yellow ripples emanated out from where it had entered the frame, and the message that had previously been there was washed away.

"What in the . . ." Aaron began, but I held up a hand.

"Look," I said. "It's rewriting itself."

I lifted it up so everyone could see:

A LESSON IN CODING: DEBUGGING 101.

And then after a moment, I flipped the frame around:

FIND THE RIGHT API.

"API?" I knew those letters rang a bell, but I couldn't quite place why. I looked to Gus for help. "What is that again? Was that in the article you read?"

Gus shook his head mournfully.

"I mean, maybe," he said. "I kind of mostly just paid attention to the part about playing video games forever."

"Oh, come on, guys," Jason said. "API stands for Application Programming—"

"Application Programming Interface!" I finished. "It's the software you need for two programs to talk to each other without glitching! Yes, *thank* you, Jason, I knew I'd heard that bef—oh."

Aaron was looking at me like I was crazy. Sammi and Laddu were looking innocently at the ceiling, or at least the vast and curving void where the ceiling would have been.

And Gus was looking at me like I had some explaining to do.

Okay, one last time, and then I never wanted to go through this again:

"Jason Alcorn has been helping me get through HIVE," I said. "While we're trapped here, he's free in the real world."

"Actually," said Jason, "it's the oppos—"

"And he's plugged into my feed," I said. "He's the one who figured out Eric Alanick was kidnapped. He's the one who helped us find the secret messages about the Bugs. And he's the only reason I was able to find you."

"Whoa, really?" Jason said excitedly.

"Well, he's *a* reason I was able to find you," I amended quickly. "So I don't want to hear any grumbling about this situation, okay? It's as weird for me as it is for you."

There was a long pause, in which Sammi continued to study the sky, and Laddu—though I was in no way sure how this was possible—appeared to be trying to whistle idly.

Finally, Gus said, "Wait, Eric Alanick was *kidnapped*?!"

"Who's Jason Elkhorn?" Aaron asked, scratching his head.

"We were getting so much done," Sammi sighed.

"Okay," Gus said, stepping from his platform to mine. "So Jason Alcorn is inside my girlfriend's head? And he's been watching this whole time without us knowing? And he's the reason you're stuck here in HIVE with the rest of us?"

"*A* reason," I repeated, but it was unclear if he heard me.

"Jason . . ." Gus began. His eyes blazed as he grabbed each of my shoulders and stared me in the face.

And then he pulled me into a hug.

"Thank you," he said.

Oh. Okay. Not what I expected. My hands wrapped tentatively around Gus's shoulders. This may sound absurd, but I couldn't tell if I was trying to hug him as me or as Jason. When Gus pulled back, though, there was nothing indecisive in his gaze.

"I always thought you were a weirdo," Gus said.

"Hey!" I said.

"I meant Jason."

"Oh. Right."

"Hey," said Jason.

"And I have, like, a thousand questions about you being in Kara's head. But if you helped get her safely to me, then I owe you more than I can say."

"I. Uh. You're welcome?" Jason said.

"And *you.*" I realized Gus was addressing me now, even though he'd been looking at me the whole time. "I've been worried sick about you all day."

"She can handle herself, you know," Sammi said. "You should see her with a plunger gun."

"Oh, sick, you guys played *Animal Flossing*?"

"Quiet, Aaron," said Gus. "Of course Kara can handle herself. But what I hated most about being separated today was not getting a chance to apologize. You had every right to be mad at me last night. I'd gotten so wrapped up in HIVE, in endless adventure games, and—and in adrenaline rushes that

I almost forgot about the greatest adventure of all. The time I spend with you."

Mercifully, Jason stayed silent for once. But as I stared up at Gus, I found myself silent as well.

I'd set out for the Apiary this morning to apologize to Gus, not the other way around. I'd wanted to prove that I got it, that I got HIVE, that I got *him*. But now that I stood here, hearing Gus try to identify the cause of our fight yesterday, I felt like something was still off. There was maybe, potentially, I quite possibly might maybe have had to admit, something that bugged me about HIVE. And about—

"*API!* Of *course!*" Aaron blurted, and Gus and I finally broke each other's gaze to look at him.

"*A Pitfallen Idol!*" Aaron continued. "You mentioned adventure games, and I realized—*Find the Right API. API* is, like, the *classic* adventure game. Maybe the Bug was telling us to go there!"

"Oh, wow," Sammi said. "*Yes.*"

"Are you two done with your cutscene or whatever?" Aaron asked, gesturing between Gus and me. "Can we go find the next Bug?"

"Yeah," Gus said, smiling. "Except—wait—if Jason's in your feed, Kara . . . when I kissed you earlier, does that mean—"

"Let's go find the next Bug," Jason said.

"Let's go find the next Bug," I said.

We went.

And I'll be honest: Now that we knew what we were looking

for, debugging was, if not easier, then certainly quicker. A standard since the earliest days of HIVE, *A Pitfallen Idol* was a game of damp and dark jungles, forbidden Incan temples, and most important, the craggy, bottomless pits that gave the game its name, and which players did not want to fall into at any cost. So when Gus pointed out that you could strip the vines from the jungle trees and use them to rappel down into the pits *on purpose*, we figured that would be exactly the sort of thing a debugger might do. And there, hidden under a rocky promontory, glowing patiently in the darkness, we found it: another bee.

We already felt like old pros by the time we returned to the Honeycomb again, hiding under a catwalk so the Drones couldn't spot us and feeding our newest Bug to the frame.

This one said:

DEBUGGING 102: A CODER'S NIGHTMARE:

And on the other side:

A CLIP IN SPACE.

"A clip?" Aaron frowned. "Like a video clip?"

"Like clipping, I think," I said. "It's when two objects in a video game pass through each other—like when your arm accidentally goes through a wall instead of bouncing off it."

"Oh, that always freaks me out," Sammi said. "So is there a game in HIVE that's notorious for clipping?"

"What about *Steampunk 1877*?" Aaron suggested. "That game's buggy as heck."

"Good guess, but no," Gus said, grinning like a player who'd just gotten the rainbow turtle shell in *Super Plumber's Backyard Barbecue Enjoyment*. "Think: What's the only game in HIVE where you begin by riding a clipper-class ship . . . in space?"

We all groaned in realization:

"*Mass Defect.*"

And so we were off again, to the worn-down, labyrinthine interior of a spaceship in the far-flung future of popular sci-fi RPG *Mass Defect*. Of course, the good ship SMS *Overcharge* was infested with mechanically enhanced space mutants, something that made searching for the next Bug even harder than before. It wasn't in the vents; it wasn't in the lowest bottom decks of the clipper ship; and it wasn't in the steaming cyborg guts of the mechanically enhanced space mutant that ambushed us in the lowest bottom decks of the clipper ship. Then Jason, with an audible eye roll, suggested:

"If you're going to play this badly, why don't you guys just look for the Bug in an open airlock?"

My eyes widened.

"Guys," I said, "I have an idea."

"Wait, no, Kara, that was a joke, you'll die. *Wait!*"

Once we'd found the Bug—which only appeared in the seventy seconds the human body could survive after throwing itself out of an airlock with no suit—the others congratulated me, but I just shrugged humbly.

"Being smart is just noticing things," I said.

"Next clue," Jason said grumpily.

The next clue:

DEBUGGING[3]:
STACK OVERFLOW.

"Geez, these are getting *really* cryptic," Gus said.

"Okay, hold on." I was desperately trying to access memories of my mom's dinner table lectures, memories I'd gotten used to blocking out over the past few years. "So stack overflow is when, like—when a programming command recurs too many times and you run out of—uh . . ."

"Guys," Sammi cut in. "Come on. Cubes. 'Stack Overflow.' It's the popular cube-based game *Stack Overflow*."

From the ensuing silence, it was clear none of us had heard of this game.

"It is, maybe, popular mostly with children," Sammi amended begrudgingly. "But the problem-solving skills it sharpens are useful to *all ages*."

"Hey," Jason said a minute later as we descended back toward the kids' section. "Have you noticed anything weird about the players in the Honeycomb right now? Like . . . that they're in the Honeycomb right now?"

He was right. Whereas our last few visits had found us alone in a sea of Drones, now signs of life had begun to crop up above and below us. A Troll here, an Anon there—something was luring players back out of the games.

As we pulled up outside *Stack Overflow*'s yellow hexagon, I spotted a Moddie on a nearby catwalk, devil horns peeking out from under her beanie. They were honestly pretty sick devil horns, which made me like her, so I called out:

"Hey! Do you know what's going on with the players right now?"

Devil Horns turned and fixed me with, in retrospect, the kind of look I might have expected from a girl in a beanie and devil horns.

"Well, we'd all been hiding in the games, *obviously*," she said. "Because it was, like, safer to stay in a game you knew you wouldn't lose than to come back out and take a gamble. But I heard from someone who heard from someone who'd just won a mission in *AATG* that there's these, like, glowing bees that you can use to get out of a game without winning, so now some of us are, like, pretty into finding those."

Whoa. The four of us looked at one another nervously.

Which we absolutely should not have done.

"Hey," Devil Horns said, noticing our shifty expressions and stepping closer to look at the frame I held closely. "What is that? Is that . . . honey?"

"Nothing," I said, trying to look very casual while still moving a large honeycomb frame behind my back. "I mean, no."

For a moment I stared her down, trying to summon the

same bluffing energy that I'd used so successfully before against Markus Fawkes.

Then Devil Horns cupped her hands to her mouth, and I remembered something crucial: Markus Fawkes was a moron.

"Hey, guys!" she yelled. "Down here! Check this out! I think I found—"

"All right, that's enough of *that*," Sammi said, and shoved us into *Stack Overflow*.

It was not much of a reprieve. Big colorful cubes fell around our heads, threatening to squash us into the surface of an immense checkered game board that stretched away to the horizon. Within moments, Devil Horns materialized a few squares away; shortly after that, more of her would-be debuggers appeared alongside her. The only bright side was that they all appeared to be as unfamiliar with the objective of *Stack Overflow* as Aaron, Gus, and me. One player in a porkpie hat reached out and attempted to touch a red cube as it fell, only to be sent flying fifty feet backward, hat and all.

Sammi, though, had no such problems. After taking only a moment to assess the selection of cubes available to her, she proceeded to—actually, I'm still not sure what it was she proceeded to do.

"Trust me," she said as she tapped one green block repeatedly and waved vaguely at another. "This is exactly the way a *Stack Overflow* expert would *never* think to play the game."

"Is . . . is that true?" I asked Jason softly.

"Beats me," he said. "I've never heard of this game in my life."

But after racking up two red-block combos and a blue-block blitz—or was it three combos and no blitz? Look, I don't know—Sammi cheered in triumph as the pile she'd created flashed an ultraviolet hue, searing our eyelids before it disappeared entirely, leaving in its absence only . . .

"The Bug!" Gus cried.

"The bee!" yelled Devil Horns. She pointed from behind the wall of cubes she had been unable to prevent from piling up around her. Luckily, the cubes acted as an accidental prison, keeping the players from reaching us as we grabbed on to the Bug. But there was no stopping them from hearing "Override initiated for game-winning protocol! You may now return to the Honeycomb," and as the golden glow overtook us, we all heard the player in the porkpie hat say, "I *knew* it! Wait till we tell—"

And then we were out.

"Yikes. We've got a head start, but not much of one," Sammi said. "*Stack Overflow*'s not that hard to figure out once you get used to it. But I can't imagine we'll have to find too many more of these, right?"

As it turned out, Sammi was wrong—we would have to find several more of these—and Sammi was right—we did not have much of a head start. Even as we moved from game to game, getting better and better at finding Bugs, we found ourselves competing with more and more players. What was supposed to be an Old West ghost town was crawling with cowpokes, tearing up the floorboards of first banks and fusty saloons—but not, crucially, looking under the trapdoor of the hangman's gallows. In an underwater palace, while we broke into the seahorse stables to steal a ride to the edge of the continental shelf, they scoured the throne room. And by the time we made our way to *Ball 20XX*, HIVE's premier basketball emulator, the players were all taking turns calling time-outs so they could search in the stands.

"Wow," Sammi said as we dug through the smelly detritus of the home team's locker room (it was a *very* realistic basketball emulator). "I guess in HIVE, the *buzz* travels fast."

"Sammi," said Gus.

"Sorry," said Sammi.

"Hey, guys, look!" Aaron said, pulling out a pair of Air Alanicks. "Do you *know* how high you can jump with these things on?"

"Aaron," said Sammi.

"Not sorry," Aaron said, slipping the shoes into his Inventory.

"Wait, guys, be quiet," I said, holding up a finger.

"Kara's right, Aaron," Gus said. "I get that this is a fun time and all, but we're trying to do something important here. Let's focus up."

"I—you're having a *fun time*?" I couldn't keep the surprise out of my voice. "Haven't we already—that's not—look, that's not what I was talking about. Be quiet and *listen*."

Aaron looked like he wanted to say something, but to his credit, he joined us all in falling silent.

Within moments, we heard footsteps closing in on the locker room, along with aggravated voices.

"The stalls," I said. *"Now."*

We rushed to hide in the bathroom at the back of the locker room. Laddu followed Sammi into a stall as she crawled up onto the tank of the toilet before pulling the door closed; Aaron took another; and Gus and I had just managed to balance ourselves on opposite sides of one toilet seat, our backs pressed against the walls, when a voice rounded the corner.

"I heard the bees were left by Eric Alanick," said the voice. "And this whole thing is some big promotional stunt."

"That's insane," said another voice. "'This whole thing' is a nightmare. What kind of promotional stunt would this be?"

"The kind Eric Alanick would do! He's a cultural disruptor! It's genius."

"Hey," Gus whispered. "Sorry for when I said this was fun. I know you must be pretty stressed. Sammi mentioned that your dad was—"

"Shh," I said. I can't believe I'm saying this, but I was starting to get tired of hearing my boyfriend apologize. Plus: "Listen."

"*I* heard," someone was saying, "that there's this crew that's been collecting them. Four kids and a bird."

"A *bird*?"

Gus and I stared at each other. Looked like Devil Horns and her crew had made it out of *Stack Overflow.*

"Now I *know* you're insane. Come on, there's nothing here—let's go."

Once they were gone, we exhaled, stepping down carefully from our hiding spot.

"We can't keep doing this," I said. "Either we find out what's going on with HIVE soon, or we might not get to at all."

"I agree," Gus said. "But how are we supposed to do that? We can't even find the Bug in this dumb basketball game."

"Uh, guys?" Aaron said from the stall to our right. "You're not gonna *believe* what's in this toilet bowl."

Two minutes later, we all stood back in the Honeycomb for what I prayed would be the last time. Aaron shook his hands furiously like he was trying to get water off them, even though they'd become dry the moment we'd left the game.

"Let us never speak of that," he said, but he didn't have to worry—already, the Bug had done its work on the frame, giving us one more clue to crack.

"I honestly have no idea what this could be about," Sammi said.

"Me too," Jason admitted. "I'm stumped."

"Kara?" Gus said. "Are you okay?"

Was I okay? I didn't know. As I flipped the frame back and forth, the words swam in front of me. Together, the two sides read:

YOU'VE FOUND ALL MANNER OF BUGS.
JUST ONE MORE, IF YOU DON'T MIND.

"Oh, you're *kidding* me," I whispered.

"What?" Gus asked. "Kara, what's going on?"

I looked up from the frame, hardly believing what I was saying as I said it:

"I know where the last Bug is," I said. "And it's in *The Skims: Mind Your Manors.*"

I told you we'd get to it.

LEVEL 22

"*This* is the game you spend all your time playing?" Sammi asked. "I mean, I guess I'm not surprised, but *wow*."

I blushed bright red, which I had to imagine clashed with my black evening gown. The silky garment stretched down to the hardwood floor of the ballroom, hiding my out-of-place boots. I'd briefly panicked upon noticing that my new look came without my honeycomb frame, but a quick pinch of my nose revealed it was still with me, just hiding in my Inventory.

Sammi's gown was a rich violet, and even longer than mine—long enough that Aaron, not for the first time since we'd entered the manor, was standing on it. As Sammi shooed him off with a wave of her right glove (the left having turned into a falconry glove for Laddu to perch on), Aaron waddled stiffly, unaccustomed to having this much starch in his trousers—not to mention his waistcoat, his tailcoat, and his chin-high collar. And wearing a Regency-era officer's uniform, Gus looked . . . Well, we didn't have time to get into how I thought Gus looked. We didn't have time to stand here at all, for already, familiar faces were streaming past us. Soon they would take their places in the middle of the ballroom and begin the festivities. There went Mr. Darkly, the incurable curmudgeon with a vast inheritance; there went Lady Susanna, the town gossip; and there now went the five famous Shadlock sisters.

In fact, I was both relieved and embarrassed to realize I knew just about everyone here—which meant we were, for now, safe among NPCs. None of the players looking for Bugs had thought to come here, presumably for the same reason there'd been no one in *Stack Overflow*—people just didn't know about this game.

Except for me.

"Lady Tilden!" said a familiar voice.

Oh no.

Mr. Knighthill, the handsome landowner who always lived two estates away from you at the start of *Mind Your Manors*, came into view. As he approached us in long, tall strides, dancers parted for him like so many waves. He stopped before us, doffed his hat, and in front of everyone—oh *no*—took my hand and kissed it. Frankly, I would have given anything to turn into a Drone right then and there.

"I didn't know you were coming to this ball," he said. "And who are your lovely companions?"

"*Some* of us are her boyfriend," Gus said, not-so-subtly puffing out his medal-encrusted chest. "So step off, buddy."

"Why, Lady Tilden!" Mr. Knighthill stepped back with a smile, all courtesy and charm. "Wait till I tell Lady Susanna this wonderful news. Pardon me, all!"

As he melted back into the dancing throng, Sammi and Aaron doubled over laughing.

"So how do you even win this game?" Aaron asked, wiping away a tear. "By securing that guy's hand in marriage or whatever?"

"I mean . . . that is one way," I admitted.

"Great," Gus said, moving forward. "So nobody would expect us to slap the sucker. Pure Bug-finding gold."

I reached out and grabbed his elbow.

"Not so fast, Officer Caveman," I said. "Causing a scandal gets you just as many points here as landing a partner."

"What if you do both at the same time?" asked Sammi thoughtfully.

"*Huge* points."

"Okay." Gus scowled, deprived of his slapping opportunity. "So what *is* the unexpected thing to do in this game? Refusing to engage in polite society at all?"

I shook my head. "Becoming a reclusive spinster is totally in the spirit of *Mind Your Manors*. Bonus points if you let your home get super dusty and weird."

Gus threw his hands up. "Is it even *possible* to lose in this game?"

"Now that you mention it," I began, "not really. I guess that's one of the reasons I love it—you can do anything you want."

"Ha, that's funny," Aaron said. "Gus only likes games he can't win at, and Kara only likes games she can't lose.

Man, sometimes it's like, do you guys even have *anything* in com— *Ow!*"

"Whoops," said Sammi, putting her armored glove back on. "Slipped off."

"Look," I said. "We're surrounded by NPCs and the most dangerous thing in this game is gout. This is the safest we've been all day, and the closest we've gotten to finding out how to fix HIVE. Let's just keep our eyes peeled and our minds open. Something *has* to turn up."

"Aaron and I will search the manor grounds," Sammi said. "You guys enjoy the dance."

"Wait, why would we split—" Aaron began, but Sammi's glove must have slipped again because he said, "Ow! Okay. Fine. Have fun, you two."

But then, as Sammi headed for the door and gestured for him to come with, Aaron paused and bit his lip. He seemed to be darting his eyes at me and deciding whether or not to say something. This was surprising behavior for Aaron Ridley, a boy who, based on all existing evidence, had never stopped to think about what he was going to say next in his life.

And it was even more surprising when he said:

"Kara, you know how this world works—can you come over here and help me fix my bow tie?"

"Aaron," Sammi said, "I'm not sure we really have time for—"

"Please?" Aaron was looking right at me. "I'd do it myself,

but I never really got the hang of doing it on my own in real life because . . . well . . . you know."

Sammi didn't know what to say to that, and neither did I, so I just stepped forward and leaned in to examine Aaron's tie.

"Take your time with it," Aaron whispered. "Make it look convincing."

"Wait, what?" Without even realizing it, I was whispering back. "Aaron, this tie is just a little crooked, I don't think you actually need—"

"Oh, I know. I'm actually sort of a bow tie expert? A couple summers ago I spent a month watching tutorials and practicing over and over again until I could do it right."

Aaron tilted his head back to give me more room to improvise, but continued at a murmur:

"It took me longer than it would take most people, but now I'm also probably way better at tying ties than most people because I've thought about it more. That's something I've noticed about my CP—it makes me not take things for granted. It's actually something I kind of like about it."

"So why—" I began, but Aaron didn't wait.

"I know you think I take things for granted, or that I'm maybe not even taking this seriously because I like HIVE more than real life. But that's not true. I don't like HIVE *more* than life. It's *different* from my real-world life, yes, and that can be fun. But what I said yesterday, *that* was true—playing these games in HIVE really does improve my hand-eye coordination, both here and in my actual body. So that's cool. But it's useless if I can't get back to that body to *use* those hands and eyes. So, no, I don't want to do this forever. And I'm really glad you've been able to guide us this far."

Once again, I was blushing, but this time it wasn't with light embarrassment; it was with real, genuine shame.

"I'm really sorry, Aaron. About what I said on the bridge, and how I—I wasn't thinking—"

"I know, and I appreciate the apology. But there's another apology you might want to make—to yourself. Cuz, I mean, in your defense, I've been covering how I'm really feeling— acting all happy-go-lucky when I'm actually pretty nervous about how this is gonna turn out. It's something I've done my whole life, and maybe I could work on being more honest. But I'm not the only one who's covering up how they're feeling. Or should I say . . . the only *ones*."

He looked at me meaningfully and then looked over my shoulder. I turned around and saw Gus, polishing the sword his uniform had come with and glowering at Mr. Knighthill's back.

I turned back to Aaron.

"Sammi's not the only one here who can help with the relationship counseling," Aaron said. And there was Aaron's wicked grin again, though this time it came with a hint of something new—something wry and hard-earned. I was just opening my mouth to say something when Aaron stepped back and blurted, "Oh, you're *done*? *Finally!* This game is so *weird*. Come on, Sammi, let's *go*!"

He squeezed my shoulder, winked, and then turned to follow Sammi out the door.

And then it was just me and Gus, and a sea of dancing nobility.

"This is all so Normal." Jason sighed.

And Jason.

"Jason," I said, "could you *please* leave us alone? For like *one* picosecond?"

"Are you kidding?" Jason asked. "I've been awake for twenty-two hours, and I burned through the last of my energy drinks at, like, five p.m. Wake me up if you and your NPC boyfriend do something useful. I'm taking a nap."

"What did he say?" Gus asked.

"He's . . . actually leaving us alone," I said, stunned. "I think he was trying to be . . . nice?"

"Is he not normally?"

I considered this. "Hard to say."

"Well, you can tell me about it later. For now, Lady Tilden . . ." Gus extended a hand. "Shall we dance?"

And yeah, maybe I needed to release some stress after an insane day, especially since the day wasn't really *after* yet; it was still very much *during*. Maybe I wanted to spite Jason—or to thank him for his small act of kindness. Maybe Gus just looked good in his officer's uniform. Actually, that last one wasn't a maybe.

Whatever the reason, I said:

"Officer Iwatani, I would love to dance."

We stepped onto the floor. I'd done this a thousand times before—the flickering candles, the murmuring gentry, the violins—and the familiarity brought me comfort. But Gus, the one unfamiliar element, managed to surprise me twice over: first with how unembarrassed he made me feel, and second with how much of a natural he was proving to be.

"I can see how this could be fun," he said as we spun smoothly across the floor.

"Where did you learn to *waltz*?" I asked.

"*Dance Pants Evolution.* Remember? They released that ballroom dancing expansion pack last year. We went for our—"

"Our fourth date," I said, smiling as the memory came flooding back. "Oh my gosh, I'd totally forgotten. I had so much fun."

"Me too." Gus grinned. "Learning to waltz? Hardest thing I'd ever done in HIVE."

"Right," I said. "So it was your favorite kind of game."

We fell silent for a moment.

I thought about Aaron, and the new honesty in his smile.

"I feel like there's something you're not saying . . ." Gus began.

"My mom gave me these boots," I said.

Stunned, Gus came to a halt in the middle of the dance floor. Then a countess twirled into him and we started up again.

"You never talk about your mom," he said.

"I know," I said. "And I love that you never force me to. Except for last night, but that's not—the point is, she gave me these. Well, she gave me the boots I wear in real life, which is why I got *these* boots in the game. She handed them down to me, and they fit me perfectly. I mean, I have to lace them really tight, but I don't mind. Anyway, she told me one of her favorite things was how we both liked to imagine worlds in our heads. It's just that her worlds were in VR, and mine were in the books I read. She said that's what the boots were for—they made her feel like she was ready to explore a new world every day. And she gave them to me so I could always feel the same way."

For a moment, there was nothing but violins.

"Kara, that's . . . that's beautiful," Gus said.

"That was two weeks before she left," I said, and the music ended.

"Come on," Gus said as the NPCs began to switch partners and prepare for the next song. "Let's get out of here."

Still holding hands, we left the ballroom and made our way through the winding halls of the manor to reach the grand entrance. It was night outside, and the stars twinkled in a sky that had never been dampened by skyscrapers or streetlights.

"Why tell me that now?" Gus asked. "About your mom?"

"Because I'm trying to figure out why I really don't like HIVE," I said.

"So you *admit*—" Gus began, but he fell quiet upon my look.

"See, as much as I hate to admit it, my mom was right," I said. "HIVE and books do the same thing—they show us new worlds, and other lives. But I guess sometimes it's hard not to feel like you, and our friends, and . . . and *everyone* have all decided this is *better* than life."

Gus nodded as we passed a line of waiting carriages.

"Yeah, but, Kara—look at Aaron. He gets to—"

"I know," I said hurriedly. "It's not *better* for him. It's just . . . different."

Gus gave me a curious look. "Well, sure. But he's not the only one. Sammi gets to explore a world where she's not so stressed all the time, and I get a world where I'm . . ."

"Where you're what?" I pressed. "Why do you always want to do everything at the highest difficulty setting? Is real life that boring?"

And I knew this next question wasn't cool, but I'd had a long day and couldn't stop myself:

"Am *I* that boring?"

"No!" Gus said, so loudly that a horse behind us huffed. "*I'm* boring," he continued, dropping his voice. "I'm not as smart as you or as cool as Sammi; I don't have Aaron's irrepressible spirit. I'm just . . . Gus. Next to you guys, I feel like a loser. So I guess at least I enjoy it when it's not my fault—when I'm doing something that *anyone* would lose at. At least then the only thing that matters is I'm trying my hardest. It makes me feel, if not as good as any of you, then at least a little better than I am."

By now we'd reached the edge of the manor grounds, and I stopped and turned to face him as realization dawned on me.

"You're the Anti-Jason," I said.

"What?"

"Jason believes he's the only real person in the universe, and that everyone else is fake and therefore expendable. Well, except Eric Alanick. And I guess me and my mom?"

"What are you—"

I understood the urge to ask follow-up questions, but I kept going:

"Meanwhile, *you* see everyone and everything else as real and exciting—which is wonderful, Gus, it really is—but you're so lost in the game that you see *yourself* as expendable. And you're *not*. So you're just making things hard for no reason. And that's not *better* than Jason's problem. It's just the same problem, but backward."

"Kara . . ." Gus said, his voice wavering.

"Sorry," I said. "Maybe that sounded harsh, but—"

"No. Kara. Look." Gus pointed over my shoulder, and I turned to see what he had seen.

A single Drone floated, lost and incongruous, through the dark and torchlit grounds.

"Where did that come from?" I asked as a trickle of dread slid slowly down my back.

"That side of the manor, over there." Gus pointed again at the shadows of the manor's east wing. "Do you know what's back there?"

"That's where the servants' entrance is."

"Do players ever generate there when they start the game?" Gus asked. His eyes were still on the Drone, which had reached the hedgerows that ringed the grounds and begun to slide along them.

"No," I said. "It's much more of an upstairs than a downstairs kind of game. People don't really interact with the servants much . . . at . . . all . . ."

I trailed off as we both realized the same thing.

"The Bug!"

I don't even remember which of us said it; I just remember that as soon as it happened, we were off at a run, me with my evening gown pulled up around my boots, Gus with a hand at his waist to stop his sword from rattling in its scabbard. We reached the servants' entrance at the side of the manor and found that its door had been left open. Quickly but carefully, we descended a dark staircase, arriving at an underground corridor where only one out of every two or three candlesticks had been lit. Light flickered inconstantly as we moved forward, and from above our heads came the sound of stomping feet and muffled music—someone had called for a jig.

Then I saw a light up ahead that wasn't inconstant at all.

"Look," I said, but Gus had already spotted the same thing. We both picked up our pace, and soon we stood in front of the entrance to a dark room. It was the servants' kitchen, a cluttered chamber lined with counters and dominated by a massive central table. Every surface was dusted in flour and laden with trays of party food, stretching backward into a shroud of darkness. The foreground of the kitchen, though, was clearly lit—not by candles or by oil lamps but by a hovering, glowing, golden Bug.

"You go find Sammi and Aaron," I said. "I'll stay here and make sure no one else comes by."

"Okay. Be safe." Gus kissed me quickly before running toward the door.

"And Gus!" I yelled, just in time for him to turn back.

"Yeah?" he asked, one foot on the staircase.

"You're a winner to me," I said.

It was hard to tell by candlelight, but his smile looked bittersweet. And then he was gone, leaving me alone.

"Wow," a voice whispered in my ear. "That was so gross."

I rolled my eyes. "Nice to have you back, Jason."

"My name's not Jason, nerd."

No.

No.

"What's the matter?" Markus Fawkes asked, stepping out of the darkness at the back of the kitchen. He spoke through a mouthful of mutton leg. "Didn't expect to see me here? I'll admit it's not my usual type of game. Good food, though."

He took one more bite of mutton and then dropped it to the

floor. It was a long way to drop. At some point since I'd last seen him, Markus had redone his avatar to be even bigger than before, and he must have won a lot of points doing *something*, because he was laden with body armor that even *Mind Your Manors* hadn't been able to find a genteel substitution for. As he closed the distance between us, Markus unleashed a sneer filled with more genuine malice than I'd seen in any mole, Drone, or mobster today. For a moment, I considered grabbing the Bug and making a quick exit, but I couldn't leave my friends here, alone in a game they didn't know how to win with a bully who appeared to have become fully unhinged.

I had to stall.

"How did you find me?" I asked.

"I've been waiting here for hours," Markus said. "After you got away last time, I thought, *Well, where might she go now?* Then I remembered—you were yakking about this game when I saw you this morning. And I figured, if *she* liked it, it would be *exactly* the kind of boring hoity-toity spot that would be easy to hide out in while the bits hit the cooling fan. You know you probably saved my life today? I only saw one other player here all day, and he was only here because he was looking for some kind of amazing Bug."

I looked around. "Is he—"

"Here? No. I wasn't going to let *him* have it, was I? I like to win. So I thanked him for his information and said he could go. He didn't want to go, but . . . I won."

The sick pride with which he said this last part was how I knew: the Drone in the garden. Markus had done that. In a game marked by its complete lack of violence or danger, Markus had done something to end a player's game for good.

And now he was right in front of me.

"Then I had some time on my hands, so I went and found the Bug," he said. "But I didn't want to leave the game before you arrived. I couldn't let you *win*. So I waited, and I waited—and thank goodness I did. I was just about to give up before *you* arrived. It's a lesson in perseverance, really. I'm aspirational."

"Inspirational," I said automatically.

Markus's sneer grew bigger.

He pounced.

I'd seen it coming just in time, and as I threw myself toward the kitchen counter, he missed me by a fraction of an inch. But for someone so megasized, Markus was surprisingly limber, and he was already rounding back on me. I reached behind me, scrabbling for something to defend myself with. My hand closed on something round and heavy, and without seeing what it was, I *swung*, which was how I wound up braining Markus Fawkes with a rolling pin. Markus stumbled to the side, almost running straight into the Bug, but at the last second he regained his balance. This was sort of a lose-lose development, for now he was stalking toward me again, my back was to the counter, and any of the playfulness in Markus's eyes had been replaced by real, red-hot fury.

Then an apple bounced off his head.

"You see that?" Aaron said from the doorway. "And to think Coach Strey won't put me on the starting lineup."

Markus snarled and spun to face this new challenger—just in time to get a face full of bird. By the time Markus had swatted Laddu back in Sammi's direction, Gus had rushed into the kitchen, removing his sword from its scabbard. But Markus was already rearing up, and Gus wasn't going to have enough time to—

"No!" I yelled, but I needn't have worried. Instead of taking the time to brandish his sword, Gus brought the blunt end of the hilt straight up and into Markus's nose. There was a distinct cracking sound, and Markus roared in pain, clutching his face and falling backward to the ground.

Now Gus tossed the sword into the air, caught it by the hilt, and brandished it down at Markus's breast. To be honest, it was all exceptionally dashing.

"Don't even think about getting up," Gus said, "unless you want to become a Drone."

Markus's hands moved away from his face. A river of red was beginning to gush down from his nose, dripping over a mask of pure contempt.

Then, as he looked up at the four of us clustering around him, something shifted. His bloody snarl melted into a smirk.

"Okay," he said. "I won't get up."

Instead, he shot his giant arm out—and grabbed the Bug.

"No!" I cried, but it was too late.

"I win." Markus grinned as the glow enveloped him. Time slowed as we waited for the voice to speak the dreaded words:

"Congratulations! You have successfully debugged HIVE. To save the head of the HIVE, please reboot."

Wait.

What?

And then the manor exploded around us.

LEVEL 23

It wasn't the type of explosion you normally think of, full of sawdust and fire. It was the explosion of a jack-in-the-box that had just been released, or a seedpod cracking open in a time-lapse video. The walls of the kitchen dropped away and the ceiling opened up, revealing the shining wood and marble surfaces of the corridors outside and above us. Then those surfaces *folded*, twisting and refracting like they'd been cranked through a kaleidoscope. Soon the walls were made of polished flooring, and the floor was made of the roof; a moment later, it shifted again, and entire wings of the manor flashed by, creaking with the strain of a thousand tons of timber, as the architecture of the entire game collapsed on itself and then recombined. A hedgerow became a wall. A corridor was made of doors. And just when I thought I'd finally snapped, had pulled a Jason, and had some massive break from reality—it ended.

We stood at the intersection of three candlelit corridors, each made of a patchwork of disparate surfaces. Down the hallway to our right, open-faced suits of armor stomped back and forth, empty inside but as vigilant as any royal knight.

Down the hallway to our left, giant axes swung slowly back and forth from the ceiling like so many lethal pendulums.

And from up the hallway immediately facing us came a living wall of all-encompassing darkness, oozing slowly toward us, getting closer and closer with every second.

"What's going on?!" Markus cried. "Where are we?!"

"Welcome to the labyrinth," said the voice of the Bug. "You are now playing on difficulty level ninety-nine. To escape the labyrinth and save the head of the HIVE, please reboot."

"Reboot *how*?" Gus asked, but the voice did not respond.

"Save the head of the HIVE," Sammi was muttering. "Save the head of . . . *the* HIVE?"

"There must be something at the end of this maze," I said. "We just have to find our way there."

"Did you hear what they said, though?" Sammi asked. "Difficulty level ninety-nine. That sounds bad."

"Please," I said, with a forced cheer that I hoped didn't sound *too* forced. "You're Sammi Khanna. Labyrinths hear about *you* and *they* say, 'That sounds bad.'"

"Labyrinths don't talk."

"This one just did," Aaron said.

"Enough!" Markus had struggled to his feet and was now backing away from us. "You're all freaks, or . . . or cheating. I don't know how you are, but—"

"Markus, be careful," Sammi said. Markus was heading straight toward the wall of shadowy darkness, which was heading straight toward him in turn.

"Of what?" Markus scoffed. "I'm not afraid of the *dark*. You're all such losers. I'm going to—"

And then his right foot went into the darkness.

Markus froze midsentence. He tried to pull his foot back out again, but it was stuck, as if the shadows were made of some solid substance.

"I—I—" He looked frantically from one of us to the other. "Help me out of here! I don't wanna be a Drone. I don't wanna lose—"

"Game over," said the voice.

And then Markus did not become a Drone.

Instead, he dissolved into a shower of pixels that scattered to the floor before disappearing from the game entirely.

And then the wall of darkness began to move even faster.

"Axes or knights?!" Gus cried.

"Knights!" I decided.

Sammi nodded, and in an instant Laddu was hurtling down the hallway, distracting the suits of armor and giving us just enough time to run past them. One of them moved fast enough to swing a sword at Aaron, but he slid to the ground like he was playing the world's most dangerous game of limbo, and Gus brought his sword up in time to match the blow. I grabbed Gus by the collar and pulled him after us until we were at the end of the hall.

At which point we were once again faced with a decision: left, right, or backward? It seemed like an easy enough choice—the path to the left was slowly narrowing, the walls sliding toward each other in a patient death vise while the path to the right was all clear. And behind us, where the suits of armor stood thwarted, the darkness continued to steal along the walls, swallowing them up inch by inch.

"Okay," Sammi said, stepping tentatively toward the right path. "I know this looks empty, but we should still be careful. I've played enough puzzle games to know appearances can be deceiving. And speaking of puzzles, Kara—you know what you said? About how being smart is just noticing things?"

"Yeah?" I said, but I was barely listening, trying as I was to follow her lead as she moved gingerly from one block of mixed-up mansion floor to the next.

"Well, I'm trying to be smart here," Sammi continued. "And if I'm being smart, I'm thinking: We weren't sent to save the head of HIVE. What they said was—"

And then the floor shot open beneath Sammi's feet.

"*No!*" I cried, leaping forward, but Gus wrapped his arms around me to stop me from meeting the same fate. Sammi scrabbled for something to hold on to, grunting in pain as her hip slammed into the edge of the trapdoor, sending her smoker skidding across the floor—but then the floor opened even wider, and Sammi dropped down into the inky blackness below.

"Game over."

And then Sammi was gone.

I cried out and beat at Gus's forearms, but he wouldn't

let go, and it wouldn't have mattered. She'd disappeared. I couldn't have imagined a worse feeling.

"Laddu?"

I ate my words as, confused and increasingly frantic, Laddu flapped around the corridor, looking for his lost human, a Sidekick without a hero.

"We have to go!" Aaron said. "The walls are closing, and we're *not* going the way Sammi went!"

He was right. The darkness was closing in on us, and the passage to our left was becoming narrower every second. But I didn't understand how you just went on from something like this.

And then Laddu showed me how. Realizing that Sammi was no longer here, Laddu did what he could—flew down, grabbed the smoker in his claws, and flew it up and deposited it into my hands.

And then he threw himself down the trapdoor, following his human to the very end.

It was the shock I needed to get me moving again. I took off down the left path, Aaron and Gus following me at a sprint. We made it without a second to spare, and behind us, the walls ground together just tight enough to be impassable for a human being but not so tight that the darkness couldn't seep through.

Now we reached a portion of the labyrinth where the threat was, rather than any sort of immediate booby trap, merely the obstacle of overwhelming choice. Six paths stretched away from us like the rays of a deadly sun. Gus picked a hall at random, but unfortunately, after several twists and turns, we hit a dead end and had to double back and try again. I would have tried to be more helpful, but even though I was once again up and moving, my mind was racing, thinking of what Sammi had said.

We weren't sent to save the head of HIVE.

To save the head of the HIVE, please reboot.

"Whoa," Aaron said, throwing his arm out just in time to stop Gus and me from plunging to our deaths. We must have found the right route because somebody sure didn't want us to take it; the floor gave way here to a massive canyon, descending forever to an unending gloom. On either side of the canyon were two ends of a drawbridge, but each end was pointing straight up. Looking around revealed no clear way to join the two ends together.

And then I looked up.

Where the previous corridors had been hemmed in by low ceilings, here the walls went up and up until they reached a height much higher than the manor had ever been. Every candlestick in the manor seemed to be here, too, joined together to create one twisted, snaking megastick that started way, way up on the wall and stretched out over the canyon, ending in—

"A switch!" Gus said. "That must control the bridge."

"But there's no way we could reach that," I said. "Unless . . ."

Aaron turned to us.

"No," Gus said instantly.

"Look," Aaron said. "I'd be lying if I said I understood half of what had happened today. I've just been along for the ride; I'm not the best person to solve what's going on. But I know *you* are." He pointed at me.

"No, I'm not!" I said. "I just—"

And then it hit me. *Save the head of the HIVE.*

"Actually," I said, stunned to my core, "I think I am."

"See? I knew it." Aaron turned to Gus. "And I know *you* will make sure she gets where she needs to go."

I looked behind us. The darkness was back.

"Aaron." Gus wasn't having any of it. "Even double jumping, I'm not sure you could reach that switch. And even if you did, you'd have nothing to jump off to reach the other side. There's no way you could do it."

"I told you," Aaron said, turning to look right into my eyes.

He pinched his nose, freezing for just a moment. When he let go, his fancy ballroom shoes had been replaced by a pair of Air Alanicks.

"I never wanted to do this forever."

And then he leaped.

And leaped again.

For a terrible moment I didn't think Aaron would make it. Then, in an equally terrible moment, he did; his outstretched fingertips just managed to reach around the edge of the switch, and he grabbed on for dear life, pulling it forward with his own momentum. With much more speed than I'd anticipated, the two ends of the drawbridge fell forward. I began to pull Gus across, but this time, it was his turn to stop.

"Aaron!" he yelled. "Jump down!"

But he'd been right the first time. There was no way for Aaron to return, no surface for him to jump off. He could only dangle off the switch, watching us as the darkness came closer than ever.

"Don't make me do this cool move for nothing, man!" Aaron yelled back. "You have to keep going!"

"No way!" Gus said, and I realized, horribly, what he was doing: having one last bickering match with his best friend while holding back tears. "I bet if you swung really hard—"

"Ugh," Aaron said, getting into the spirit of it. "If you're going to be like this, I'll take care of it myself."

And then he let go of the switch and plunged into the canyon.

Gus leaned over the railing and opened his mouth like he was trying to yell, but nothing came out. There was only that awful announcement:

"Game over."

We had lost another friend to the darkness.

And then the edge of the bridge was enveloped in shadows, and I was forcing Gus onward, farther into the labyrinth.

And then, once we'd run down a particularly long stretch of corridor, I forced Gus to stop.

"I can't believe he did that," Gus was saying. "That stupid, stubborn, wrongheaded—"

"Actually, Aaron was right," I said, bending down and lifting up my gown. "So was Sammi. Help me take off my shoes."

"I—what?" Gus, shocked as he was, didn't have the fight left in him to resist. He just bent down and helped me pull my right foot out of its boot, like a reverse Cinderella. If I was correct, that would be all I needed—but running in just one boot and an evening gown sounded like no fun for anyone, so I quickly moved on to untying the left boot as well.

"The original message said we were saving 'the head of HIVE,'" I explained as Gus held the boot down and I began to wriggle out of it. "Which would be Eric Alanick. But whoever was writing on the frames had a thirty-six-character limit— they told us that themselves. And both times the voice spoke just now, it told us to save the head of *the* HIVE."

"Kara, what are you talking about?" Gus said, looking up at me with confusion in his eyes.

"Don't think about Bugs," I said. "Think about bees. Don't think about HIVE. Think about *hives*. Who is the head of the hive?"

Gus screwed his face up in concentration.

"The head of the hive . . ." he said. "The head of the hive is the . . . the . . . *no way*."

"That's right," I said. "The head of the hive is the queen."

As I helped Gus to his feet with one hand, I held up my right boot with the other—and flipped it upside down.

"And the queen of HIVE," I said, "is the person who gave me these boots."

There, on the bottom of my trusty boots, the ones I'd bought from the HIVE store because I thought they looked so much like my mom's—never once thinking to question why that might be so—was an elaborate design of treads. Not just a design, in fact—a labyrinth. At the back of the heel were a bunch of right angles; then farther on, a burst of six lines, like a deadly sun; and then just beyond that, a big circle, as if there were a canyon in the tread of the boots.

I didn't know when. I didn't know why. But somehow, my mother had left me countless messages all across HIVE. And now, when I needed it most, she had provided me with a map of the maze.

All I'd had to do was reboot.

If I was reading the map right, we were almost to the end of the labyrinth—which was good because we'd used up all the time we had, and the wall of shadows was ten feet away and closing in.

"Follow me!" I said.

We darted up one corridor and down another, dodging arrows and axes, ducking under bursts of flame and tiptoeing across the narrowest of ledges. I held the boot up all the way, consulting it for each twist and turn. Soon enough, we reached what seemed to be the end—the very last line of tread, up at the tip of the toe. There was just one more curve, up on our left.

Cautiously, we stepped around it.

Rapidly, we stepped back.

I peeked my head back around the lip of the wall. Beyond it was a door, hexagonal in shape, ringed by some eye-straining shade of neon black. And between us and that door was . . .

"Was that a Bug?" Gus asked. "Or a, a Drone, or—"

I shook my head. This was bigger than any Bug, and meaner and more jittery than any Drone. Its stinger was sharper. Its movements were quicker. Its wings were as long as my arms— no, longer.

There were no two ways about it: It was a wasp. And it was the last thing between us and freedom.

"We need a distraction," I said, turning back to face Gus— and stopping when I saw the odd expression on his face.

"No," Gus said. "You need a distraction."

I almost dropped my boot.

"Gus—" I began.

"Look," he said. "We both just saw how this goes down, so let's speed-run through it. You're going to tell me why I shouldn't do it, why we should both make it to the end. I'm going to tell you what we both know: that you're the only one who *can* make it to the end. You're the one who *has* to. You're here for a reason, Kara. You're going to save your mom *and* your dad, *and* everyone else in HIVE, too. I was right all along: You're a winner."

I threw a boot at Gus Iwatani's head.

"Are you *dense*?" I hissed as he ducked it easily. "Didn't you listen to a word I said tonight? You're not a loser, I'm not a winner—stop *talking* like that! I hate it! I—"

I choked on my words, wiping my hand across my eyes. Who had designed digital avatars to cry, anyway? It was stupid. Everything in HIVE was stupid.

Even the things I loved.

"If you dissolve and go away forever," I continued, "don't come back!"

Gus just pulled me close and kissed me one last time.

"You're right," he said.

And then he stepped back, revealing himself fully to the wasp around the corner.

"Right now, I feel like a winner." He grinned.

And then the wasp shot forward, tackling him to the ground.

I couldn't look. I could only run while the wasp was distracted, trying not to trip over my gown, straining to see through my tears. I grabbed on to the handle of the hexagonal door, expecting at the last moment for it to be locked, for all this to be for nothing—but it swung inward as easily as pressing an on switch.

Beyond it lay a white void.

I ran into the void, slamming the door shut behind me and then falling against it, breathing in ragged, wet gasps.

Then even the door vanished and I fell to the floor—a floor

that looked like the walls, which looked like the ceiling, which looked like nothing, forever and ever in all directions.

"Welcome to the loading screen," said the voice.

"The head of HIVE will be with you soon."

And then I was alone.

PART THREE

LEVEL 24

In an eternal white void, I sat, and I cried, and I waited for the loading screen to go away.

And waited.

And waited, and waited.

Loading screens. You know how it is.

Eventually, I cried myself out, and my sadness turned to numbness, then to boredom, then to outright irritation. I wrapped my arms around my legs and hunched up in a sulky ball. How long was this going to take? Why even put me through this at all? What heretofore undiscovered part of HIVE could be so impressive that it took this long to load?

On some level, I knew that these cranky questions were just a way to mask the deep grief and loneliness I felt. I missed my family. I missed my friends. Heck, I even missed—

"Kara?"

I shot straight upright.

"Jason?" I asked. "You—you can hear me? You're still with me?"

"Uh, yeah," he said. "And apparently I'm the only one. What

happened while I was asleep? Where'd everybody go? Where'd . . .
everything go?"

I filled him in on all the details: that we'd found the last
Bug, and that Markus Fawkes had come back one last time.
That it seemed like my mom had been leaving the messages
the whole time—but that by following them, I'd lost everyone
I cared about.

"Whoa," Jason said when I was done. "That sounds . . .
intense. Sorry."

"Thanks," I said tentatively, but I remained on guard. With
Jason, there was always a catch.

"But if it makes you feel any better," he went on, "they're
not really—"

"*I knew it!*" I exploded. "I *knew* you were going to say something *ridiculous* and *delusional* about how everything I care
about is pointless because none of it's *real*! Well, news flash,
you jerk—my *feelings* are real! The pain I'm going through
is real! And if you can't understand that, then you're less real
than anyone I know!"

There was silence in the void.

Then:

"I was going to say," Jason began slowly, "that they're not
really gone for certain. You didn't see them dissolve like
Markus did, right? And we don't really know what's been happening to anyone since the Update dropped. If we fix it, they
might be okay."

"Oh."

I tugged abashedly at the edge of my dress.

"So are you saying—"

"Look, can I tell you why . . . *how* I got here?"

I gestured broadly at the loading screen. "I'm not going anywhere. Knock yourself out."

"Okay." Jason took a deep breath.

"My parents were always neglectful. They left me alone a lot—at the library, yes, which you knew, but elsewhere, too. The park. The playground. Heck, even the power plant. Places much less safe than the Bullworth Library Reading Room. They were addicts."

From the way he said it, the irony did not seem to be lost on Jason, the biggest HIVE addict I knew. Or maybe it was lost on him. Things that were obvious to me were not always obvious to Jason, and vice versa.

"That's how I wound up at the mall by myself the first day they were offering the free HIVE demo," Jason said. "I was fourteen—okay, I was thirteen—but when I offered to start working at the arcade in exchange for free access to HIVE, Mr. Wamengatch said yes.

"I hadn't moved in yet, but it was like I'd gained a new home. Or actually, given my parents, it was like I'd gained a home, period. And the more time I spent in HIVE, the higher up the Honeycomb I went. Part of it was just that I loved the games: They kept getting weirder and harder the farther up I climbed, and learning how to play them made me proud. But mostly, I just liked how few people were up there. HIVE was really taking off at that time—this is around when they turned the arcade into an Apiary—which meant there were a lot more Normals filling up the bottom of the Honeycomb. Then the middle. Then, more and more often, the top. So I kept going up. And up, and up. And then one day, someone was in my last safe game, the one I thought no one else would play."

"Was it *Frisbee, but Bad*?" I asked, unable to stop myself.

"What—how did you know that?"

"Saw it earlier." I shrugged. "Continue."

"Well—yes. Anyway. I wanted one place that was just mine. One place no one else would think to go. And when I went as far up into HIVE as it was possible to go, I found it."

"Terms and Conditions."

"Exactly," Jason said. "And in all the years I spent there—all the years until today—*no one* ever went in there. They all assumed it was boring. Not me, though. To me, it was fascinating. I read everything I could, and went through all the doors to all the little mini-libraries like the one you saw—though I never thought to open the beehives, credit where it's due."

"Thank y—"

"So anyway, slowly but surely I worked my way to the back of the library. Which is where I found it—the weirdest door of them all."

"The back door?"

"Yep," Jason said. "Except that's not what it was called. You couldn't see it today because it was covered by all the . . .

well, you couldn't see it today. But when I first approached it, there was a little label on the door. BOREDOM SIMULATOR. And I stepped through it."

"And?" If I'd had a seat to sit on, I'd have been on the edge of it.

"I woke up in the Apiary," Jason said. "It popped me right back out into Bullworth. Our world. The Boredom Simulator."

"I . . ." I honestly didn't know where to begin. "Jason, it's a joke. A gag. Like when someone tells you to hit F4 and your window closes. Or an egress."

"What's an egress?"

I shifted backward onto my palms. "Carnival workers used to say, 'This way to the egress,' or 'Step here to see the amazing egress.' And then you go through this whole tent and you get to the back and you find out *egress* is just a fancy word for *exit*."

There was a long silence in which I could practically feel Jason staring at me.

"What?" I huffed. "I read. You pick stuff up."

"Well," Jason said at last. "I thought it was just an egress, too. Then I got home."

Something in the way he said it made me shiver, even though it was perfectly room temperature in the void. Void temperature?

"What was at home?" I asked.

"Nothing. My parents had disappeared." Jason relayed this info the same way he'd relayed everything else—flatly, like he was reading an old news article that had worn out with age. But I thought I detected the slightest pause before he continued.

"And not just like they'd done before," he said. "I waited, but they never came back. They were gone for good."

"Jason," I said quietly. "That's . . . that's terrible. I'm so sorry. I know that when my mom left, I felt—"

"No, it's okay," Jason said. "Because I figured it out. They'd gone home. Their real home, the one in the real world. All those times growing up when they'd disappear—I thought it was because they were addicts, but those times were the only times they were getting sober. Because those were the times they left HIVE."

"By HIVE," I said slowly, "you mean . . ."

"The world where you and I grew up, yes. The day my parents left was the day they got back to the real world and got clean. I don't know if it was their choice or not. My guess is, something about me getting close to the truth scared someone way up top, and they found my parents and brought them home. But they forgot to find me. So I decided then and there that I would keep reading everything in Terms and Conditions, and I would do what it takes to find the one true door to the real world, and find them. Until this Update today, when everything went out of whack, and I went through the Boredom Simulator door just one more time to see if it would still work. It did. But now I can't get back in again. I was even trying to drive back to my old home, to see if maybe this all meant they'd come back . . . until I ran into you. And now here we are."

And then he was done, and we both sat there in silence.

"Jason . . ." I said at last.

"Yeah?" he said, and I could tell already he was feeling defensive, and I wished I didn't have to be the one to make him feel that way. But I couldn't not say it. It wouldn't have been honest to keep quiet, and it wouldn't have been doing my duty to him as a fellow human being, or as a friend.

Curse my need to help everyone.

"It just doesn't make sense," I said. "How would your using the Boredom Simulator trigger your parents leaving? It's a terrible coincidence, I admit, but that's the only thing it can be. And surely if you'd read that much of Terms and Conditions, you'd have found something by now revealing that our world wasn't real. Or you'd have some memories of the 'real world' where you'd been born, or . . . or . . ."

"Stop it!" Jason said. "Stop trying to confuse me! I'm just telling you what happened to me!"

And there it was—that voice crack I knew so well. For the first time since he'd started telling this story, Jason's emotions were seeping through. But I didn't think that was a bad thing—far from it. I was pretty sure it meant I was starting to get through to him.

"Jason, I get why it's easier to think that none of it's real, or that everyone's against you," I said. "I felt that way a few times myself after my mom left. But other people *aren't* against you. They're real, and they're going through as much pain as you are, and you can help them, which means they can help you."

"Who's gone through *half* the pain I have?" Jason spat.

"I mean," I said, trying not to sound too flippant. "I think I . . . literally have?"

"You don't count!" Jason said. "You're real!"

"That's it, though, Jason," I said. "I'm real. My friends were—*are*—real, too. And I think on some level you know that, or you wouldn't have helped us as much as you did today. Deep down, you care about other people. That's not bad. That's good."

"I'm so sick of this," Jason said. "I'm sick of you. I should never have helped you get here—and where even *is* here, anyway? I went to sleep for two minutes and you *clearly* messed *everything* up without me. I bet this isn't even a loading screen. You're just going to be stuck here forever, and that's your problem because I'm done helping you. I'm done *talking* to you. Enjoy forever, I'm—"

"Loading completed," said a voice, ringing out across the nothing.

And then the nothing went away.

I'd expected somewhere astounding, an insanely elaborate lair full of opulence and eye-popping detail to justify just how long it had taken to get here.

Instead, I sat in what appeared to be a corporate meeting

room—like my dad's office, but with a slightly more minimalist decorator. There was a whiteboard on the wall and a little plastic water bottle next to me. My chair was wheely.

My *Mind Your Manors* evening gown was gone, replaced by a default Honeycomb suit, though the smoker was still clipped to my belt, under the table.

It was a very boring table.

But the person who sat across it was not very boring at all.

"Kara—" Jason gasped, suddenly much less combative. "That thing I said about not talking to you . . ."

"I know," I said. "No worries. Please stick around."

"Okay. I, uh. I will."

Across the table, my new companion stood up.

"Hello, Kara," said Eric Alanick.

LEVEL 25

"How are you, Kara?" asked the founder and head architect of the most successful and popular big-tech company in the history of the free market. "Are you doing okay? Need some water? I mean, you don't, because it's HIVE, but have some, anyway."

"I. Uh." My brain appeared to be stuck back in the loading screen.

"You should be asking if *he's* okay!" Jason cried, snapping me out of it. "He's being held *hostage* in his *own* invention!"

"I should be asking if you're okay!" I blurted, just trying to keep up. "You're being held—hostage?"

As I'd said it, Eric Alanick's eyebrows had shot up. Now he laughed.

"Kara," he said. "Whatever gave you *that* idea?"

Up close, you could really see why people said he might have been a vampire. He was even paler and more handsome in person than he was on-screen—or, I guess, his avatar was. His black hair was expertly coiffed, with just enough gray in the temples to add a hint of sophistication. He wore a black blazer and a white shirt in much the same style that Gus had—just rumpled enough to make him look the perfect mix of classy and cool. And as he sank back down into his chair, he moved with the fluidity and ease of someone who had never once felt out of place in any room.

And, I realized with a sinking feeling, he certainly did not move like a hostage.

"But . . . that apology video you were forced to record today . . ." I began. "And—and those world leaders we saw in Terms and Conditions . . . they said you were tied up."

Again, Eric burst out laughing. He seemed genuinely delighted by my company. It would have been flattering if it hadn't all felt so upside down.

"I *was* tied up," he said, smiling. "The day of a new Update is always immensely busy for me, and today was no exception— quite the opposite, in fact. And if you think that apology video seemed forced, you've got me dead to rights. If I had my way, we'd move forward and never look back. Move fast and break things, that's my motto, and that's how you rise to the top of any industry. But"—and here he sighed heavily—"some of my *shareholders* thought it might be best if we mollified the consumer base a bit before moving into Phase Two."

"What—what is he talking about?" Jason stammered. "Ask him how to get to the real world. Ask him if he knows my—"

But Jason was just so much static to me now, as the full horror of Eric's words dawned on me, rising over the horizon of my mind like a bloodred star.

"You did this all on purpose," I said. "The Update. The

people trapped in HIVE. The Drones. Everything. You *planned* it. And you got people to *help* you."

"Very important, powerful people, yes." Eric grinned. "And you might just be one of them."

My eyes flickered to the door of the corporate meeting room—and as soon as they did, possibly even sooner, Eric Alanick *blurred* and went from sitting at the table to standing in front of the door, faster than humanly possible.

"Cool, right?" Eric beamed. "My world, my rules."

He moved to lock the door, and then stopped.

"Wait," he said. "Watch this."

He snapped his fingers, and the door locked on its own.

"I love that," he said, still beaming as he crossed back to the table. He was moving at a human speed again, but I couldn't see him the same way anymore. Which seemed perfectly fine by him as he sat back down and leaned forward to address me.

"Kara," he said. "I've been following you all day. Not at first—I had no idea I should be following you at first—but then I began hearing stories, from those world leaders you mentioned in Terms and Conditions, and from a pair of Drones in *Ain't Auto Theft Grand* that had some very odd player behavior to report. From there I noticed what you and your friends were doing. I noticed you were *smart*. And because you're so smart, I'm going to give you a chance to answer a question: Do you know what HIVE needs a lot of?"

I thought hard. I had no interest in impressing this creep, but I couldn't deny that the question intrigued me. Jason, for his part, had fallen deathly silent; I didn't think he was enjoying meeting his hero very much.

Did HIVE need a lot of players? No, the *company* needed a lot of players. HIVE itself—the High Integrity Virtual Environment—needed . . .

"Power," I said.

Eric slapped the table. "Ding ding ding!" he said. "You *are* smart. Every bit your mother's daughter. HIVE needs—"

But I had already leaped out of my seat. "*Mom!* Is she—"

Eric blurred again. The force with which he shoved me back into my wheely chair felt like being pushed from the very top of the Honeycomb and accelerating all the way until I hit the bottom—but in less than a fraction of a second. The chair shot back across the carpet and slammed into the wall, followed shortly by my head, which hit the wall *hard*. I hadn't even finished crying out when Eric blurred again and was back where he'd been sitting, as if nothing had changed.

"I was *talking*," Eric whined. "Don't *interrupt*. So. HIVE needs an *insane* amount of power—like, just to operate one pod, let alone an entire Apiary, let alone hundreds of thousands of Apiaries across the world."

"Which world?" Jason asked quietly, but from the hopeless tone in his voice, I could tell he already knew.

"And power costs money," Eric said. "Don't get me wrong, we do all right—we do great, actually. But there was always going to be a cap someday. There was always going to come a time when we just couldn't get enough power to keep up with the massive, massive demand for HIVE. And that day is coming sooner than you think."

The back of my head throbbed fiercely, and when I spoke, it was through gritted teeth:

"So what does this have to do with the Update?"

"Smart question! Smart again!"

Eric smiled wide, like I was a particularly witty journalist at a press conference, and not a girl he had just attacked.

"The human brain is the most efficient processor there is. I mean, even just a cat's brain can hold a thousand times more data than a powerful server—and act on it a million times faster. The human genome—the thing that runs your entire body, your entire life—executes its programs with less input than a laptop. And remember laptops? They were real, real stupid."

"Hey," Jason protested weakly, and in that moment I had the most absurd image of him sitting cross-legged on the floor of the Bullworth Apiary, his entire world falling apart before his eyes, and nevertheless finding the sheer cussedness required to defend his ancient laptop. In a way I couldn't describe, my heart swelled for him in that moment.

Eric, unaware of all this, kept going, picking up excitement as he did.

"So the solution was obvious," he said. "It occurred to us years ago. Why pay to generate the power that helps keep players' brains happy in HIVE—when we could just *use players' brains themselves*? We got to work on the technology right away. And in the meantime, we began paving the way for players to have the best possible user experience in this exciting new business model. In this new world."

He moved up from the table, apparently not to get anything, but just because he was so giddy that he needed to pace around the room. I had the sense that he'd had to keep these things to himself for a very long time, and that he wasn't a man who liked keeping big news to himself. Now that he had a (literal) captive audience, he was going to make the most of it.

"Do you know what a hive *really* is?" he asked, and then held up a finger before I could speak. "This one, you don't have to answer. You're going to say it's a bee's nest."

I had intended to say nothing of the sort.

"But that's wrong," Eric said. "A nest is a structure a bee builds for itself. That's natural. *Hive* is the word for the thing humans make to trap the bees in. It's unnatural—it's a prison—but the bees learn to love it. And then the humans extract the resource they want—the honey. I love beekeeping, for the record. That's real. Got super into it in college—you know, before I dropped out. Your mother did, too; that's one of the first things we bonded over."

He looked at me quickly to see if I would react, but I didn't take the bait.

"So that's how HIVE became what it is," he said. "An actual hive. Phase One this morning was all about sealing the exits. And when we start Phase Two tonight, we won't be extracting honey. We'll be extracting energy. Of course, honey is sugar and sugar is energy, so it's— Oh, I'm getting into the weeds again. I always do this; I'm such a geek."

He stopped pacing just long enough to turn and face me.

"But for real—do you know what they call the hexagons in a beehive?" he asked, grinning, like he was about to pull off a particularly neat trick. "They're called cells."

"You want to keep everyone in HIVE forever so you can use their brains to . . . keep everyone in HIVE forever," I said. "You're insane."

I probably shouldn't have said this to the all-powerful man with a hair-trigger temper, but he just waved a hand dismissively.

"Visionaries are always misunderstood in their time," he said blithely. "But here's the thing: I really think people *will* understand. They'll *love* it. Like bees. Nobody wants to leave HIVE anyway, not really."

"What about the outside world?" I pointed out. "The real world? It'll crumble."

"Who cares!" Eric threw his hands up, grinning. "They'll never need it again!"

"What about people's *bodies*?"

"Doesn't matter," he said. "People are in HIVE now. And today, the day of the Update, more people entered Apiary pods than on any other day in recorded HIVE history, so, you know. They'll actually be quite comfortable."

"What about the people who *aren't* in pods?" I could feel the rage swelling, imagining Sheila the bus driver, and all her passengers, and everyone like them across the world. "They don't have the nutrient feeds or the temperature-controlled chambers. They'll *die*."

Eric shrugged.

"Move fast and break things," he said, like this was a perfectly reasonable explanation—no—a noble one.

And if I hadn't known it before, I knew now: Eric Alanick may not have been a vampire, but he was, undoubtedly, a monster.

"People will never go along with this," I said.

"But they already *have*." Eric leaned forward onto the table, looking into my eyes with real concern as if it was of the utmost importance to him that I understood. "My shareholders. My investors. Those bigwigs you saw. They were all dying to get on board. Of course, they seem to have misunderstood—they thought they'd be allowed to toast with me during Phase One and then leave HIVE before Phase Two begins, and that's simply not going to happen. But everyone's going to like it eventually. Everyone belongs in HIVE."

And now here was my last and weakest defense:

"They'll get bored," I said. "No one wants to play a game *forever*."

I felt silly even as I said it, but Eric just shook his head.

"You know, it's actually interesting," he said. "I'm glad you brought it up. Winning a game is a relatively recent idea. The first games—the games that made everyone want more games, forever—were the ones you could never win. Ever. And that's what we're returning to. If you want a picture of the future, imagine a ball bouncing back and forth between two lines, faster and faster. Forever."

And that's when I really felt in my bones that he was right. I'd learned it from Gus, and from Jason, and from everyone who wished they could live in HIVE. No one was going to stop this. Eric was going to win.

"You know," Eric began, "there was *one* person who tried to stop me."

I looked up at him. Surely he didn't mean—

"And now that you've so rudely rejected my pitch deck," Eric said, "there are two. Which is a shame—I'd hoped to recruit you; the company always needs fresh, dynamic young thinkers like yourself. You know you caused quite a stir today? Inspiring all those players to move from game to game—it actually made us delay starting Phase Two by a couple of hours. It's harder to catalyze the energy in people's brains when they're moving around, you see. That's why we've been trying a pilot program where we pacify players' brains before converting them, by turning them into—"

"Drones," I said.

"Ding ding ding! You'd make great competition, Kara. Which means I'm going to keep you as locked up tight as my other competition. It's just good business practice."

He blurred to the door again, and with a snap, it unlocked.

"Come on, princess," he said. "Your queen is in another castle."

I got up from my chair. In any other world but this one, I would have traveled less than zero feet with a man who called me princess. But if he was taking me where I thought he was taking me, he wouldn't have been able to shake me loose if he tried.

He led me out of the meeting room and across what appeared to be an open-plan office, littered with skateboards, encouraging Post-it notes, and generous snack bars.

"Where is everyone?" I asked.

"Oh, this floor tried to unionize right before the Update," Eric said. "Which was actually good, because I needed more Drones. Of course, I'm all full up on Drones now! You know how it goes."

He stopped in front of a door made out of steamed glass and clearly labeled THE QUEEN'S CELL. My heart began to beat faster, but Eric had one last question for me.

"By the way," he said, "a few minutes ago—when you first entered the office—who were you talking to?"

Now my heart was doing a tarantella. Eric didn't know about Jason. And for some reason, it felt crucial to me to keep it that way.

"Oh, I just—I talk to myself," I said. "When I'm nervous, or . . . or . . ."

Eric held up a hand, regarding me closely. I had a terrible thought: If Eric Alanick was all-powerful here in HIVE, could he even read my mind?

Then he said, "Say no more. I do the same thing. You know

it's a sign of intelligence? My meditation guy taught me that. Dang, Kara—you really could have been a great add to my team. And people are always saying I need to be supporting more women in tech—but I just find it's so *inconvenient*. Case in point."

He swung the door open. Before I could react to what was inside, he'd blurred again, pushing me in, slamming the door shut, and snapping it locked.

"I have to go activate Phase Two!" he called cheerily through the door. "You girls get along—you're here forever!"

And then he was gone, leaving me in the room.

Leaving *us* in the room.

Everything I'd been thinking about, intentionally not thinking about, and then thinking about not thinking about, over and over in loops, for the past several minutes, days, months, and years, all came crashing down on my head at once.

And when I finally opened my mouth to speak, that crashing sounded like two words:

"Hi, Mom."

LEVEL 26

I'd imagined this moment for years. How angry I'd be. The things I would say. I'd practiced my speeches in the shower, in the car, even while sitting in the Apiary lobby waiting to pick up Gus for a ride home. I'd dreamed of the hurt I'd unleash, the irrefutable points I'd make, the way I'd pick a fight.

The way I'd win.

Now the subject of all those imagined speeches stood before me. Under me, really—I was short, yes, but I got that from her, and the small staircase that descended from the doorway down into the Queen's Cell meant that for once, I had not just the moral but the literal high ground. I towered over her. There would never be a better moment to make my mother pay.

I ran down the steps two at a time and threw my arms around her in the tightest hug I could possibly give.

"Kara!" Mom cried, wrapping her arms around me even tighter in return. "You did it; you found me!"

"Mom, Mom," I was gasping over her, "I thought—I didn't—"

"Shh. It's okay." Mom ran her thumbs across my cheeks,

wonder in her brown eyes, eyes that looked just like mine—to say nothing of her hair, hair I recognized as precisely Dark Umber. "You've grown so much. You're beautiful."

I realized then that it hadn't just been years for me—it had been years for her, too. There was so much I wanted to tell her.

"Mom," I said. "Since you left . . ."

But she stopped me right there.

"I never left. Honey, I would never, never leave. I was taken."

"But . . . the letter you left for the family—"

"You got a *letter*? In the *mail*? Surely your dad recognized it wasn't my handwriting."

I hung my head, realizing how foolish I'd been to ever believe my mom could have done something so callous.

"It was . . . left in HIVE," I said. "Saying that you didn't have time for us anymore. *Because* of HIVE."

"Oh, honey." Mom hugged me again. "You must have been *furious*. Well, so was I. Eric told the board what he was planning to do all those years ago and I was the only one who objected. I threatened to go to the authorities right then and there, so the way they saw it, they had no choice—they locked me up, and I've been here ever since."

She gestured around, and for the first time, I really took in our surroundings. As prison cells went, it wasn't too bad. It was the kind of office you saw in startup brochures—a pinball machine in one corner; a set of jump ropes and yoga balls in another; and there, on the far side of the room . . .

"They gave you a computer?" I asked, incredulous.

"Eric knew I was his best coder," Mom said, unable to keep the note of pride out of her voice. "He couldn't afford to lose me. So he gave me this programming rig—with as many safeguards as he could think of. He did his absolute best to make sure I couldn't leave any messages for anyone in the games."

She smiled. "Good thing I'm absolutely better."

"The messages in the Hive Simulator," I said. "And the Bugs."

"Exactly. Hidden away in places no one else would think to look. Waiting for the day someone would come find me. It's a bit dramatic that it wound up happening *today*—and when Eric found out what I'd done, he was able to corrupt my labyrinth, making it far more difficult than it was ever supposed to be. But it looks like it all worked out, right?"

I felt a pang in my chest as I wondered whether or not I should tell her what had happened in the labyrinth. But I never got the chance because at that moment, she looked down.

"And—you got the *boots*!" she cried, ecstatic. "Oh, it was a long shot, but when Eric asked me to add some items to the HIVE store, I thought, *What the heck. This could be my only chance, and he'll never suspect it. He's too arrogant.*"

"You think *that* was a long shot?" I exclaimed. "How could you have known I would even get to Terms and Conditions in the first place?"

Mom looked at me, amused. "Honey, it's a library. You were going to get there eventually."

The tears threatened to return.

"No, don't cry," Mom said hurriedly. "This is amazing. I'm so proud of you, honey; you did incredible."

"But," I said. "Eric is going to start Phase Two, and then everyone will—"

"I know." Mom sighed. "I would stop it if I could. But with this programming rig I can only reach the marginal things— the store, the mini-libraries, the leftover bits of dead code from years ago, scattered across HIVE. A pair of boots here, a Drone-proof smoker there, obscure little Bugs in some of the games I knew you played with your friends—I've been able to leave clues for you, but I'm just absolutely unable to shut down Eric's code."

"How is he going to do it?" I asked. "And *when*?"

"Oh, I know exactly how he'll do it," Mom said darkly. "He'll activate this Update the same way he does every Update: with a quick visit to Terms and Conditions, so he can say that he's read the new ones before the Update begins. The one thing buying us time is that he can't just zap his way through the Honeycomb like he does through here. He has to ride that platform all the way up from the Business District."

I nodded. I'd learned just this morning how long that trip took.

Then I realized:

"Wait. I spent an hour in that loading screen just to reach a *regular office in the Business District*?"

"You did *what*?" Mom rolled her eyes. "*Ugh*. He must have

built a back door function into the labyrinth. He used to do that to our investors in real life all the time—make them wait an hour just to meet him. Some tip he read in a business self-help book about how to be the biggest man in the room."

"Arrgh!" I roared so loud that Mom jumped.

"I can't believe we're stuck here because of that—that *lunatic*!" I said. "And you know what the worst part is? He's not even *unique*!"

Mom stood back as I picked up pace and energy. You could tell she'd spent a few years without seeing a teenage tantrum up close and personal, but there was no stopping me now.

"I'm so *sick* of men like Eric Alanick!" I yelled. "Eric, and Markus, and *everyone* who thinks life is a game, and they *must* be the main characters, so everyone else is either a threat or just doesn't exist! Because if you're the winner, then everyone else *has to* be the loser. I'm sick of there being winners and losers at all! You know my favorite thing about books? Nobody flipping *wins* a book! You just *enjoy* it! And now we're all going to be stuck here in this *dumb* world, and all there ever will be is winners, and losers, and HIVE, and—"

I stopped dead in my tracks.

"Wait," I said.

"What is it?" Mom asked.

"What if . . ." I tested out the idea carefully. "What if Jason was right?"

"What?"

"What?" said Jason, still in my ear.

"I don't know who you're talking about," my mom said.

"Jason Alcorn," I said. I guess we *were* doing this one more time.

"The . . . boy I used to drive home from the library?"

"Told you," I muttered. "She was there and you just never noticed."

"Sorry," Jason said, "I was busy *not having parents.*"

"What?" Mom said again.

"Sorry. Yes, Mom—the boy from the library. After you left he hit a, uh, really rough patch." I just decided to go for it. "He got addicted to HIVE and began to think that NPCs were real people and real people were NPCs."

"I sure did!" Jason said, with a fairly reasonable level of manic cheer for someone whose whole worldview had been shattered less than half an hour ago.

"Oh, no, that's terrible," Mom said. "Wait, and—and you think he's *right*?"

"Well, no," I said. "Not about everything—but what if he was right about one big thing in particular?"

As quickly as I could, I told Mom my plan. When I was done, she regarded me with a mixture of pride and sadness.

"Honestly, honey? I love that idea. It's bizarre and outside the box and everything I wanted to encourage in you and other players when I put those Bugs in the crazy places I did. But it's like I said—we can't do anything without a way for me to bypass the security protocols on this rig. We'd need someone on the outside. As long as we're in here, we're sealed off."

"What about Jason?" I suggested.

"What about him?"

"What about me?" he said.

"Oh, right, sorry." I pointed at my head. "Jason's in here. I mean, he's *not* in here. He's in my feed, but he's sitting in the Bullworth Apiary, in the real world, with an old programming rig of his own, using some freaky hacker magic to keep himself hooked up into the pod that I'm in right now."

Mom stared at me, processing this information. And then she sat down at her rig and began to tie her hair back into a messy topknot.

"Jason," she said. "Can you hear me?"

"Yes," Jason said, and it was the most genuinely excited I'd heard him sound about anything all day.

"Oh—yes," I repeated, after there was a pause in the Queen's Cell.

"Okay." Mom booted up her monitor. "Are you operating on an Anaconda system?"

"Actually," Jason said as I repeated his every word, "it's a Mocha language processor with a VDMI plug-in."

Mom laughed. "Oh, that's old-school. *Respect.*"

"Th-thank you," Jason said, and I could *hear* him blushing.

"Don't be weird," I said.

"What?"

"Not you, Mom."

"Jason, honey," Mom said, already on to the next thought, "I need you to type in a request-access function for Kara's pod. Can you do that?"

There was a pause during which I imagined Jason must have been typing at lightning speed, after which he said: "Done."

"Great. You should be looking at a password menu. I'm going to give you some top-secret access info about HIVE that no one else has. Are you ready for that?"

"I have never been more ready for anything," Jason said, his voice trembling, "in my entire life."

"Fantastic," she said. "Because if my math is correct, we have just under twenty minutes. Here's what you're going to do . . ."

Just under twenty minutes later, right as my brain began to hurt from relaying technobabble from one plane of reality to another, Mom yelled, "And . . . *execute!*"

"Done!" Jason said.

"Done!" I repeated.

For a moment, all three of us cheered.

But then the moment passed.

"So now what?" Jason asked. "Do we just wait?"

"Yes," Mom said. "And hope we were fast enough."

"Actually, if the plan worked," I said, "then I think I have an idea of how to get us out of here."

I pinched my nose briefly, finding a powerset that had been

lying dormant all day in my Inventory, and then returned to the Queen's Cell.

"*Now* we wait," I said.

We waited.

If our plan had gone through, right now, things would be getting chaotic in the Honeycomb. The part of me that had grown up on books, that had come to expect a certain standard of narrative tension, wanted to hear the first rumblings of that chaos—the shouting, the confusion, the signs something was coming. But sealed off in this sterile office environment, the only way we would have heard anything like that was if someone came into our hexagon.

Someone came into our hexagon.

From outside the smoked-glass door of the Queen's Cell, I heard yelling as people ran into the office, so desperate to find cover that they never suspected they were running into the headquarters of the very virtual reality they'd become trapped in.

Then a deafening roar signaled the arrival of the thing they were running from.

"It worked!" I said.

"It worked." Mom beamed.

Sounds of commotion filled the open-plan offices of HIVE: the shattering of a snack bar being decimated, and the shrieking of hiding players as something huge and destructive lumbered ever closer to the Queen's Cell.

And then the door was blown off its hinges in a burst of

flame, and I saw a face I hadn't seen since yesterday—a.k.a., a lifetime ago—in *Family Feudalism*.

A face with two big, smoking nostrils and a lot of scales.

"What is *happening*?" Jason cried.

"What's happening is we just changed HIVE forever," I said, grinning wildly. "And I have control over dragons."

LEVEL 27

When I'd first entered the Honeycomb this morning, I'd been confused, afraid, and alone in a crowd of frustrated players who were rapidly descending into chaos.

Now chaos had officially descended. Chaos had arrived in a way that made the morning's faint gestures at chaos look like a finger-painted portrait of a happy family and a smiling sun. This chaos now threw buckets of paint at the walls and, upon running out of paint, promptly attacked you with the bucket.

But I didn't care. Because my mom and I were riding a dragon.

This was what we'd done:

"Jason couldn't tell who was real and who was part of HIVE," I'd said, snapping my fingers as the thoughts came rushing to me. "And some of his arguments were so good that sometimes, I couldn't tell, either. He thought we were some form of NPC that's been given the freedom to travel between games."

"But NPCs can't travel between games," Mom said, frowning. "Except for—"

"Sidekicks!" Jason and I said at the same time.

"Exactly!" I said. "NPCs with agency. NPCs who can go anywhere with us, who have the capacity to surprise us, to inspire wonder and love. I should know. A bird saved my life, like, eight times today. So maybe Jason was right to envision a world where people are just like Sidekicks, but he got the point of it backward. It doesn't mean that we don't matter. It means that *everyone* matters—players, NPCs, *everyone*. We should *all* be given the chance to surprise one another. To act freely. To imagine entirely new ways of playing. After all, Eric said it himself—his worst nightmare right now is for players to act unpredictably, moving from game to game at random."

"So what are you suggesting?" Mom asked.

"I'm suggesting," I began, a devious smile growing on my face, "that we make it so *everyone* can move from game to game."

And in just under twenty minutes, that's what we did.

The results were beautiful to see, and not just because I was watching them on dragonback. If the Drones had had trouble keeping down the mob earlier today, now they were entirely hopeless in the face of the combined onslaught of every single game in HIVE unleashed into the Honeycomb at once. *Mass Defect* space mutants vaulted from one platform to another, slamming into Drones with their steel bodies and sending them careening down into catwalks. Mobsters and cowboys fought one another until they were accosted by silvery sentinels, at which point they formed wary truces and teamed up against their common enemy. And at the sound of an explosion, I turned to see Tom A. Toehead bursting out of a bridge, defying all physics as he sucked a Drone down and away from a pair of cowering kids with wings.

And all the while we soared up, up, up, toward Terms and Conditions, racing against the clock and hoping that we'd caused enough confusion to give Eric Alanick a loading screen headache of his own.

And speaking of loading screens: Once again, everything went white. Blinded by the bright light, our dragon roared and reared back, nearly turning upside down and dropping us to our dooms. But I pulled tight on the makeshift reins I'd made out of Mom's captor-supplied jump rope, and the dragon came to a halt, its huge red wings flapping with enough force to keep us floating in the air. When the whiteness faded, it did so to reveal a thousand recurring faces on the walls of the Honeycomb.

"Not this again," I groaned.

"Valued HIVE users," said Eric Alanick. "Please, listen to me."

It was a far cry from how he'd appeared in his first video this morning. He looked more impatient now, his hair mussed up from hands being run through it. But any pleasure I might have gotten from seeing him stressed out was diminished by the sight of what was behind him—the endless scrolls of Terms and Conditions.

"He's already there," I said. "We're too late."

"No," Mom said. "We'd know if we were. We *must* have slowed him down. Look—he's frantic."

"I understand we are facing further technical malfunctions," Eric said, "but I ask you all to stay calm. Remember, we're all in this together! Go back into your games—and stay there! Play on!"

But the same trick wasn't going to work twice. Whereas before people had been willing to hear him out at least a little, now the crowd turned against him instantly.

"Is this guy insane?"

"I'm tired of this!"

"Where is he, anyway? I don't recognize that game!"

I saw an opening and took it.

"He's in Terms and Conditions!" I yelled. "Follow me if you want to give him a piece of your mind!"

Sometimes, it paid to be a girl riding a big scary dragon. The word spread faster than a curable disease in *Mind Your Manors*. As we took off again, racing up the top half of the Honeycomb, we were quickly joined by a bizarre mishmash of players, Sidekicks, and newly escaped game characters who got swept up in all the commotion.

But we all froze into a holding position when we reached the top of the Honeycomb and saw an army of Drones blocking the way to Terms and Conditions like a phalanx.

"Don't worry," I said, reaching to my belt. "I got this."

I pulled out Sammi's smoker—or really, I supposed, my mom's smoker—and with an immense satisfaction, I gave it one big puff.

Nothing came out.

"Kara!" Mom said. "Your smoker's run out!"

"What? But—I thought it couldn't run out!"

"Of course it can! It's not a renewable resource!"

"But—but earlier there was barely any left, and it still worked—I thought it was, like, magic?"

"Yes! The magic was that it worked because you had some left!"

"Oh. Well." I gulped as the Drones began to lower down toward us. "So now what are we going to . . ."

And then they arrived: the *weird* games.

Zombie horses with rolling eyes charged across the air, levitating like ghosts and throwing themselves at the Drones, trying to push them apart in the world's most macabre version of red rover. Cloaked figures shrouded in shadows summoned balls of black energy that blasted the Drones into nothingness upon impact. And from one catwalk, I saw a pale kid in gym shorts and knee-high tube socks throwing a disc with razor blades that flew at a terrifying speed, lopping the head off a Drone and embedding itself in a steel strut above.

"*Frisbee, but Bad,*" I breathed, eyes wide with delight.

"Come on!" Jason said. "Now's your chance!"

He was right. We weren't going to get a better moment than this. I snapped the jump rope, and the dragon surged forward, blowing enough fire to scatter the remaining Drones and fly us snoutfirst into the hexagon marked TERMS AND CONDITIONS.

It was dimly lit and dangerously quiet. We were back.

"He's not here," I said, looking around for Eric Alanick and finding nothing.

"He'll be farther back," Mom said. "Deeper in the library."

"Sorry, ma'am," I said, patting the dragon on the nose as we got off. "This is as far as you can go."

The dragon just huffed, releasing a puff of flame dangerously close to a row of scrolls.

"Should we have brought a dragon into a library?" I asked.

"We'll worry about it later," Mom said. "Come on, let's go down my aisle."

"Your aisle?"

She pointed at the sign above the Hive Simulator hexagon as we passed it. "K–S. Kimi Swift. Did you not get that?"

"Oh, come *on*." Despite the insanity of the situation, I smiled. "Not everyone's got terminal programmer brain, *Mom*."

"Reunited for ten minutes and already my teenage daughter is embarrassed of me. I swear . . ."

"Can we *focus*?" Jason said.

"We're focusing!" I said, and Mom nodded and led us farther into the library.

In the aisles around us, we heard the sounds of the others who had made it past the Drone wall. There seemed to be more than a few NPCs in that number—in some distant aisle, monkeys chattered excitedly; in another, a horse whinnied. Players had also followed us and were clearly stunned to find themselves in a corner of HIVE they had truly never seen before. I heard scrolls firing off in all directions, and then calls of outrage:

"Wait, I agreed to *what*, now?"

"Hold on, they have copyright over my *brain waves*?"

I'd thought we might be headed to the rear of the library, where the back door was, but Mom was leading us to a new wing, one where the shelves read UPDATE 9.1. UPDATE 9.1.5. UPDATE . . .

"So how are we actually going to stop Eric when we find him?" I asked as we rounded a corner.

"Well, the Update is made up of a group of patches, all of which have to load," Mom said. "That'll be going slower than he expected—thanks to us—but it won't take forever. Once it's ready to go, all he'll have to do is read through the new set of Terms and Conditions and mark them as accepted."

"Okay, but I've seen how long those scrolls are," I said. "That might buy us a few minutes, right?"

"Are you kidding?" Mom said. "No one reads the Terms and Conditions—especially not him. He's just going to scroll through them and click yes."

"Oh. Right. Well, at least he won't have the superpowers he had down in his office, right?"

Mom shook her head ruefully. "Wrong again. He's only depowered out in the Honeycomb. In here, he's as dangerous as he's ever been."

"Oh. Great. Kinda makes me wish I'd kept our dragon."

"We'll figure something out," Mom said. "We'll have to. Because I think we're just about . . ."

"Here."

Eric stood proudly in front of the newest Update shelf. A hexagon on the end of the aisle blinked bright green, sending an unmistakable signal: loading complete.

The good news was, Eric wasn't holding the Terms and Conditions scroll he would need to start Phase Two. It lay on the ground, unrolled but ignored.

The bad news was, this was because Eric was holding my father and brother, one arm wrapped around each neck.

"Dad!" I cried as Mom gasped "Kyle!," Kyle yelled *"Mom?!,"* and Dad, of course, said nothing.

"Look who I found sneaking around up here," Eric said through a rictus smile. "Turns out they've been hiding up here all day in one of the mini-libraries. Kara, I don't think they even knew you came and went while they were here. They must have come out just now when they thought the coast was clear, but the coast—was very much—not—*clear*!"

He squeezed on their windpipes with each word, only to release them. Kyle gasped for air, and I had a horrible flashback. Just yesterday, I had watched Markus Fawkes do exactly this in the chemistry classroom with Jason, for the exact same thing: more power in HIVE. Markus and Eric really were cut from the same cloth.

But this time, I couldn't just run at him—he was inhumanly

fast, and Dad and Kyle would feel the punishing consequences of my actions before I had even closed half the distance. Running toward Eric was exactly what he would expect.

So . . .

I ran away.

I darted into the nearest aisle of shelves. Just as I'd hoped, I heard the twin cries of *"Oof!"* that signaled my dad and brother had been dropped to the ground—ungracefully, perhaps, but still alive and now free from Eric's clutches.

Of course, that meant that a millisecond later he was coming up behind me in the aisle—but I'd been running my hands along the spines from the moment I entered. I didn't know what it felt like to run into a wall of exploding scrolls at two hundred miles an hour, but I had to imagine it was at least something of a shock because Eric deblurred with a roar, his feet flying out from under him. He slammed into the opposite shelf as he fell to the ground, triggering a whole host of other explosions and burying him under a layer of paper.

That wasn't going to keep him down long, but it wouldn't have to—here, now, came the cavalry. Those chattering monkeys I'd heard earlier raced down the aisle toward me and Eric. They were looking furious and feral, and followed by some equally unfriendly-looking players. I doubled back and returned the way I'd come, running over Eric's body as I did so. Sadly I'd lost my boots in the labyrinth, but even just in my stocking feet, it felt satisfying to hear him grunt in pain and surprise as my foot came down on his chest. Disoriented, he threw his arms out to catch me but caught only the business end of a macaque's jaws.

Then I was out of the aisle, back to where Mom was helping Dad and Kyle up to their feet.

"Get out of here!" I yelled.

"But—" Kyle began.

"I've got this!" I said. *"Go!"*

"Let her," said Mom. "She knows what she's doing."

And without another moment's hesitation, she grabbed Dad's and Kyle's hands and pulled them away and up an aisle that led back toward the front of the library.

Which was good because based on the monkey that had just been sent flying into the passageway, Eric was back on his feet again. I bent down just long enough to snatch up the unrolled Terms and Conditions scroll, and then I was off again, heading into the maze of shelves. I could hear Eric snarling in fury as he ran to catch up with me, but no amount of strength or speed could make up for him not knowing where I was, and as long as I was running shoeless, my footfalls were harder to trace.

If there was anything I knew, it was how to be quiet in a library.

"Jason," I whispered. "Do you know how to get to—"

"Next two lefts," Jason said, reading my mind. "Then straight two, then a right."

I obeyed. In that moment, I knew that I could trust Jason entirely. And soon enough, I reached my destination.

The hexagon I saw now was colored the same bright black as the one that had led me out of the labyrinth and into Eric Alanick's clutches. This one, though, was completely unguarded. Any Drones that had been posted here had since been diverted to deal with the siege outside, leaving the door wide open, the label clearly visible: BOREDOM SIMULATOR.

I could have leaped through it right now, reemerging into the Bullworth Apiary, safe from HIVE forever.

Instead, I planted my feet where I stood and turned to wait for Eric Alanick.

He must have guessed after a while where I was headed because soon there was a blur, and there he stood. Blazer torn. Flesh bitten. Chest heaving and face contorted with pure, unvarnished hatred.

I held up the scroll I'd been clutching close to my chest. It hadn't been easy to run with, unraveled to its full length as it was.

"Looking for this?" I said.

His eyes narrowed.

"Because if you want it," I said, "we're going to have to come to an agreement. I want my family safe. I want my friends brought back. And—"

And then Eric *flickered*, like for a second he had ceased to exist, and then suddenly reappeared. It wasn't until the wind had stopped blowing around my face that I realized: My hand was both empty and bleeding. He'd snatched the scroll out of it so fast that he'd cut my palm open.

"This is so *disappointing*," Eric spat. "Honestly, I thought you were a thought leader, I really did. A *winner*. But you just overplayed your hand. *Terrible* negotiation move."

As he spoke, he moved his grip rapidly down the scroll, barely glancing at it as he fed it upward, until the length of it was trailing out in front of him and the very bottom, with its dotted line, was clutched in his bloodstained fingers.

And then he looked right back up at me.

"If you're going to win, you don't have *time* for diplomacy," he sneered. "You don't have *time* to think about others. Move fast. *Break* things. Disrupt. Level up. *Update*."

In place of ink, he pressed his bloody thumb into the square where a signature would have gone.

"I accept these terms." He leered triumphantly.

And then he dropped the scroll to the ground and waited. Eric hadn't been a small man to begin with, but he'd never seemed bigger than right now, chest pumped up in anticipation, head back, nostrils flared in sheer animal pride, as he basked in the fruition of all he had worked toward: the completion of the Update. The swallowing of every mind in HIVE into a spiral of eternal profit growth, unchained from the real world's limits on power or wealth. Game over; he'd won.

And yet.

Nothing happened.

The chest deflated slightly.

The nostrils shrank and the eyebrows furrowed.

I smiled.

"Maybe," I said, "you should at least make time to read the Terms and Conditions? Like, what if you'd looked at them, and noticed they were just legal text from some random scroll that'd been pulled off a shelf and swapped out with the real thing? Wouldn't that totally just, like . . . *disrupt* your day?"

And then I pulled my non-injured hand from behind my back, revealing the scroll I'd been holding the whole time—the real one as opposed to the one I'd grabbed while I was on the run, the one that I'd let Eric take from me.

Eric Alanick looked back and forth from the scroll on the ground to the one in my hands, uncomprehending. But before he could react, I'd pressed my own bloody palm onto the signature line.

"I *don't* accept your Terms and Conditions," I said. "Please cancel this Update."

And I knew what Eric was going to do next. I knew it because it's what I would have done, what I had done just yesterday, what someone playing to win would do. He charged. But I'd already flung myself to the floor.

Eric Alanick flew over me and right into the Boredom Simulator, throwing himself out of HIVE through the cruel joke door that had locked people out of HIVE permanently just this morning—the door of Eric Alanick's own making.

And as the scroll and I fell, a voice proclaimed:

"The Update in progress has been canceled. HIVE will return to its last save point."

I had just enough time to worry about what that meant before the floor rushed up at me.

I never hit the floor.

LEVEL 28

Sometimes when you win a video game, you get a really cool reward. Maybe you get to see a beautiful, lavishly animated cutscene. Maybe you get a chance to put your name at the top of a high-score list. Maybe you even unlock a whole new part of the game that you never suspected was there, and fireworks shoot off over a magnificent castle as you hurry on to the next new world.

Or maybe you find yourself suspended in another white void, with your immediate family, a crowd of strangers, several macaque monkeys, one zombie horse, and a dragon.

Maybe it's the best reward you ever could have imagined.

Because of the family part, to be clear. Not the zombie horse or dragon.

"Kara!" Mom cried. She was the first of us to regain her bearings, and she threw her arms around me even as I was still dizzy from my dramatic final move against Eric Alanick. Frankly, I was grateful for the support in standing up, and even more so when my mother's arms were joined by Kyle's, and then—silently, but with a strength of grip that spoke volumes—my dad's.

"This is so sweet," Jason said.

"Hi, Jason. Everyone, Jason is in this group hug, too," I announced.

"Wait, *what*?" Kyle asked.

"Hi, Jason," Mom and Dad chorused.

"No, seriously, though," Kyle continued. "What happened back there?"

"What's happening *here*?" I asked, looking around—or trying my best to do so from within a dense thicket of Tilden-Swifts. Behind Dad's head, my dragon looked one way and then the other, clearly just as confused as I was. "Mom, this void—are we back in Alanick's lobby? Was this all for nothing?"

Mom shook her head fiercely. "No, honey," she said. "You did it. This is a fail-safe we patched in a long time ago for bodies coming out of deep HIVE stasis—so, for pretty much everyone in HIVE right now. It means we're being let out of HIVE—but slowly, so that it isn't a fatal shock to our systems. It's a depressurization process, like how divers have to stop halfway up to the surface so they don't get the bends. Though the NPCs aren't normally supposed to be here. I guess after what we just did to HIVE's core functions, 'normal' isn't so normal anymore."

"Whoa," Kyle said, awestruck. "So we won't be buzzed when we get out?"

"Oh, no." Mom grimaced. "We are all going to be *so* buzzed. And I am quite possibly about to be the most buzzed anyone has ever been."

And then she beamed at me and squeezed me one more time.

"But we're going to be alive. Thanks to you, Kara."

"Thanks to you both, it seems," Dad mumbled, finally detaching from the group hug to step back and look at Mom. And I didn't know what was more shocking: the fact that Dad was suddenly being so demonstrative (you know, for Dad), or the way Mom was suddenly blushing brighter than a bashful lighthouse.

"Honey," she said, taking Dad's hand in hers, and then grabbing Kyle's as well. "Kyle. I understand you probably hate me for what—I mean, you must have thought—you must both have so many questions—"

"Honestly, not really." Kyle shrugged. "Eric Alanick kind of explained a lot to Dad and me while he had us held hostage. That guy *really* likes to talk about himself."

I nodded. "He really does."

Mom laughed. "He *really* does."

"Well, then, *I* have questions," I jumped in, before Mom and Dad could return to making goo-goo eyes at each other. "How did you guys get here, anyway? I was worried we'd lost you forever in *Brawl of Duty*."

"Oh my gosh, you wouldn't have *believed* it," Kyle said. "Dad is *incredible*."

Mom smiled loopily at Dad.

"I'd believe it," she said.

Well, so much for that.

"Okay, you two get five more minutes of being like this," I

said, but on the inside I felt a warmth I hadn't felt in years. It was like that incendiary explosion of emotions I used to feel whenever I saw my mom's name on a patch note, but without all the sharp shrapnel of negativity attached.

Really, it was less like a bomb and more like fireworks.

Speaking of fireworks: It was at this point that the dragon, increasingly irritated by this strange new world that had such loud food in it, reared up and blew a jet of flame into the eternal nothingness that stood in for the sky. As players around us shrieked and scattered in all directions, the dragon fell back to all fours and began whipping its neck left and right, presumably looking to eat its feelings.

"Kara!" Mom cried. "Do you still have control over dragons?"

I had no idea, but I was like my mom right up to the end— I just had to stick my nose in and help. Even as Kyle yelled "Wait!" and Dad reached out for me, I ran directly toward the dragon (amazing how attitudes can change in one short day), hollering: "Stop! Wait! Don't eat any—"

And then, with a small *b-doop* that sounded for all the world like a handheld device shutting down, the dragon popped out of existence.

"Body," I finished.

"Whoa," Kyle said. "You *do* have control over dragons."

"I don't think that was me," I said, turning to face my family. Over their shoulders, I watched as a zombie horse disappeared from view with another *b-doop*, leaving the two monkeys that had been climbing on top of it to fall through the sudden nothingness before blinking out of sight themselves.

"Extraneous programming must be shutting down," Mom said, looking around. Players were cautiously reapproaching us as NPCs flickered out one by one. "The depressurization process is advancing. We don't have much longer here together; we could all get ejected at any moment. We need to—"

"Cherish the remaining moments we have together?"

"Talk logistics," Mom said. "If we play this right, we'll have as many more moments together as you want."

She caught Dad's eye and blushed again.

"I mean," she said, "if you even still want—"

"Logistics!" Kyle and I cried.

"Right, right." Mom turned to us, her hand unconsciously patting at her already-knotted hair. "Based on hints I've gotten from Eric over the past four years and geographic metadata I've found in my own code, I have reason to believe I'm being kept in the storage unit of a HIVE server farm somewhere off I-95, in some sort of super-pod with a muscle stimulator and a beefed-up nutrient feed. As soon as it is safe for you to drive, and *not a second sooner*, I want you to come find me. Though no rush, really. I'm not planning on going anywhere."

I couldn't help it: I laughed out loud. Those fireworks I'd been feeling in my stomach were multiplying, making me giddy, almost turning me delirious. Hearing Mom talk about the real world was having the unanticipated effect of making the world feel, well, real. After what had felt like an eternity trapped in HIVE, I was about to emerge into a world unlike any I had ever known—and my mom was going to be in that world with me.

And just like that, the laughter turned to tears.

"Kara?" Mom asked. "Is everything all right?"

"No, yes, I'm fine, I'm fine," I said. "I just—don't know what to say—"

"I do," Dad said, and as one, the three other members of the family turned to him, stunned, as if to say: *You do? You do?*

"I . . ." Dad began.

And then:

B-doop.

He was gone.

"Dad!" I cried.

"No, no, it's fine!" Mom said. "It's good! It's happening! It means we're getting out of here!"

And, indeed, player after player had begun to vanish around us, sending up a chorus of *b-doop*s that was as funny as it was frightening.

"This is crazy," Kyle said. "I wonder when I'm going to—"

B-doop.

It was just me and Mom now.

"I'll see you soon, honey." Mom smiled, but I couldn't wait that long. I threw myself around her, getting one last hug—no, one *more* hug—which would be followed by many, but my brain just couldn't convince my body of that right now. I was laughing, panicked, tearful, and elated all at the same time, and it didn't matter because my mom was hugging me and I was hugging her back.

"We'll find you, Mom," I said. "We'll get there as soon as we can. I found you once, and I'll find you again. Just hold on. Just—"

B-doop.

LEVEL 29

This is how popular HIVE was: A plurality of the world had been trapped in it for nearly twenty-four hours. It had caused a crisis of global proportions. It had attempted to swallow humanity into itself forever.

And it was *still* all anyone wanted to talk about at the Bullworth High cafeteria lunch table the following Monday.

"I just still can't believe Eric Alanick was *evil*," Gus said. "Like totally, crazy-pants *evil*."

"I can," Aaron said, through a mouthful of stuffed-crust pizza. "Guy was a vampire. Come on."

"Okay, *whatever*," Gus said. "I'm just glad they caught him before he made it to his private jet. Apparently the guy was so buzzed from all that time in HIVE, they found him crawling across the tarmac."

"We were all buzzed, Gus," said Sammi, moving in to steal a pepper slice. "I seem to remember you face-planting the moment our pod doors opened, screaming about wasps."

"Yeah, but. Come on." Gus shifted in his seat defensively. "It's a funnier image when it's corporate bigwig *Eric Alanick*."

"Fair." Sammi crunched into the contraband pepper, and then got an idea. "Hey—talk about a *final boss*, am I right?"

"Sammi."

"Sorry."

"I thought it was funny, Sammi," said Jason.

"*Thank* you, Jason." Sammi beamed. "You know, I don't know if I've said this enough, but I'm really so glad you joined us for lunch today."

As a sign of inclusiveness and respect, she stole a pepper slice from his tray as well. And if he wasn't too pale for color to ever pass his cheeks, it might almost have looked like Jason had maybe, possibly, blushed.

"Thanks," he said. "I mean it—thank you, guys. I don't want to be rude, but I'm sort of new to having friends—and I know you guys are sort of old to it—I mean, you're all each other's friends—I mean, I just hope it's not too weird that I—"

This was my cue to put a bookmark in my book, close it, and put it down on the table.

All eyes turned to me.

"Jason," I said. "Everything about this is weird. Two days ago, you didn't know we existed. Literally. Then we all went through an insane ordeal together, most of us died, and then we came back, and we are all just trying to act like that is normal."

The table was deathly silent.

"But you can't be new to having friends," I said, rolling my eyes, "because we've been friends since we were six. And the only way you can be rude is by forgetting that. Okay?"

Jason smiled, and I saw the same thing I'd seen when I'd fallen gasping out of a pod chamber not thirty hours ago, prompting him to come running toward me with concern on his face.

I saw someone who really and truly cared about other people.

"Okay," he said. "Thanks."

"Well, Kara," said Sammi. "While we aren't pretending everything is normal—how are things with your mom?"

"Hey!" Aaron whined. "That's the kind of thing that I normally ask, and then someone kicks me for being rude!"

"It's a post-Update world, my friend." Sammi shrugged.

"It's good," I said. "Things with my mom are good."

And I smiled.

Because they really were. No—they were great.

Those first few moments back in the Apiary had been overwhelming, to say the least. It turned out that HIVE returning to its last save point meant returning everyone to how they'd been before Phase One of the Update had begun that morning. People who'd become Drones were restored to their full selves; my friends were pulled back from whatever digital abyss they'd been consigned to; and most pressingly, everyone who had been trapped was once again free to remove themselves from HIVE.

Which they did. En masse.

I was the first one in our Apiary to exit, and Jason had rushed to my side, propped my back up against the side of the chamber, and wet my dry, gasping lips with a bottle of water—oh, no, that was energy drink. Okay, he was trying to revive me with neon-green energy drink. Cool. Still, I'd been grateful, spluttering it down like an astronaut who'd just crawled out of their reentry craft.

Then, down the row from us, another pod door had popped open.

Then another, and another, and another.

Soon the entire Apiary was filled with people hugging one another, helping one another off the ground like a mutual support society of baby deer, and disbelievingly swapping notes on the insanity they had all just survived.

Jason and I just looked at each other and laughed like crazy people. We'd done it. We'd really done it. I couldn't wait to tell—

"Kara!"

"Kyle!" I yelled. "Kyle, I'm over here!"

As the only non-buzzed person in the room, Jason had gotten up and run to find my brother, throwing his arm over his shoulders and carrying him to me, which was especially touching considering Jason weighed about ninety pounds less than my brother. Or than anyone, really.

"Wait, Kara!" That was the unmistakable sound of Sammi's listen-to-me yell. "We're over here! We're here, too!"

"I can only carry one of you at a time!" Jason wheezed, but he dropped Kyle at my side and went off to find her.

While Jason rounded us up, I grabbed Kyle's hand. "Are you okay? Is Dad—"

"Yeah, yeah, he should be at home—oh, hold on, I think he's calling me," Kyle said, reaching into his pocket with a still-shaking hand and holding his phone up to his ear with considerable effort.

"Hello? Dad? Yes, no, we're fine—no, *don't* drive to come get us! Stay at home until you can stand, *obviously*. Kara, tell him he can't drive."

I would very much have liked to do that, but at that moment, my own phone started buzzing.

"What—is he calling my phone, too?" I asked. "Hold on a second, let me just—"

I stopped, staring at the words on my phone: UNKNOWN NUMBER.

And then I answered the call.

"Mom?" I asked, hoping against hope. "Are you okay?!"

"Well, it's definitely a storage unit," Mom said, her voice unspeakably bemused. "And I am *definitely* the most buzzed anyone has ever been. But from my very comfortable spot here on the floor, I was able to open the circuit board of this pod and turn it into a GPS-slash-cell-phone, so. See you soon?"

I babbled promises to find her, and Kyle shouted one or two things over my ear as well in a very sweet but unhelpful way, and then Jason dropped Sammi next to me and ran back to get Aaron and Gus, and Sammi demanded to know what she'd missed since the labyrinth, and the conversation *really* took off from there.

On the whole, there were much worse places to be after Update Day, as it came to be called, than safe with your friends and loved ones in an Apiary. We were spared the worst of the chaos in those first few hours after the world was freed. (*After* you *freed the world*, a tiny voice in my head tended to whisper. *How cool is* that? *We probably shouldn't dwell on it or anything, seems like it might go to our head, but, like, come* on.) In those urgent initial moments of recovery, emergency services received more incoming calls than they'd ever gotten before during peacetime while half their staff were heavily buzzed themselves. And as the late hours of Saturday night turned into Sunday morning, the news just kept pouring in: Eric Alanick had been arrested. He'd been arrested by someone high up in international affairs, who'd been there in Terms and Conditions that day and decided to spill the beans in case it helped him to avoid getting arrested himself. He got arrested himself, and then everyone else he mentioned was collared as well—including, you know, the president of the United States. The vice president was claiming they knew nothing about it, but every news organization was having an absolute field day.

But none of that mattered because the Tilden-Swifts were having a home day.

All four of them.

Well, four and a guest.

As Gus, Aaron, and Sammi called their families to let them know they were okay, Kyle and I made plans to find Mom as soon as we were good to drive again. Then Jason had said, "You know I'm good to drive right *now*, right?"

And so Jason, Kyle, and I were off in Jason's car, following Mom's signal to where Eric Alanick had left her all those years ago, which was, indeed, in a rented storage unit only a few hours south of the city. She was, as she'd mentioned, *heavily* whammied after several uninterrupted years in HIVE, and I found myself glad we had taken Jason's burrow of a car, since it meant we were able to wrap Mom up in some of Jason's blankets and give her a comfy spot in the back seat to recover.

"Jason, dear," Mom said, craning her neck around slowly as we drove north again. "Do you live in your car?"

"No," Jason said quickly.

"Oh, good."

"I live in the Apiary."

"Oh—*no*, Jason, that is *not allowed*. You're coming home with us."

And he did, the sun just beginning to rise again as we pulled into the driveway, where Dad had been waiting up for us, having never technically left the house that weekend.

And then everyone was finally home.

Gus had called a lot of times that day. So had Sammi, and I'd even gotten one or two texts from Aaron, which oddly had been the closest I'd come to returning someone's communication:

Just practiced pitching with my little sister. Not as good as with the apple, Aaron had sent. *But better than I was before. And if I'd stayed stuck in HIVE, I could've been the world's best pitcher, and I still couldn't have hugged my sister after. So. Not sorry.*

But I didn't respond to him, or to anyone.

It was a day for family.

And then somehow, against all odds, in the face of unprecedented historical and political scandal, Monday was a day for school. Mom had asked Jason if he would be needing a ride to school, and when Jason had said that, honestly, he tended to spend the first few periods of the day at the Apiary, Mom had asked again if Jason. Would be needing. A ride. To school. He'd gotten the hint, and all day he'd been glued to my side, like he was my foreign exchange student and I was the host introducing him to our culture. In a way, I kind of was—I was introducing him to the culture of real life. It was actually sort of fun. My friend of ten years wasn't so bad, once I got to know him.

And so here we all sat at the lunch table, technically having our first group meeting since the Apiary. No one had known what to say when we'd all sat down—but then Markus Fawkes had walked by, seen us, and run out of the cafeteria so fast that a hall monitor had chased after him, and we'd all burst out laughing. It appeared that being briefly and functionally nonexistent had finally drilled some humility into him, which was going to make the rest of the school year a lot easier.

Speaking of.

Gus and I still hadn't really talked about what had happened between us in the labyrinth; to be honest, I didn't know when we would, or what we might say. We'd all learned a lot about ourselves in a very short amount of time, and we could pretend it was normal for this lunch period, but sooner or later we'd have to face what we'd said and done.

But now as I sat here, watching Aaron ask Jason to tell him all about the craziest things he'd found at the top of the Honeycomb, and watching Sammi continue to steal food from both of them, and feeling Gus lean over and give my hand one quick, silent squeeze, I knew that nothing was going to break this group up. We'd be helping and teasing and irritating and delighting one another for a long time to come. Maybe we would even play more HIVE together—I'd heard that the first few people daring enough to go back into the Honeycomb in the last couple of days had found an entirely different world, one in which games seeped into other games and all the old ways of winning and losing had been rewritten entirely.

That sounded like a world I would love to explore.

ACKNOWLEDGMENTS

It feels like I have been writing this book for many years. Accordingly, thanks and acknowledgments are due to many people.

I am deeply indebted to my editor, Orlando Dos Reis, whose persistence and perceptiveness have saved this book time and again. Among (many) other things, he helped me get into Kara's head, got this book off the ground, and brought it home. Thank you.

Thanks are also due to the entire team at Scholastic, who brought me such joy with every stage of this book's formation, from art to copyediting, that I have now become even more annoying at parties because I can not stop talking about any of it. I am also grateful to David Levithan, whose advice restarted this book when it glitched. Truly, your help was the equivalent of unplugging the controller, dusting it off, and plugging it back in again; may every writer be so lucky as to have such an incredible cheat code in their arsenal. Or a player's guide, because you were a guide? This metaphor is getting away from me.

My sincere thanks to both Pasquale Toscano and Jennifer Keelan-Chaffins; Aaron and this book are both better off because of your time and thoughtfulness. Thanks as well to Dan Fitzpatrick and Jacob Rienstra, for fielding unexpected questions about video games and programming, respectively. And then there are those who consulted on this book without knowing it. In particular, I owe thanks to Greta, Danna, Nita, Gianina, and Julianna, all of whom were major inspirations for Kara. And I didn't even plan that name thing. Wild!

Many people either had to hear about this book incessantly for years, or in some cases watch, for hours at a time, as it got dragged kicking and screaming into existence. A non-exhaustive but very heartfelt list would include (deep breath, from the top): Devon, Dan, Nora, Micah, Moulie, Mark, Neil, Gianina, Jack, Jules, Aleja, Elizabeth, Lydia, Matt, Brice, Bugra, Dylan, Jon, Billy, Nico, Andrew, Nick, David, Chris, and the Q train. If I have forgotten anyone, please excuse my lack of RAM. Let me know and you will be included in the next Update's patch notes.

And, of course, thank you to my family, who got me here and helped me stay here. In many ways, they are the reason this book exists. But let's get specific about one particular way: They supported me as I ransacked book fairs, libraries, and (in my brother's case) hard-earned private property for years. Mom was constantly on book fair duty; Dad is the reason I was able to bike to the library; and countless uncles and aunts contributed books to the effort as well (one in particular knocked it out of the park with *The Amazing Maurice and His Educated Rodents*). As a result, I was introduced to all the great, empowering action-adventure books I read and reread growing up, along with their authors, to whom this book is one big, breathless tribute: Eoin Colfer, Vivian Vande Velde, Scott Westerfeld, Diane Duane, Terry Pratchett, and too many more to name. They all deserve thanks, as well.

And if you're reading this: Thank you, too. Now that you've finished your first playthrough, you can actually go back and reread this book with all the side quests unlocked.

If I'm lucky, you'll enjoy it half as much as I did.

ABOUT THE AUTHOR

M. C. Ross is an author and playwright living in New York City. He is almost too good at *Tetris*. For more information, please visit mcrosswrites.com.